THE COUNT
OF MONTE CRISTO
VOL IV.

BY

ALEXANDRE DUMAS

British Library Cataloguing-in-Publication Data
A catalogue record for this book is available from the
British Library

Contents

Alexandre Dumas

Alexandre Dumas was born in Villers-Cotterêts, France in 1802. His parents were poor, but their heritage and good reputation – Alexandre's father had been a general in Napoleon's army – provided Alexandre with opportunities for good employment. In 1822, Dumas moved to Paris to work for future king Louis Philippe I in the Palais Royal. It was here that he began to write for magazines and the theatre.

In 1829 and 1830 respectively, Dumas produced the plays *Henry III and His Court* and *Christine,* both of which met with critical acclaim and financial success. As a result, he was able to commit himself full-time to writing. Despite the turbulent economic times which followed the Revolution of 1830, Dumas turned out to have something of an entrepreneurial streak, and did well for himself in this decade. He founded a production studio that turned out hundreds of stories under his creative direction, and began to produce serialised novels for newspapers which were widely read by the French public. It was over the next two decades, as a now famous and much loved author of romantic and adventuring sagas, that Dumas produced his best-known works – the D'Artagnan romances, including

The Three Musketeers, in 1844, and *The Count of Monte Cristo,* in 1846.

Dumas made a lot of money from his writing, but he was almost constantly penniless as a result of his extravagant lifestyle and love of women. In 1851 he fled his creditors to Belgium, and then Russia, and then Italy, not returning to Paris until 1864. Dumas died in Puys, France, in 1870, at the age of 68. He is now enshrined in the Panthéon of Paris alongside fellow authors Victor Hugo and Emile Zola. Since his death, his fiction has been translated into almost a hundred languages, and has formed the basis for more than 200 motion pictures.

CHAPTER 74.
THE VILLEFORT FAMILY VAULT.

Two days after, a considerable crowd was assembled, towards ten o'clock in the morning, around the door of M. de Villefort's house, and a long file of mourning-coaches and private carriages extended along the Faubourg Saint-Honore and the Rue de la Pepiniere. Among them was one of a very singular form, which appeared to have come from a distance. It was a kind of covered wagon, painted black, and was one of the first to arrive. Inquiry was made, and it was ascertained that, by a strange coincidence, this carriage contained the corpse of the Marquis de Saint-Meran, and that those who had come thinking to attend one funeral would follow two. Their number was great. The Marquis de Saint-Meran, one of the most zealous and faithful dignitaries of Louis XVIII. and King Charles X., had preserved a great number of friends, and these, added to the personages whom the usages of society gave Villefort a claim on, formed a considerable body.

Due information was given to the authorities, and permission obtained that the two funerals should take place at the same time. A second hearse, decked with the same funereal pomp, was brought to M. de Villefort's door, and the coffin removed into it from the post-wagon. The two

3

bodies were to be interred in the cemetery of Pere-la-Chaise, where M. de Villefort had long since had a tomb prepared for the reception of his family. The remains of poor Renee were already deposited there, and now, after ten years of separation, her father and mother were to be reunited with her. The Parisians, always curious, always affected by funereal display, looked on with religious silence while the splendid procession accompanied to their last abode two of the number of the old aristocracy—the greatest protectors of commerce and sincere devotees to their principles. In one of the mourning-coaches Beauchamp, Debray, and Chateau-Renaud were talking of the very sudden death of the marchioness. "I saw Madame de Saint-Meran only last year at Marseilles, when I was coming back from Algiers," said Chateau-Renaud; "she looked like a woman destined to live to be a hundred years old, from her apparent sound health and great activity of mind and body. How old was she?"

"Franz assured me," replied Albert, "that she was sixty-six years old. But she has not died of old age, but of grief; it appears that since the death of the marquis, which affected her very deeply, she has not completely recovered her reason."

"But of what disease, then, did she die?" asked Debray.

"It is said to have been a congestion of the brain, or apoplexy, which is the same thing, is it not?"

"Nearly."

"It is difficult to believe that it was apoplexy," said Beauchamp. "Madame de Saint-Meran, whom I once saw, was short, of slender form, and of a much more nervous than sanguine temperament; grief could hardly produce apoplexy in such a constitution as that of Madame de Saint-Meran."

"At any rate," said Albert, "whatever disease or doctor may have killed her, M. de Villefort, or rather, Mademoiselle Valentine,—or, still rather, our friend Franz, inherits a magnificent fortune, amounting, I believe, to 80,000 livres per annum."

"And this fortune will be doubled at the death of the old Jacobin, Noirtier."

"That is a tenacious old grandfather," said Beauchamp. "Tenacem propositi virum. I think he must have made an agreement with death to outlive all his heirs, and he appears likely to succeed. He resembles the old Conventionalist of '93, who said to Napoleon, in 1814, 'You bend because your empire is a young stem, weakened by rapid growth. Take the Republic for a tutor; let us return with renewed strength to the battle-field, and I promise you 500,000 soldiers, another Marengo, and a second Austerlitz. Ideas do not become extinct, sire; they slumber sometimes, but only revive the stronger before they sleep entirely.' Ideas and men appeared the same to him. One thing only puzzles me, namely, how Franz d'Epinay will like a grandfather who cannot be separated from his wife. But where is Franz?"

"In the first carriage, with M. de Villefort, who considers him already as one of the family."

Such was the conversation in almost all the carriages; these two sudden deaths, so quickly following each other, astonished every one, but no one suspected the terrible secret which M. d'Avrigny had communicated, in his nocturnal walk to M. de Villefort. They arrived in about an hour at the cemetery; the weather was mild, but dull, and in harmony with the funeral ceremony. Among the groups which flocked towards the family vault, Chateau-Renaud recognized Morrel, who had come alone in a cabriolet, and walked silently along the path bordered with yew-trees. "You here?" said Chateau-Renaud, passing his arms through the young captain's; "are you a friend of Villefort's? How is it that I have never met you at his house?"

"I am no acquaintance of M. de Villefort's," answered Morrel, "but I was of Madame de Saint-Meran." Albert came up to them at this moment with Franz.

"The time and place are but ill-suited for an introduction," said Albert; "but we are not superstitious. M. Morrel, allow me to present to you M. Franz d'Epinay, a delightful travelling companion, with whom I made the tour of Italy. My dear Franz, M. Maximilian Morrel, an excellent friend I have acquired in your absence, and whose name you will hear me mention every time I make any allusion to affection, wit, or amiability." Morrel hesitated for a moment; he feared it would be hypocritical to accost in a friendly manner the man whom he was tacitly opposing, but his oath and the gravity of the circumstances recurred to his memory; he struggled to conceal his emotion and bowed to Franz. "Mademoiselle de Villefort is in deep sorrow, is she not?" said Debray to Franz.

"Extremely," replied he; "she looked so pale this morning, I scarcely knew her." These apparently simple words pierced Morrel to the heart. This man had seen Valentine, and spoken to her! The young and high-spirited officer required all his strength of mind to resist breaking his oath. He took the arm of Chateau-Renaud, and turned towards the vault, where the attendants had already placed the two coffins. "This is a magnificent habitation," said Beauchamp, looking towards the mausoleum; "a summer and winter palace. You will, in turn, enter it, my dear d'Epinay, for you will soon be numbered as one of the family. I, as a philosopher, should like a little country-house, a cottage down there under the trees, without so many free-stones over my poor body. In dying, I will say to those around me what Voltaire wrote to Piron: 'Eo rus, and all will be over.' But come, Franz, take courage, your wife is an heiress."

"Indeed, Beauchamp, you are unbearable. Politics has made you laugh at everything, and political men have made you disbelieve everything. But when you have the honor of associating with ordinary men, and the pleasure of leaving politics for a moment, try to find your affectionate heart, which you leave with your stick when you go to the Chamber."

"But tell me," said Beauchamp, "what is life? Is it not a hall in Death's anteroom?"

"I am prejudiced against Beauchamp," said Albert, drawing Franz away, and leaving the former to finish his philosophical dissertation with Debray. The Villefort vault formed a square of white stones, about twenty feet high; an interior partition separated the two families, and each apartment had its entrance door. Here were not, as in other tombs, ignoble drawers, one above another, where thrift bestows its dead and labels them like specimens in a museum; all that was visible within the bronze gates was a gloomy-looking room, separated by a wall from the vault itself. The two doors before mentioned were in the middle of this wall, and enclosed the Villefort and Saint-Meran coffins. There grief might freely expend itself without being disturbed by the trifling loungers who came from a picnic party to visit Pere-la-Chaise, or by lovers who make it their rendezvous.

The two coffins were placed on trestles previously prepared for their reception in the right-hand crypt belonging to the Saint-Meran family. Villefort, Franz, and a few near relatives alone entered the sanctuary.

As the religious ceremonies had all been performed at the door, and there was no address given, the party all separated; Chateau-Renaud, Albert, and Morrel, went one way, and Debray and Beauchamp the other. Franz remained with M. de Villefort; at the gate of the cemetery, Morrel made an excuse to wait; he saw Franz and M. de Villefort get into the same mourning coach, and thought this meeting forboded evil. He then returned to Paris, and although in the same carriage with Chateau-Renaud and Albert, he did not hear one word of their conversation. As Franz was about to take leave of M. de Villefort, "When shall I see you again?" said the latter.

"At what time you please, sir," replied Franz.

"As soon as possible."

"I am at your command, sir; shall we return together?"

"If not unpleasant to you."

"On the contrary, I shall feel much pleasure." Thus, the future father and son-in-law stepped into the same carriage, and Morrel, seeing them pass, became uneasy. Villefort and Franz returned to the Faubourg Saint-Honore. The procureur, without going to see either his wife or his daughter, went at once to his study, and, offering the young man a chair,—"M. d'Epinay," said he, "allow me to remind you at this moment,—which is perhaps not so ill-chosen as at first sight may appear, for obedience to the wishes of the departed is the first offering which should be made at their tomb,—allow me then to remind you of the wish expressed by Madame de Saint-Meran on her death-bed, that Valentine's wedding might not be deferred. You know the affairs of the deceased are in perfect order, and her will bequeaths to Valentine the entire property of the Saint-Meran family; the notary showed me the documents yesterday, which will enable us to draw up the contract immediately. You may call on the notary, M. Deschamps, Place Beauveau, Faubourg Saint-Honore, and you have my authority to inspect those deeds."

"Sir," replied M. d'Epinay, "it is not, perhaps, the moment for Mademoiselle Valentine, who is in deep distress, to think of a husband; indeed, I fear"—

"Valentine will have no greater pleasure than that of fulfilling her grandmother's last injunctions; there will be no obstacle from that quarter, I assure you."

"In that case," replied Franz, "as I shall raise none, you may make arrangements when you please; I have pledged my word, and shall feel pleasure and happiness in adhering to it."

"Then," said Villefort, "nothing further is required. The contract was to have been signed three days since; we shall find it all ready, and can sign it to-day."

"But the mourning?" said Franz, hesitating.

"Don't be uneasy on that score," replied Villefort; "no ceremony will be neglected in my house. Mademoiselle de Villefort may retire during the prescribed three months to her estate of Saint-Meran; I say hers, for she inherits it to-day. There, after a few days, if you like, the civil marriage shall be celebrated without pomp or ceremony. Madame de Saint-Meran wished her daughter should be married there. When that is over, you, sir, can return to Paris, while your wife passes the time of her mourning with her mother-in-law."

"As you please, sir," said Franz.

"Then," replied M. de Villefort, "have the kindness to wait half an hour; Valentine shall come down into the drawing-room. I will send for M. Deschamps; we will read and sign the contract before we separate, and this evening Madame de Villefort shall accompany Valentine to her estate, where we will rejoin them in a week."

"Sir," said Franz, "I have one request to make."

"What is it?"

"I wish Albert de Morcerf and Raoul de Chateau-Renaud to be present at this signature; you know they are my witnesses."

"Half an hour will suffice to apprise them; will you go for them yourself, or shall you send?"

"I prefer going, sir."

"I shall expect you, then, in half an hour, baron, and Valentine will be ready." Franz bowed and left the room. Scarcely had the door closed, when M. de Villefort sent to tell Valentine to be ready in the drawing-room in half an hour, as he expected the notary and M. d'Epinay and his witnesses. The news caused a great sensation throughout the house; Madame de Villefort would not believe it, and Valentine was thunderstruck. She looked around for help, and would have gone down to her grandfather's room, but on the stairs she met M. de Villefort, who took her arm and led her into the drawing-room. In the anteroom, Valentine met Barrois, and looked despairingly at the old servant. A moment later, Madame de Villefort entered the drawing-room with her little Edward. It was evident that she had shared the grief of the family, for she was pale and looked fatigued. She sat down, took Edward on her knees, and from time to time pressed this child, on whom her affections appeared centred, almost convulsively to her bosom. Two carriages were soon heard to enter the court yard. One was the notary's; the other, that of Franz and his friends. In a moment the whole party was assembled. Valentine was so pale one might trace the blue veins from her temples, round her eyes and down her cheeks. Franz was deeply affected. Chateau-Renaud and Albert looked at each other with amazement; the ceremony which was just concluded had not appeared more sorrowful than did that which was about to begin. Madame de Villefort had placed herself in the shadow behind a velvet curtain, and as she constantly bent over her child, it was difficult to read the expression of her face. M. de Villefort was, as usual, unmoved.

The notary, after having according to the customary method arranged the papers on the table, taken his place in an armchair, and raised his spectacles, turned towards Franz:

"Are you M. Franz de Quesnel, baron d'Epinay?" asked he, although he knew it perfectly.

"Yes, sir," replied Franz. The notary bowed. "I have, then, to inform you, sir, at the request of M. de Villefort, that your projected marriage with Mademoiselle de Villefort has changed the feeling of M. Noirtier towards his grandchild, and that he disinherits her entirely of the fortune he would have left her. Let me hasten to add," continued he, "that the testator, having only the right to alienate a part of his fortune, and having alienated it all, the will will not bear scrutiny, and is declared null and void."

"Yes," said Villefort; "but I warn M. d'Epinay, that during my life-time my father's will shall never be questioned, my position forbidding any doubt to be entertained."

"Sir," said Franz, "I regret much that such a question has been raised in the presence of Mademoiselle Valentine; I have never inquired the amount of her fortune, which, however limited it may be, exceeds mine. My family has sought consideration in this alliance with M. de Villefort; all I seek is happiness." Valentine imperceptibly thanked him, while two silent tears rolled down her cheeks. "Besides, sir," said Villefort, addressing himself to his future son-in-law, "excepting the loss of a portion of your hopes, this unexpected will need not personally wound you; M. Noirtier's weakness of mind sufficiently explains it. It is not because Mademoiselle Valentine is going to marry you that he is angry, but because she will marry, a union with any other would have caused him the same sorrow. Old age is selfish, sir, and Mademoiselle de Villefort has been a faithful companion to M. Noirtier, which she cannot be when she becomes the Baroness d'Epinay. My father's melancholy state prevents our speaking to him on any subjects, which the weakness of his mind would incapacitate him from understanding, and I am perfectly convinced that at the present time, although, he knows that his granddaughter is going to be married, M. Noirtier has even forgotten the name of his intended grandson." M. de Villefort had scarcely said this, when the door opened, and Barrois appeared.

"Gentlemen," said he, in a tone strangely firm for a servant speaking to his masters under such solemn circumstances,—"gentlemen, M. Noirtier de Villefort wishes to speak immediately to M. Franz de Quesnel, baron d'Epinay;" he, as well as the notary, that there might be no mistake in the person, gave all his titles to the bride-groom elect.

Villefort started, Madame de Villefort let her son slip from her knees, Valentine rose, pale and dumb as a statue. Albert and Chateau-Renaud exchanged a second look, more full of amazement than the first. The notary looked at Villefort. "It is impossible," said the procureur. "M. d'Epinay cannot leave the drawing-room at present."

"It is at this moment," replied Barrois with the same firmness, "that M. Noirtier, my master, wishes to speak on important subjects to M. Franz d'Epinay."

"Grandpapa Noirtier can speak now, then," said Edward, with his habitual quickness. However, his remark did not make Madame de Villefort even smile, so much was every mind engaged, and so solemn was the situation. Astonishment was at its height. Something like a smile was perceptible on Madame de Villefort's countenance. Valentine instinctively raised her eyes, as if to thank heaven.

"Pray go, Valentine," said; M. de Villefort, "and see what this new fancy of your grandfather's is." Valentine rose quickly, and was hastening joyfully towards the door, when M. de Villefort altered his intention.

"Stop," said he; "I will go with you."

"Excuse me, sir," said Franz, "since M. Noirtier sent for me, I am ready to attend to his wish; besides, I shall be happy to pay my respects to him, not having yet had the honor of doing so."

"Pray, sir," said Villefort with marked uneasiness, "do not disturb yourself."

"Forgive me, sir," said Franz in a resolute tone. "I would not lose this opportunity of proving to M. Noirtier how wrong it would be of him to encourage feelings of dislike to me, which I am determined to conquer, whatever they may be, by my devotion." And without listening to Villefort he arose, and followed Valentine, who was running down-stairs with the joy of a shipwrecked mariner who finds a rock to cling to. M. de Villefort followed them. Chateau-Renaud and Morcerf exchanged a third look of still increasing wonder.

CHAPTER 75.
A SIGNED STATEMENT.

Noirtier was prepared to receive them, dressed in black, and installed in his arm-chair. When the three persons he expected had entered, he looked at the door, which his valet immediately closed.

"Listen," whispered Villefort to Valentine, who could not conceal her joy; "if M. Noirtier wishes to communicate anything which would delay your marriage, I forbid you to understand him." Valentine blushed, but did not answer. Villefort, approaching Noirtier—"Here is M. Franz d'Epinay," said he; "you requested to see him. We have all wished for this interview, and I trust it will convince you how ill-formed are your objections to Valentine's marriage."

Noirtier answered only by a look which made Villefort's blood run cold. He motioned to Valentine to approach. In a moment, thanks to her habit of conversing with her grandfather, she understood that he asked for a key. Then his eye was fixed on the drawer of a small chest between the windows. She opened the drawer, and found a key; and, understanding that was what he wanted, again watched his eyes, which turned toward an old secretary which had been neglected for many years and was supposed to contain nothing but useless documents. "Shall I open the secretary?" asked Valentine.

"Yes," said the old man.

"And the drawers?"

"Yes."

"Those at the side?"

"No."

"The middle one?"

"Yes." Valentine opened it and drew out a bundle of papers. "Is that what you wish for?" asked she.

"No."

She took successively all the other papers out till the drawer was empty. "But there are no more," said she. Noirtier's eye was fixed on the dictionary. "Yes, I understand, grandfather," said the young girl.

He pointed to each letter of the alphabet. At the letter S the old man stopped her. She opened, and found the word "secret."

"Ah, is there a secret spring?" said Valentine.

"Yes," said Noirtier.

"And who knows it?" Noirtier looked at the door where the servant had gone out. "Barrois?" said she.

"Yes."

"Shall I call him?"

"Yes."

Valentine went to the door, and called Barrois. Villefort's impatience during this scene made the perspiration roll from his forehead, and Franz was stupefied. The old servant came. "Barrois," said Valentine, "my grandfather has told me to open that drawer in the secretary, but there is a secret spring in it, which you know—will you open it?"

Barrois looked at the old man. "Obey," said Noirtier's intelligent eye. Barrois touched a spring, the false bottom came out, and they saw a bundle of papers tied with a black string.

"Is that what you wish for?" said Barrois.

"Yes."

"Shall I give these papers to M. de Villefort?"

"No."

"To Mademoiselle Valentine?"

"No."

"To M. Franz d'Epinay?"

"Yes."

Franz, astonished, advanced a step. "To me, sir?" said he.

"Yes." Franz took them from Barrois and casting a glance at the cover, read:—

"'To be given, after my death, to General Durand, who shall bequeath the packet to his son, with an injunction to preserve it as containing an important document.'

"Well, sir," asked Franz, "what do you wish me to do with this paper?"

"To preserve it, sealed up as it is, doubtless," said the procureur.

"No," replied Noirtier eagerly.

"Do you wish him to read it?" said Valentine.

"Yes," replied the old man. "You understand, baron, my grandfather wishes you to read this paper," said Valentine.

"Then let us sit down," said Villefort impatiently, "for it will take some time."

"Sit down," said the old man. Villefort took a chair, but Valentine remained standing by her father's side, and Franz before him, holding the mysterious paper in his hand. "Read," said the old man. Franz untied it, and in the midst of the most profound silence read:

"'Extract from the Report of a meeting of the Bonapartist Club in the Rue Saint-Jacques, held February 5th, 1815.'"

Franz stopped. "February 5th, 1815!" said he; "it is the day my father was murdered." Valentine and Villefort were dumb; the eye of the old man alone seemed to say clearly, "Go on."

"But it was on leaving this club," said he, "my father disappeared." Noirtier's eye continued to say, "Read." He resumed:—

"'The undersigned Louis Jacques Beaurepaire, lieutenant-colonel of artillery, Etienne Duchampy, general of brigade, and Claude Lecharpal, keeper of woods and forests, Declare, that on the 4th of February, a letter arrived from the Island of Elba, recommending to the kindness and the confidence of the Bonapartist Club, General Flavien de Quesnel, who having served the emperor from 1804. to 1814 was supposed to be devoted to the interests of the Napoleon dynasty, notwithstanding the title of baron which Louis XVIII. had just granted to him with his estate of Epinay.

"'A note was in consequence addressed to General de Quesnel, begging him to be present at the meeting next day, the 5th. The note indicated neither the street nor the number of the house where the meeting was to be held; it bore no signature, but it announced to the general that some one would call for him if he would be ready at nine o'clock. The meetings were always held from that time till midnight. At nine o'clock the president of the club presented himself; the general was ready, the president informed him that one of the conditions of his introduction was that he should be eternally ignorant of the place of meeting, and that he would allow his eyes to be bandaged, swearing that he would not endeavor to take off the bandage. General de Quesnel accepted the condition, and promised on his honor not to seek to discover the road they took. The general's carriage was ready, but the president told him it was impossible for him to use it, since it was useless to blindfold the master if the coachman knew through what streets he went. "What must be done then?" asked the general.—"I have my carriage here," said the president.

""""Have you, then, so much confidence in your servant that you can intrust him with a secret you will not allow me to know?"

""""Our coachman is a member of the club," said the president; "we shall be driven by a State-Councillor."

""""Then we run another risk," said the general, laughing, "that of being upset." We insert this joke to prove that the general was not in the least compelled to attend the meeting, but that he came willingly. When they were seated in the carriage the president reminded the general of his promise to allow his eyes to be bandaged, to which he made no opposition. On the road the president thought he saw the general make an attempt to remove the handkerchief, and reminded him of his oath. "Sure enough," said the general. The carriage stopped at an alley leading out of the Rue Saint-Jacques. The general alighted, leaning on the arm of the president, of whose dignity he was not aware, considering him simply as a member of the club; they went through the alley, mounted a flight of stairs, and entered the assembly-room.

"'The deliberations had already begun. The members, apprised of the sort of presentation which was to be made that evening, were all in attendance. When in the middle of the room the general was invited to remove his bandage, he did so immediately, and was surprised to see so many well-known faces in a society of whose existence he had till then been ignorant. They questioned him as to his sentiments, but he contented himself with answering, that the letters from the Island of Elba ought to have informed them'"—

Franz interrupted himself by saying, "My father was a royalist; they need not have asked his sentiments, which were well known."

"And hence," said Villefort, "arose my affection for your father, my dear M. Franz. Opinions held in common are a ready bond of union."

"Read again," said the old man. Franz continued:—

"'The president then sought to make him speak more explicitly, but M. de Quesnel replied that he wished first to know what they wanted with him. He was then informed of the contents of the letter from the Island of Elba, in which he was recommended to the club as a man who would be likely to advance the interests of their party. One paragraph spoke of the return of Bonaparte and promised another letter and further details, on the arrival of the Pharaon belonging to the shipbuilder Morrel, of Marseilles, whose captain was entirely devoted to the emperor. During all this time, the general, on whom they thought to have relied as on a brother, manifested evidently signs of discontent and repugnance. When the reading was finished, he remained silent, with knitted brows.

""''Well," asked the president, "what do you say to this letter, general?"

""''I say that it is too soon after declaring myself for Louis XVIII. to break my vow in behalf of the ex-emperor." This answer was too clear to permit of any mistake as to his sentiments. "General," said the president, "we acknowledge no King Louis XVIII., or an ex-emperor, but his majesty the emperor and king, driven from France, which is his kingdom, by violence and treason."

""''Excuse me, gentlemen," said the general; "you may not acknowledge Louis XVIII., but I do, as he has made me a baron and a field-marshal, and I shall never forget that for these two titles I am indebted to his happy return to France."

""''Sir," said the president, rising with gravity, "be careful what you say; your words clearly show us that they are deceived concerning you in the Island of Elba, and have deceived us! The communication has been made to you in consequence of the confidence placed in you, and which does you honor. Now we discover our error; a title and promotion attach you to the government we wish to overturn. We will not constrain you to help us; we enroll no one against his conscience, but we will compel you to act generously, even if you are not disposed to do so."

""'You would call acting generously, knowing your conspiracy and not informing against you, that is what I should call becoming your accomplice. You see I am more candid than you.""'

"Ah, my father!" said Franz, interrupting himself. "I understand now why they murdered him." Valentine could not help casting one glance towards the young man, whose filial enthusiasm it was delightful to behold. Villefort walked to and fro behind them. Noirtier watched the expression of each one, and preserved his dignified and commanding attitude. Franz returned to the manuscript, and continued:—

""'Sir," said the president, "you have been invited to join this assembly—you were not forced here; it was proposed to you to come blindfolded—you accepted. When you complied with this twofold request you well knew we did not wish to secure the throne of Louis XVIII., or we should not take so much care to avoid the vigilance of the police. It would be conceding too much to allow you to put on a mask to aid you in the discovery of our secret, and then to remove it that you may ruin those who have confided in you. No, no, you must first say if you declare yourself for the king of a day who now reigns, or for his majesty the emperor."

""'I am a royalist," replied the general; "I have taken the oath of allegiance to Louis XVIII., and I will adhere to it." These words were followed by a general murmur, and it was evident that several of the members were discussing the propriety of making the general repent of his rashness.

"'The president again arose, and having imposed silence, said,—"Sir, you are too serious and too sensible a man not to understand the consequences of our present situation, and your candor has already dictated to us the conditions which remain for us to offer you." The general, putting his hand on his sword, exclaimed,—"If you talk of honor, do not begin by disavowing its laws, and impose nothing by violence."

""'And you, sir," continued the president, with a calmness still more terrible than the general's anger, "I advise you not to touch your sword." The general looked around him with slight uneasiness; however he did not yield, but calling up all his fortitude, said,—"I will not swear."

""'Then you must die," replied the president calmly. M. d'Epinay became very pale; he looked round him a second time, several members of the club were whispering, and getting their arms from under their cloaks. "General," said the president, "do not alarm yourself; you are among men of honor who will use every means to convince you before resorting to the last extremity, but as you have said, you are among conspirators, you are in possession of our secret, and you must restore it to us." A significant silence followed these words, and as the general did not reply,—"Close the doors," said the president to the door-keeper.

"'The same deadly silence succeeded these words. Then the general advanced, and making a violent effort to control his feelings,—"I have a son," said he, "and I ought to think of him, finding myself among assassins."

""""General," said the chief of the assembly, "one man may insult fifty—it is the privilege of weakness. But he does wrong to use his privilege. Follow my advice, swear, and do not insult." The general, again daunted by the superiority of the chief, hesitated a moment; then advancing to the president's desk,—"What is the form, said he.

""""It is this:—'I swear by my honor not to reveal to any one what I have seen and heard on the 5th of February, 1815, between nine and ten o'clock in the evening; and I plead guilty of death should I ever violate this oath.'" The general appeared to be affected by a nervous tremor, which prevented his answering for some moments; then, overcoming his manifest repugnance, he pronounced the required oath, but in so low a tone as to be scarcely audible to the majority of the members, who insisted on his repeating it clearly and distinctly, which he did.

""""Now am I at liberty to retire?" said the general. The president rose, appointed three members to accompany him, and got into the carriage with the general after bandaging his eyes. One of those three members was the coachman who had driven them there. The other members silently dispersed. "Where do you wish to be taken?" asked the president.—"Anywhere out of your presence," replied M. d'Epinay. "Beware, sir," replied the president, "you are no longer in the assembly, and have only to do with individuals; do not insult them unless you wish to be held responsible." But instead of listening, M. d'Epinay went on,—"You are still as brave in your carriage as in your assembly because you are still four against one." The president stopped the coach. They were at that part of the Quai des Ormes where the steps lead down to the river. "Why do you stop here?" asked d'Epinay.

""""Because, sir," said the president, "you have insulted a man, and that man will not go one step farther without demanding honorable reparation."

""""Another method of assassination?" said the general, shrugging his shoulders.

""""Make no noise, sir, unless you wish me to consider you as one of the men of whom you spoke just now as cowards, who take their weakness for a shield. You are alone, one alone shall answer you; you have a sword by your side, I have one in my cane; you have no witness, one of these gentlemen will serve you. Now, if you please, remove your bandage." The general tore the handkerchief from his eyes.

"At last," said he, "I shall know with whom I have to do."
They opened the door and the four men alighted.'"

Franz again interrupted himself, and wiped the cold
drops from his brow; there was something awful in hearing
the son read aloud in trembling pallor these details of his
father's death, which had hitherto been a mystery. Valentine
clasped her hands as if in prayer. Noirtier looked at Villefort
with an almost sublime expression of contempt and pride.
Franz continued:—

"'It was, as we said, the fifth of February. For three
days the mercury had been five or six degrees below freezing
and the steps were covered with ice. The general was stout
and tall, the president offered him the side of the railing to
assist him in getting down. The two witnesses followed. It
was a dark night. The ground from the steps to the river
was covered with snow and hoarfrost, the water of the
river looked black and deep. One of the seconds went for a
lantern in a coal-barge near, and by its light they examined
the weapons. The president's sword, which was simply, as he
had said, one he carried in his cane, was five inches shorter
than the general's, and had no guard. The general proposed
to cast lots for the swords, but the president said it was he
who had given the provocation, and when he had given it he
had supposed each would use his own arms. The witnesses
endeavored to insist, but the president bade them be silent.
The lantern was placed on the ground, the two adversaries

took their stations, and the duel began. The light made the two swords appear like flashes of lightning; as for the men, they were scarcely perceptible, the darkness was so great.

"'General d'Epinay passed for one of the best swordsmen in the army, but he was pressed so closely in the onset that he missed his aim and fell. The witnesses thought he was dead, but his adversary, who knew he had not struck him, offered him the assistance of his hand to rise. The circumstance irritated instead of calming the general, and he rushed on his adversary. But his opponent did not allow his guard to be broken. He received him on his sword and three times the general drew back on finding himself too closely engaged, and then returned to the charge. At the third he fell again. They thought he slipped, as at first, and the witnesses, seeing he did not move, approached and endeavored to raise him, but the one who passed his arm around the body found it was moistened with blood. The general, who had almost fainted, revived. "Ah," said he, "they have sent some fencing-master to fight with me." The president, without answering, approached the witness who held the lantern, and raising his sleeve, showed him two wounds he had received in his arm; then opening his coat, and unbuttoning his waistcoat, displayed his side, pierced with a third wound. Still he had not even uttered a sigh. General d'Epinay died five minutes after.'"

Franz read these last words in a voice so choked that they were hardly audible, and then stopped, passing his hand over his eyes as if to dispel a cloud; but after a moment's silence, he continued:—

"'The president went up the steps, after pushing his sword into his cane; a track of blood on the snow marked his course. He had scarcely arrived at the top when he heard a heavy splash in the water—it was the general's body, which the witnesses had just thrown into the river after ascertaining that he was dead. The general fell, then, in a loyal duel, and not in ambush as it might have been reported. In proof of this we have signed this paper to establish the truth of the facts, lest the moment should arrive when either of the actors in this terrible scene should be accused of premeditated murder or of infringement of the laws of honor.

"'Signed, Beaurepaire, Deschamps, and Lecharpal.'"

When Franz had finished reading this account, so dreadful for a son; when Valentine, pale with emotion, had wiped away a tear; when Villefort, trembling, and crouched in a corner, had endeavored to lessen the storm by supplicating glances at the implacable old man,—"Sir," said d'Epinay to Noirtier, "since you are well acquainted with all these details, which are attested by honorable signatures,— since you appear to take some interest in me, although you have only manifested it hitherto by causing me sorrow, refuse me not one final satisfaction—tell me the name of the president of the club, that I may at least know who killed my father." Villefort mechanically felt for the handle of the door; Valentine, who understood sooner than anyone her grandfather's answer, and who had often seen two scars upon his right arm, drew back a few steps. "Mademoiselle," said Franz, turning towards Valentine, "unite your efforts with mine to find out the name of the man who made me an orphan at two years of age." Valentine remained dumb and motionless.

"Hold, sir," said Villefort, "do not prolong this dreadful scene. The names have been purposely concealed; my father himself does not know who this president was, and if he knows, he cannot tell you; proper names are not in the dictionary."

"Oh, misery," cried Franz: "the only hope which sustained me and enabled me to read to the end was that of knowing, at least, the name of him who killed my father! Sir, sir," cried he, turning to Noirtier, "do what you can—make me understand in some way!"

"Yes," replied Noirtier.

"Oh, mademoiselle,—mademoiselle!" cried Franz, "your grandfather says he can indicate the person. Help me,—lend me your assistance!" Noirtier looked at the dictionary. Franz took it with a nervous trembling, and repeated the letters of the alphabet successively, until he came to M. At that letter the old man signified "Yes."

"M," repeated Franz. The young man's finger, glided over the words, but at each one Noirtier answered by a negative sign. Valentine hid her head between her hands. At length, Franz arrived at the word MYSELF.

"Yes!"

"You?" cried Franz, whose hair stood on end; "you, M. Noirtier—you killed my father?"

"Yes!" replied Noirtier, fixing a majestic look on the young man. Franz fell powerless on a chair; Villefort opened the door and escaped, for the idea had entered his mind to stifle the little remaining life in the heart of this terrible old man.

CHAPTER 76.
PROGRESS OF CAVALCANTI
THE YOUNGER.

Meanwhile M. Cavalcanti the elder had returned to his service, not in the army of his majesty the Emperor of Austria, but at the gaming-table of the baths of Lucca, of which he was one of the most assiduous courtiers. He had spent every farthing that had been allowed for his journey as a reward for the majestic and solemn manner in which he had maintained his assumed character of father. M. Andrea at his departure inherited all the papers which proved that he had indeed the honor of being the son of the Marquis Bartolomeo and the Marchioness Oliva Corsinari. He was now fairly launched in that Parisian society which gives such ready access to foreigners, and treats them, not as they really are, but as they wish to be considered. Besides, what is required of a young man in Paris? To speak its language tolerably, to make a good appearance, to be a good gamester, and to pay in cash. They are certainly less particular with a foreigner than with a Frenchman. Andrea had, then, in a fortnight, attained a very fair position. He was called count, he was said to possess 50,000 livres per annum; and his father's immense riches, buried in the quarries of Saravezza, were a constant theme. A learned man, before whom the last circumstance was mentioned as a fact, declared he had seen the quarries in question, which gave great weight to assertions hitherto somewhat doubtful, but which now assumed the garb of reality.

Such was the state of society in Paris at the period we bring before our readers, when Monte Cristo went one evening to pay M. Danglars a visit. M. Danglars was out, but the count was asked to go and see the baroness, and he accepted the invitation. It was never without a nervous shudder, since the dinner at Auteuil, and the events which followed it, that Madame Danglars heard Monte Cristo's name announced. If he did not come, the painful sensation became most intense; if, on the contrary, he appeared, his noble countenance, his brilliant eyes, his amiability, his polite attention even towards Madame Danglars, soon dispelled every impression of fear. It appeared impossible to the baroness that a man of such delightfully pleasing manners should entertain evil designs against her; besides, the most corrupt minds only suspect evil when it would answer some interested end—useless injury is repugnant to every mind. When Monte Cristo entered the boudoir,—to which we have already once introduced our readers, and where the baroness was examining some drawings, which her daughter passed to her after having looked at them with M. Cavalcanti,—his presence soon produced its usual effect, and it was with smiles that the baroness received the count, although she had been a little disconcerted at the announcement of his name. The latter took in the whole scene at a glance.

The baroness was partially reclining on a sofa, Eugenie sat near her, and Cavalcanti was standing. Cavalcanti, dressed in black, like one of Goethe's heroes, with varnished shoes and white silk open-worked stockings, passed a white and tolerably nice-looking hand through his light hair, and so displayed a sparkling diamond, that in spite of Monte Cristo's advice the vain young man had been unable to resist putting on his little finger. This movement was accompanied by killing glances at Mademoiselle Danglars, and by sighs launched in the same direction. Mademoiselle Danglars was still the same—cold, beautiful, and satirical. Not one of these glances, nor one sigh, was lost on her; they might have been said to fall on the shield of Minerva, which some philosophers assert protected sometimes the breast of Sappho. Eugenie bowed coldly to the count, and availed herself of the first moment when the conversation became earnest to escape to her study, whence very soon two cheerful and noisy voices being heard in connection with occasional notes of the piano assured Monte Cristo that Mademoiselle Danglars preferred to his society and to that of M. Cavalcanti the company of Mademoiselle Louise d'Armilly, her singing teacher.

It was then, especially while conversing with Madame Danglars, and apparently absorbed by the charm of the conversation, that the count noticed M. Andrea Cavalcanti's solicitude, his manner of listening to the music at the door he dared not pass, and of manifesting his admiration. The banker soon returned. His first look was certainly directed towards Monte Cristo, but the second was for Andrea. As for his wife, he bowed to her, as some husbands do to their wives, but in a way that bachelors will never comprehend, until a very extensive code is published on conjugal life.

"Have not the ladies invited you to join them at the piano?" said Danglars to Andrea. "Alas, no, sir," replied Andrea with a sigh, still more remarkable than the former ones. Danglars immediately advanced towards the door and opened it.

The two young ladies were seen seated on the same chair, at the piano, accompanying themselves, each with one hand, a fancy to which they had accustomed themselves, and performed admirably. Mademoiselle d'Armilly, whom they then perceived through the open doorway, formed with Eugenie one of the tableaux vivants of which the Germans are so fond. She was somewhat beautiful, and exquisitely formed—a little fairy-like figure, with large curls falling on her neck, which was rather too long, as Perugino sometimes makes his Virgins, and her eyes dull from fatigue. She was said to have a weak chest, and like Antonia in the "Cremona Violin," she would die one day while singing. Monte Cristo cast one rapid and curious glance round this sanctum; it was the first time he had ever seen Mademoiselle d'Armilly, of whom he had heard much. "Well," said the banker to his daughter, "are we then all to be excluded?" He then led the young man into the study, and either by chance or manoeuvre the door was partially closed after Andrea, so that from the place where they sat neither the Count nor the baroness could see anything; but as the banker had accompanied Andrea, Madame Danglars appeared to take no notice of it.

The count soon heard Andrea's voice, singing a Corsican song, accompanied by the piano. While the count smiled at hearing this song, which made him lose sight of Andrea in the recollection of Benedetto, Madame Danglars was boasting to Monte Cristo of her husband's strength of mind, who that very morning had lost three or four hundred thousand francs by a failure at Milan. The praise was well deserved, for had not the count heard it from the baroness, or by one of those means by which he knew everything, the baron's countenance would not have led him to suspect it. "Hem," thought Monte Cristo, "he begins to conceal his losses; a month since he boasted of them." Then aloud,— "Oh, madame, M. Danglars is so skilful, he will soon regain at the Bourse what he loses elsewhere."

"I see that you participate in a prevalent error," said Madame Danglars. "What is it?" said Monte Cristo.

"That M. Danglars speculates, whereas he never does."

"Truly, madame, I recollect M. Debray told me—apropos, what is become of him? I have seen nothing of him the last three or four days."

"Nor I," said Madame Danglars; "but you began a sentence, sir, and did not finish."

"Which?"

"M. Debray had told you"—

"Ah, yes; he told me it was you who sacrificed to the demon of speculation."

"I was once very fond of it, but I do not indulge now."

"Then you are wrong, madame. Fortune is precarious; and if I were a woman and fate had made me a banker's wife, whatever might be my confidence in my husband's good fortune, still in speculation you know there is great risk. Well, I would secure for myself a fortune independent of him, even if I acquired it by placing my interests in hands unknown to him." Madame Danglars blushed, in spite of all her efforts. "Stay," said Monte Cristo, as though he had not observed her confusion, "I have heard of a lucky hit that was made yesterday on the Neapolitan bonds."

"I have none—nor have I ever possessed any; but really we have talked long enough of money, count, we are like two stockbrokers; have you heard how fate is persecuting the poor Villeforts?"

"What has happened?" said the count, simulating total ignorance.

"You know the Marquis of Saint-Meran died a few days after he had set out on his journey to Paris, and the marchioness a few days after her arrival?"

"Yes," said Monte Cristo, "I have heard that; but, as Claudius said to Hamlet, 'it is a law of nature; their fathers died before them, and they mourned their loss; they will die before their children, who will, in their turn, grieve for them.'"

"But that is not all."

"Not all!"

"No; they were going to marry their daughter"—

"To M. Franz d'Epinay. Is it broken off?"

"Yesterday morning, it appears, Franz declined the honor."

"Indeed? And is the reason known?"

"No."

"How extraordinary! And how does M. de Villefort bear it?"

"As usual. Like a philosopher." Danglars returned at this moment alone. "Well," said the baroness, "do you leave M. Cavalcanti with your daughter?"

"And Mademoiselle d'Armilly," said the banker; "do you consider her no one?" Then, turning to Monte Cristo, he said, "Prince Cavalcanti is a charming young man, is he not? But is he really a prince?"

"I will not answer for it," said Monte Cristo. "His father was introduced to me as a marquis, so he ought to be a count; but I do not think he has much claim to that title."

"Why?" said the banker. "If he is a prince, he is wrong not to maintain his rank; I do not like any one to deny his origin."

"Oh, you are a thorough democrat," said Monte Cristo, smiling.

"But do you see to what you are exposing yourself?" said the baroness. "If, perchance, M. de Morcerf came, he would find M. Cavalcanti in that room, where he, the betrothed of Eugenie, has never been admitted."

"You may well say, perchance," replied the banker; "for he comes so seldom, it would seem only chance that brings him."

"But should he come and find that young man with your daughter, he might be displeased."

"He? You are mistaken. M. Albert would not do us the honor to be jealous; he does not like Eugenie sufficiently. Besides, I care not for his displeasure."

"Still, situated as we are"—

"Yes, do you know how we are situated? At his mother's ball he danced once with Eugenie, and M. Cavalcanti three times, and he took no notice of it." The valet announced the Vicomte Albert de Morcerf. The baroness rose hastily, and was going into the study, when Danglars stopped her. "Let her alone," said he. She looked at him in amazement. Monte Cristo appeared to be unconscious of what passed. Albert entered, looking very handsome and in high spirits. He bowed politely to the baroness, familiarly to Danglars, and affectionately to Monte Cristo. Then turning to the baroness: "May I ask how Mademoiselle Danglars is?" said he.

"She is quite well," replied Danglars quickly; "she is at the piano with M. Cavalcanti." Albert retained his calm and indifferent manner; he might feel perhaps annoyed, but he knew Monte Cristo's eye was on him. "M. Cavalcanti has a fine tenor voice," said he, "and Mademoiselle Eugenie a splendid soprano, and then she plays the piano like Thalberg. The concert must be a delightful one."

"They suit each other remarkably well," said Danglars. Albert appeared not to notice this remark, which was, however, so rude that Madame Danglars blushed.

"I, too," said the young man, "am a musician—at least, my masters used to tell me so; but it is strange that my voice never would suit any other, and a soprano less than any." Danglars smiled, and seemed to say, "It is of no consequence." Then, hoping doubtless to effect his purpose, he said,—"The prince and my daughter were universally admired yesterday. You were not of the party, M. de Morcerf?"

"What prince?" asked Albert. "Prince Cavalcanti," said Danglars, who persisted in giving the young man that title.

"Pardon me," said Albert, "I was not aware that he was a prince. And Prince Cavalcanti sang with Mademoiselle Eugenie yesterday? It must have been charming, indeed. I regret not having heard them. But I was unable to accept your invitation, having promised to accompany my mother to a German concert given by the Baroness of Chateau-Renaud." This was followed by rather an awkward silence. "May I also be allowed," said Morcerf, "to pay my respects to Mademoiselle Danglars?" "Wait a moment," said the banker, stopping the young man; "do you hear that delightful cavatina? Ta, ta, ta, ti, ta, ti, ta, ta; it is charming, let them finish—one moment. Bravo, bravi, brava!" The banker was enthusiastic in his applause.

"Indeed," said Albert, "it is exquisite; it is impossible to understand the music of his country better than Prince Cavalcanti does. You said prince, did you not? But he can easily become one, if he is not already; it is no uncommon thing in Italy. But to return to the charming musicians— you should give us a treat, Danglars, without telling them there is a stranger. Ask them to sing one more song; it is so delightful to hear music in the distance, when the musicians are unrestrained by observation."

Danglars was quite annoyed by the young man's indifference. He took Monte Cristo aside. "What do you think of our lover?" said he.

"He appears cool. But, then your word is given."

"Yes, doubtless I have promised to give my daughter to a man who loves her, but not to one who does not. See him there, cold as marble and proud like his father. If he were rich, if he had Cavalcanti's fortune, that might be pardoned. Ma foi, I haven't consulted my daughter; but if she has good taste"—

"Oh," said Monte Cristo, "my fondness may blind me, but I assure you I consider Morcerf a charming young man who will render your daughter happy and will sooner or later attain a certain amount of distinction, and his father's position is good."

"Hem," said Danglars.

"Why do you doubt?"

"The past—that obscurity on the past."

"But that does not affect the son."

"Very true."

"Now, I beg of you, don't go off your head. It's a month now that you have been thinking of this marriage, and you must see that it throws some responsibility on me, for it was at my house you met this young Cavalcanti, whom I do not really know at all."

"But I do."

"Have you made inquiry?"

"Is there any need of that! Does not his appearance speak for him? And he is very rich."

"I am not so sure of that."

"And yet you said he had money."

"Fifty thousand livres—a mere trifle."

"He is well educated."

"Hem," said Monte Cristo in his turn.

"He is a musician."

"So are all Italians."

"Come, count, you do not do that young man justice."

"Well, I acknowledge it annoys me, knowing your connection with the Morcerf family, to see him throw himself in the way." Danglars burst out laughing. "What a Puritan you are!" said he; "that happens every day."

"But you cannot break it off in this way; the Morcerfs are depending on this union."

"Indeed."

"Positively."

"Then let them explain themselves; you should give the father a hint, you are so intimate with the family."

"I?—where the devil did you find out that?"

"At their ball; it was apparent enough. Why, did not the countess, the proud Mercedes, the disdainful Catalane, who will scarcely open her lips to her oldest acquaintances, take your arm, lead you into the garden, into the private walks, and remain there for half an hour?"

"Ah, baron, baron," said Albert, "you are not listening— what barbarism in a megalomaniac like you!"

"Oh, don't worry about me, Sir Mocker," said Danglars; then turning to the count he said, "but will you undertake to speak to the father?"

"Willingly, if you wish it."

"But let it be done explicitly and positively. If he demands my daughter let him fix the day—declare his conditions; in short, let us either understand each other, or quarrel. You understand—no more delay."

"Yes, sir, I will give my attention to the subject."

"I do not say that I await with pleasure his decision, but I do await it. A banker must, you know, be a slave to his promise." And Danglars sighed as M. Cavalcanti had done half an hour before. "Bravi, bravo, brava!" cried Morcerf, parodying the banker, as the selection came to an end. Danglars began to look suspiciously at Morcerf, when some one came and whispered a few words to him. "I shall soon return," said the banker to Monte Cristo; "wait for me. I shall, perhaps, have something to say to you." And he went out.

The baroness took advantage of her husband's absence to push open the door of her daughter's study, and M. Andrea, who was sitting before the piano with Mademoiselle Eugenie, started up like a jack-in-the-box. Albert bowed with a smile to Mademoiselle Danglars, who did not appear in the least disturbed, and returned his bow with her usual coolness. Cavalcanti was evidently embarrassed; he bowed to Morcerf, who replied with the most impertinent look possible. Then Albert launched out in praise of Mademoiselle Danglars' voice, and on his regret, after what he had just heard, that he had been unable to be present the previous evening. Cavalcanti, being left alone, turned to Monte Cristo.

"Come," said Madame Danglars, "leave music and compliments, and let us go and take tea."

"Come, Louise," said Mademoiselle Danglars to her friend. They passed into the next drawing-room, where tea was prepared. Just as they were beginning, in the English fashion, to leave the spoons in their cups, the door again opened and Danglars entered, visibly agitated. Monte Cristo observed it particularly, and by a look asked the banker for an explanation. "I have just received my courier from Greece," said Danglars.

"Ah, yes," said the count; "that was the reason of your running away from us."

"Yes."

"How is King Otho getting on?" asked Albert in the most sprightly tone. Danglars cast another suspicious look towards him without answering, and Monte Cristo turned away to conceal the expression of pity which passed over his features, but which was gone in a moment. "We shall go together, shall we not?" said Albert to the count.

"If you like," replied the latter. Albert could not understand the banker's look, and turning to Monte Cristo, who understood it perfectly,—"Did you see," said he, "how he looked at me?"

"Yes," said the count; "but did you think there was anything particular in his look?"

"Indeed, I did; and what does he mean by his news from Greece?"

"How can I tell you?"

"Because I imagine you have correspondents in that country." Monte Cristo smiled significantly.

"Stop," said Albert, "here he comes. I shall compliment Mademoiselle Danglars on her cameo, while the father talks to you."

"If you compliment her at all, let it be on her voice, at least," said Monte Cristo.

"No, every one would do that."

"My dear viscount, you are dreadfully impertinent." Albert advanced towards Eugenie, smiling. Meanwhile, Danglars, stooping to Monte Cristo's ear, "Your advice was excellent," said he; "there is a whole history connected with the names Fernand and Yanina."

"Indeed?" said Monte Cristo.

"Yes, I will tell you all; but take away the young man; I cannot endure his presence."

"He is going with me. Shall I send the father to you?"

"Immediately."

"Very well." The count made a sign to Albert and they bowed to the ladies, and took their leave, Albert perfectly indifferent to Mademoiselle Danglars' contempt, Monte Cristo reiterating his advice to Madame Danglars on the prudence a banker's wife should exercise in providing for the future. M. Cavalcanti remained master of the field.

CHAPTER 77.
HAIDEE.

Scarcely had the count's horses cleared the angle of the boulevard, than Albert, turning towards the count, burst into a loud fit of laughter—much too loud in fact not to give the idea of its being rather forced and unnatural. "Well," said he, "I will ask you the same question which Charles IX. put to Catherine de Medicis, after the massacre of Saint Bartholomew, 'How have I played my little part?'"

"To what do you allude?" asked Monte Cristo.

"To the installation of my rival at M. Danglars'."

"What rival?"

"Ma foi, what rival? Why, your protege, M. Andrea Cavalcanti!"

"Ah, no joking, viscount, if you please; I do not patronize M. Andrea—at least, not as concerns M. Danglars."

"And you would be to blame for not assisting him, if the young man really needed your help in that quarter, but, happily for me, he can dispense with it."

"What, do you think he is paying his addresses?"

"I am certain of it; his languishing looks and modulated tones when addressing Mademoiselle Danglars fully proclaim his intentions. He aspires to the hand of the proud Eugenie."

"What does that signify, so long as they favor your suit?"

"But it is not the case, my dear count: on the contrary. I am repulsed on all sides."

"What!"

"It is so indeed; Mademoiselle Eugenie scarcely answers me, and Mademoiselle d'Armilly, her confidant, does not speak to me at all."

"But the father has the greatest regard possible for you," said Monte Cristo.

"He? Oh, no, he has plunged a thousand daggers into my heart, tragedy-weapons, I own, which instead of wounding sheathe their points in their own handles, but daggers which he nevertheless believed to be real and deadly."

"Jealousy indicates affection."

"True; but I am not jealous."

"He is."

"Of whom?—of Debray?"

"No, of you."

"Of me? I will engage to say that before a week is past the door will be closed against me."

"You are mistaken, my dear viscount."

"Prove it to me."

"Do you wish me to do so?"

"Yes."

"Well, I am charged with the commission of endeavoring to induce the Comte de Morcerf to make some definite arrangement with the baron."

"By whom are you charged?"

"By the baron himself."

"Oh," said Albert with all the cajolery of which he was capable. "You surely will not do that, my dear count?"

"Certainly I shall, Albert, as I have promised to do it."

"Well," said Albert, with a sigh, "it seems you are determined to marry me."

"I am determined to try and be on good terms with everybody, at all events," said Monte Cristo. "But apropos of Debray, how is it that I have not seen him lately at the baron's house?"

"There has been a misunderstanding."

"What, with the baroness?"

"No, with the baron."

"Has he perceived anything?"

"Ah, that is a good joke!"

"Do you think he suspects?" said Monte Cristo with charming artlessness.

"Where have you come from, my dear count?" said Albert.

"From Congo, if you will."

"It must be farther off than even that."

"But what do I know of your Parisian husbands?"

"Oh, my dear count, husbands are pretty much the same everywhere; an individual husband of any country is a pretty fair specimen of the whole race."

"But then, what can have led to the quarrel between Danglars and Debray? They seemed to understand each other so well," said Monte Cristo with renewed energy.

"Ah, now you are trying to penetrate into the mysteries of Isis, in which I am not initiated. When M. Andrea Cavalcanti has become one of the family, you can ask him that question." The carriage stopped. "Here we are," said Monte Cristo; "it is only half-past ten o'clock, come in."

"Certainly I will."

"My carriage shall take you back."

"No, thank you; I gave orders for my coupe to follow me."

"There it is, then," said Monte Cristo, as he stepped out of the carriage. They both went into the house; the drawing-room was lighted up—they went in there. "You will make tea for us, Baptistin," said the count. Baptistin left the room without waiting to answer, and in two seconds reappeared, bringing on a waiter all that his master had ordered, ready prepared, and appearing to have sprung from the ground, like the repasts which we read of in fairy tales. "Really, my dear count," said Morcerf, "what I admire in you is, not so much your riches, for perhaps there are people even wealthier than yourself, nor is it only your wit, for Beaumarchais might have possessed as much,—but it is your manner of being served, without any questions, in a moment, in a second; it is as if they guessed what you wanted by your manner of ringing, and made a point of keeping everything you can possibly desire in constant readiness."

"What you say is perhaps true; they know my habits. For instance, you shall see; how do you wish to occupy yourself during tea-time?"

"Ma foi, I should like to smoke."

Monte Cristo took the gong and struck it once. In about the space of a second a private door opened, and Ali appeared, bringing two chibouques filled with excellent latakia. "It is quite wonderful," said Albert.

"Oh no, it is as simple as possible," replied Monte Cristo. "Ali knows I generally smoke while I am taking my tea or coffee; he has heard that I ordered tea, and he also knows that I brought you home with me; when I summoned him he naturally guessed the reason of my doing so, and as he comes from a country where hospitality is especially manifested through the medium of smoking, he naturally concludes that we shall smoke in company, and therefore brings two chibouques instead of one—and now the mystery is solved."

"Certainly you give a most commonplace air to your explanation, but it is not the less true that you—Ah, but what do I hear?" and Morcerf inclined his head towards the door, through which sounds seemed to issue resembling those of a guitar.

"Ma foi, my dear viscount, you are fated to hear music this evening; you have only escaped from Mademoiselle Danglars' piano, to be attacked by Haidee's guzla."

"Haidee—what an adorable name! Are there, then, really women who bear the name of Haidee anywhere but in Byron's poems?"

"Certainly there are. Haidee is a very uncommon name in France, but is common enough in Albania and Epirus; it is as if you said, for example, Chastity, Modesty, Innocence,— it is a kind of baptismal name, as you Parisians call it."

"Oh, that is charming," said Albert, "how I should like to hear my countrywomen called Mademoiselle Goodness, Mademoiselle Silence, Mademoiselle Christian Charity! Only think, then, if Mademoiselle Danglars, instead of being called Claire-Marie-Eugenie, had been named Mademoiselle Chastity-Modesty-Innocence Danglars; what a fine effect that would have produced on the announcement of her marriage!"

"Hush," said the count, "do not joke in so loud a tone; Haidee may hear you, perhaps."

"And you think she would be angry?"

"No, certainly not," said the count with a haughty expression.

"She is very amiable, then, is she not?" said Albert.

"It is not to be called amiability, it is her duty; a slave does not dictate to a master."

"Come; you are joking yourself now. Are there any more slaves to be had who bear this beautiful name?"

"Undoubtedly."

"Really, count, you do nothing, and have nothing like other people. The slave of the Count of Monte Cristo! Why, it is a rank of itself in France, and from the way in which you lavish money, it is a place that must be worth a hundred thousand francs a year."

"A hundred thousand francs! The poor girl originally possessed much more than that; she was born to treasures in comparison with which those recorded in the 'Thousand and One Nights' would seem but poverty."

"She must be a princess then."

"You are right; and she is one of the greatest in her country too."

"I thought so. But how did it happen that such a great princess became a slave?"

"How was it that Dionysius the Tyrant became a schoolmaster? The fortune of war, my dear viscount,—the caprice of fortune; that is the way in which these things are to be accounted for."

"And is her name a secret?"

"As regards the generality of mankind it is; but not for you, my dear viscount, who are one of my most intimate friends, and on whose silence I feel I may rely, if I consider it necessary to enjoin it—may I not do so?"

"Certainly; on my word of honor."

"You know the history of the Pasha of Yanina, do you not?"

"Of Ali Tepelini? [*] Oh, yes; it was in his service that my father made his fortune."

"True, I had forgotten that."

* Ali Pasha, "The Lion," was born at Tepelini, an Albanian village at the foot of the Klissoura Mountains, in 1741. By diplomacy and success in arms he became almost supreme ruler of Albania, Epirus, and adjacent territory. Having aroused the enmity of the Sultan, he was proscribed and put to death by treachery in 1822, at the age of eighty.— Ed.

"Well, what is Haidee to Ali Tepelini?"

"Merely his daughter."

"What? the daughter of Ali Pasha?"

"Of Ali Pasha and the beautiful Vasiliki."

"And your slave?"

"Ma foi, yes."

"But how did she become so?"

"Why, simply from the circumstance of my having bought her one day, as I was passing through the market at Constantinople."

"Wonderful! Really, my dear count, you seem to throw a sort of magic influence over all in which you are concerned; when I listen to you, existence no longer seems reality, but a waking dream. Now, I am perhaps going to make an imprudent and thoughtless request, but"—

"Say on."

"But, since you go out with Haidee, and sometimes even take her to the opera"—

"Well?"

"I think I may venture to ask you this favor."

"You may venture to ask me anything."

"Well then, my dear count, present me to your princess."

"I will do so; but on two conditions."

"I accept them at once."

"The first is, that you will never tell any one that I have granted the interview."

"Very well," said Albert, extending his hand; "I swear I will not."

"The second is, that you will not tell her that your father ever served hers."

"I give you my oath that I will not."

"Enough, viscount; you will remember those two vows, will you not? But I know you to be a man of honor." The count again struck the gong. Ali reappeared. "Tell Haidee," said he, "that I will take coffee with her, and give her to understand that I desire permission to present one of my friends to her." Ali bowed and left the room. "Now, understand me," said the count, "no direct questions, my dear Morcerf; if you wish to know anything, tell me, and I will ask her."

"Agreed." Ali reappeared for the third time, and drew back the tapestried hanging which concealed the door, to signify to his master and Albert that they were at liberty to pass on. "Let us go in," said Monte Cristo.

Albert passed his hand through his hair, and curled his mustache, then, having satisfied himself as to his personal appearance, followed the count into the room, the latter having previously resumed his hat and gloves. Ali was stationed as a kind of advanced guard, and the door was kept by the three French attendants, commanded by Myrtho. Haidee was awaiting her visitors in the first room of her apartments, which was the drawing-room. Her large eyes were dilated with surprise and expectation, for it was the first time that any man, except Monte Cristo, had been accorded an entrance into her presence. She was sitting on a sofa placed in an angle of the room, with her legs crossed under her in the Eastern fashion, and seemed to have made for herself, as it were, a kind of nest in the rich Indian silks which enveloped her. Near her was the instrument on which she had just been playing; it was elegantly fashioned, and worthy of its mistress. On perceiving Monte Cristo, she arose and welcomed him with a smile peculiar to herself, expressive at once of the most implicit obedience and also of the deepest love. Monte Cristo advanced towards her and extended his hand, which she as usual raised to her lips.

Albert had proceeded no farther than the door, where he remained rooted to the spot, being completely fascinated by the sight of such surpassing beauty, beheld as it was for the first time, and of which an inhabitant of more northern climes could form no adequate idea.

"Whom do you bring?" asked the young girl in Romaic, of Monte Cristo; "is it a friend, a brother, a simple acquaintance, or an enemy."

"A friend," said Monte Cristo in the same language.

"What is his name?"

"Count Albert; it is the same man whom I rescued from the hands of the banditti at Rome."

"In what language would you like me to converse with him?"

Monte Cristo turned to Albert. "Do you know modern Greek," asked he.

"Alas, no," said Albert; "nor even ancient Greek, my dear count; never had Homer or Plato a more unworthy scholar than myself."

"Then," said Haidee, proving by her remark that she had quite understood Monte Cristo's question and Albert's answer, "then I will speak either in French or Italian, if my lord so wills it."

Monte Cristo reflected one instant. "You will speak in Italian," said he. Then, turning towards Albert,—"It is a pity you do not understand either ancient or modern Greek, both of which Haidee speaks so fluently; the poor child will be obliged to talk to you in Italian, which will give you but a very false idea of her powers of conversation." The count made a sign to Haidee to address his visitor. "Sir," she said to Morcerf, "you are most welcome as the friend of my lord and master." This was said in excellent Tuscan, and with that soft Roman accent which makes the language of Dante as sonorous as that of Homer. Then, turning to Ali, she directed him to bring coffee and pipes, and when he had left the room to execute the orders of his young mistress she beckoned Albert to approach nearer to her. Monte Cristo and Morcerf drew their seats towards a small table, on which were arranged music, drawings, and vases of flowers. Ali then entered bringing coffee and chibouques; as to M. Baptistin, this portion of the building was interdicted to him. Albert refused the pipe which the Nubian offered him. "Oh, take it—take it," said the count; "Haidee is almost as civilized as a Parisian; the smell of an Havana is disagreeable to her, but the tobacco of the East is a most delicious perfume, you know."

Ali left the room. The cups of coffee were all prepared, with the addition of sugar, which had been brought for Albert. Monte Cristo and Haidee took the beverage in the original Arabian manner, that is to say, without sugar. Haidee took the porcelain cup in her little slender fingers and conveyed it to her mouth with all the innocent artlessness of a child when eating or drinking something which it likes. At this moment two women entered, bringing salvers filled with ices and sherbet, which they placed on two small tables appropriated to that purpose. "My dear host, and you, signora," said Albert, in Italian, "excuse my apparent stupidity. I am quite bewildered, and it is natural that it should be so. Here I am in the heart of Paris; but a moment ago I heard the rumbling of the omnibuses and the tinkling of the bells of the lemonade-sellers, and now I feel as if I were suddenly transported to the East; not such as I have seen it, but such as my dreams have painted it. Oh, signora, if I could but speak Greek, your conversation, added to the fairy-scene which surrounds me, would furnish an evening of such delight as it would be impossible for me ever to forget."

"I speak sufficient Italian to enable me to converse with you, sir," said Haidee quietly; "and if you like what is Eastern, I will do my best to secure the gratification of your tastes while you are here."

"On what subject shall I converse with her?" said Albert, in a low tone to Monte Cristo.

"Just what you please; you may speak of her country and of her youthful reminiscences, or if you like it better you can talk of Rome, Naples, or Florence."

"Oh," said Albert, "it is of no use to be in the company of a Greek if one converses just in the same style as with a Parisian; let me speak to her of the East."

"Do so then, for of all themes which you could choose that will be the most agreeable to her taste." Albert turned towards Haidee. "At what age did you leave Greece, signora?" asked he.

"I left it when I was but five years old," replied Haidee.

"And have you any recollection of your country?"

"When I shut my eyes and think, I seem to see it all again. The mind can see as well as the body. The body forgets sometimes—but the mind never forgets."

"And how far back into the past do your recollections extend?"

"I could scarcely walk when my mother, who was called Vasiliki, which means royal," said the young girl, tossing her head proudly, "took me by the hand, and after putting in our purse all the money we possessed, we went out, both covered with veils, to solicit alms for the prisoners, saying, 'He who giveth to the poor lendeth to the Lord.' Then when our purse was full we returned to the palace, and without saying a word to my father, we sent it to the convent, where it was divided amongst the prisoners."

"And how old were you at that time?"

"I was three years old," said Haidee.

"Then you remember everything that went on about you from the time when you were three years old?" said Albert.

"Everything."

"Count," said Albert, in a low tone to Monte Cristo, "do allow the signora to tell me something of her history. You prohibited my mentioning my father's name to her, but perhaps she will allude to him of her own accord in the course of the recital, and you have no idea how delighted I should be to hear our name pronounced by such beautiful lips." Monte Cristo turned to Haidee, and with an expression of countenance which commanded her to pay the most implicit attention to his words, he said in Greek,—"Tell us the fate of your father; but neither the name of the traitor nor the treason." Haidee sighed deeply, and a shade of sadness clouded her beautiful brow.

"What are you saying to her?" said Morcerf in an undertone.

"I again reminded her that you were a friend, and that she need not conceal anything from you."

"Then," said Albert, "this pious pilgrimage in behalf of the prisoners was your first remembrance; what is the next?"

"Oh, then I remember as if it were but yesterday sitting under the shade of some sycamore-trees, on the borders of a lake, in the waters of which the trembling foliage was reflected as in a mirror. Under the oldest and thickest of these trees, reclining on cushions, sat my father; my mother was at his feet, and I, childlike, amused myself by playing with his long white beard which descended to his girdle, or with the diamond-hilt of the scimitar attached to his girdle. Then from time to time there came to him an Albanian who said something to which I paid no attention, but which he always answered in the same tone of voice, either 'Kill,' or 'Pardon.'"

"It is very strange," said Albert, "to hear such words proceed from the mouth of any one but an actress on the stage, and one needs constantly to be saying to one's self, 'This is no fiction, it is all reality,' in order to believe it. And how does France appear in your eyes, accustomed as they have been to gaze on such enchanted scenes?"

"I think it is a fine country," said Haidee, "but I see France as it really is, because I look on it with the eyes of a woman; whereas my own country, which I can only judge of from the impression produced on my childish mind, always seems enveloped in a vague atmosphere, which is luminous

65

or otherwise, according as my remembrances of it are sad or joyous."

"So young," said Albert, forgetting at the moment the Count's command that he should ask no questions of the slave herself, "is it possible that you can have known what suffering is except by name?"

Haidee turned her eyes towards Monte Cristo, who, making at the same time some imperceptible sign, murmured,—"Go on."

"Nothing is ever so firmly impressed on the mind as the memory of our early childhood, and with the exception of the two scenes I have just described to you, all my earliest reminiscences are fraught with deepest sadness."

"Speak, speak, signora," said Albert, "I am listening with the most intense delight and interest to all you say."

Haidee answered his remark with a melancholy smile. "You wish me, then, to relate the history of my past sorrows?" said she.

"I beg you to do so," replied Albert.

"Well, I was but four years old when one night I was suddenly awakened by my mother. We were in the palace of Yanina; she snatched me from the cushions on which I was sleeping, and on opening my eyes I saw hers filled with tears. She took me away without speaking. When I saw her weeping I began to cry too. 'Hush, child!' said she. At other times in spite of maternal endearments or threats, I had with a child's caprice been accustomed to indulge my feelings of sorrow or anger by crying as much as I felt inclined; but on this occasion there was an intonation of such extreme terror in my mother's voice when she enjoined me to silence, that I ceased crying as soon as her command was given. She bore me rapidly away.

"I saw then that we were descending a large staircase; around us were all my mother's servants carrying trunks, bags, ornaments, jewels, purses of gold, with which they were hurrying away in the greatest distraction.

"Behind the women came a guard of twenty men armed with long guns and pistols, and dressed in the costume which the Greeks have assumed since they have again become a nation. You may imagine there was something startling and ominous," said Haidee, shaking her head and turning pale at the mere remembrance of the scene, "in this long file of slaves and women only half-aroused from sleep, or at least so they appeared to me, who was myself scarcely awake. Here and there on the walls of the staircase, were reflected gigantic shadows, which trembled in the flickering light of the pine-torches till they seemed to reach to the vaulted roof above.

"'Quick!' said a voice at the end of the gallery. This voice made every one bow before it, resembling in its effect the wind passing over a field of wheat, by its superior strength forcing every ear to yield obeisance. As for me, it made me tremble. This voice was that of my father. He came last, clothed in his splendid robes and holding in his hand the carbine which your emperor presented him. He was leaning on the shoulder of his favorite Selim, and he drove us all before him, as a shepherd would his straggling flock. My father," said Haidee, raising her head, "was that illustrious man known in Europe under the name of Ali Tepelini, pasha of Yanina, and before whom Turkey trembled."

Albert, without knowing why, started on hearing these words pronounced with such a haughty and dignified accent; it appeared to him as if there was something supernaturally gloomy and terrible in the expression which gleamed from the brilliant eyes of Haidee at this moment; she appeared like a Pythoness evoking a spectre, as she recalled to his mind the remembrance of the fearful death of this man, to the news of which all Europe had listened with horror. "Soon," said Haidee, "we halted on our march, and found ourselves on the borders of a lake. My mother pressed me to her throbbing heart, and at the distance of a few paces I saw my father, who was glancing anxiously around. Four marble steps led down to the water's edge, and below them was a boat floating on the tide.

"From where we stood I could see in the middle of the lake a large blank mass; it was the kiosk to which we were going. This kiosk appeared to me to be at a considerable distance, perhaps on account of the darkness of the night, which prevented any object from being more than partially discerned. We stepped into the boat. I remember well that the oars made no noise whatever in striking the water, and when I leaned over to ascertain the cause I saw that they were muffled with the sashes of our Palikares. [*] Besides the rowers, the boat contained only the women, my father, mother, Selim, and myself. The Palikares had remained on the shore of the lake, ready to cover our retreat; they were kneeling on the lowest of the marble steps, and in that manner intended making a rampart of the three others, in case of pursuit. Our bark flew before the wind. 'Why does the boat go so fast?' asked I of my mother.

* Greek militiamen in the war for independence.—Ed.

"'Silence, child! Hush, we are flying!' I did not understand. Why should my father fly?—he, the all-powerful—he, before whom others were accustomed to fly—he, who had taken for his device, 'They hate me; then they fear me!' It was, indeed, a flight which my father was trying to effect. I have been told since that the garrison of the castle of Yanina, fatigued with long service"—

Here Haidee cast a significant glance at Monte Cristo, whose eyes had been riveted on her countenance during the whole course of her narrative. The young girl then continued, speaking slowly, like a person who is either inventing or suppressing some feature of the history which he is relating.

"You were saying, signora," said Albert, who was paying the most implicit attention to the recital, "that the garrison of Yanina, fatigued with long service"—

"Had treated with the Serasker [*] Koorshid, who had been sent by the sultan to gain possession of the person of my father; it was then that Ali Tepelini—after having sent to the sultan a French officer in whom he reposed great confidence—resolved to retire to the asylum which he had long before prepared for himself, and which he called kataphygion, or the refuge."

"And this officer," asked Albert, "do you remember his name, signora?" Monte Cristo exchanged a rapid glance with the young girl, which was quite unperceived by Albert. "No," said she, "I do not remember it just at this moment; but if it should occur to me presently, I will tell you." Albert was on the point of pronouncing his father's name, when Monte Cristo gently held up his finger in token of reproach; the young man recollected his promise, and was silent.

* A Turkish pasha in command of the troops of a province.—

Ed.

"It was towards this kiosk that we were rowing. A ground-floor, ornamented with arabesques, bathing its terraces in the water, and another floor, looking on the lake, was all which was visible to the eye. But beneath the ground-floor, stretching out into the island, was a large subterranean cavern, to which my mother, myself, and the women were conducted. In this place were together 60,000. pouches and 200 barrels; the pouches contained 25,000,000 of money in gold, and the barrels were filled with 30,000. pounds of gunpowder.

"Near the barrels stood Selim, my father's favorite, whom I mentioned to you just now. He stood watch day and night with a lance provided with a lighted slowmatch in his hand, and he had orders to blow up everything—kiosk, guards, women, gold, and Ali Tepelini himself—at the first signal given by my father. I remember well that the slaves, convinced of the precarious tenure on which they held their lives, passed whole days and nights in praying, crying, and groaning. As for me, I can never forget the pale complexion and black eyes of the young soldier, and whenever the angel of death summons me to another world, I am quite sure I shall recognize Selim. I cannot tell you how long we remained in this state; at that period I did not even know what time meant. Sometimes, but very rarely, my father summoned me and my mother to the terrace of the palace; these were hours of recreation for me, as I never saw anything in the dismal cavern but the gloomy countenances of the slaves and Selim's fiery lance. My father was endeavoring to pierce with his eager looks the remotest verge of the horizon, examining attentively every black speck which appeared on the lake, while my mother, reclining by his side, rested her head on his shoulder, and I played at his feet, admiring everything I saw with that unsophisticated innocence of childhood which throws a charm round objects insignificant in themselves, but which in its eyes are invested with the greatest importance. The heights of Pindus towered above us; the castle of Yanina rose white and angular from the blue waters of the lake, and the immense masses of black vegetation which, viewed in the distance, gave the idea of lichens clinging to the rocks, were in reality gigantic fir-trees and myrtles.

"One morning my father sent for us; my mother had been crying all the night, and was very wretched; we found the pasha calm, but paler than usual. 'Take courage, Vasiliki,' said he; 'to-day arrives the firman of the master, and my fate will be decided. If my pardon be complete, we shall return triumphant to Yanina; if the news be inauspicious, we must fly this night.'—'But supposing our enemy should not allow us to do so?' said my mother. 'Oh, make yourself easy on that head,' said Ali, smiling; 'Selim and his flaming lance will settle that matter. They would be glad to see me dead, but they would not like themselves to die with me.'

"My mother only answered by sighs to consolations which she knew did not come from my father's heart. She prepared the iced water which he was in the habit of constantly drinking,—for since his sojourn at the kiosk he had been parched by the most violent fever,—after which she anointed his white beard with perfumed oil, and lighted his chibouque, which he sometimes smoked for hours together, quietly watching the wreaths of vapor that ascended in spiral clouds and gradually melted away in the surrounding atmosphere. Presently he made such a sudden movement that I was paralyzed with fear. Then, without taking his eyes from the object which had first attracted his attention, he asked for his telescope. My mother gave it him, and as she did so, looked whiter than the marble against which she leaned. I saw my father's hand tremble. 'A boat!— two!—three!' murmured my, father;—'four!' He then arose, seizing his arms and priming his pistols. 'Vasiliki,' said he to my mother, trembling perceptibly, 'the instant approaches which will decide everything. In the space of half an hour we shall know the emperor's answer. Go into the cavern with Haidee.'—'I will not quit you,' said Vasiliki; 'if you die, my lord, I will die with you.'—'Go to Selim!' cried my father. 'Adieu, my lord,' murmured my mother, determining quietly to await the approach of death. 'Take away Vasiliki!' said my father to his Palikares.

"As for me, I had been forgotten in the general confusion; I ran toward Ali Tepelini; he saw me hold out my arms to him, and he stooped down and pressed my forehead with his lips. Oh, how distinctly I remember that kiss!—it was the last he ever gave me, and I feel as if it were still warm on my forehead. On descending, we saw through the lattice-work several boats which were gradually becoming more distinct to our view. At first they appeared like black specks, and now they looked like birds skimming the surface of the waves. During this time, in the kiosk at my father's feet, were seated twenty Palikares, concealed from view by an angle of the wall and watching with eager eyes the arrival of the boats. They were armed with their long guns inlaid with mother-of-pearl and silver, and cartridges in great numbers were lying scattered on the floor. My father looked at his watch, and paced up and down with a countenance expressive of the greatest anguish. This was the scene which presented itself to my view as I quitted my father after that last kiss. My mother and I traversed the gloomy passage leading to the cavern. Selim was still at his post, and smiled sadly on us as we entered. We fetched our cushions from the other end of the cavern, and sat down by Selim. In great dangers the devoted ones cling to each other; and, young as I was, I quite understood that some imminent danger was hanging over our heads."

Albert had often heard—not from his father, for he never spoke on the subject, but from strangers—the description of the last moments of the vizier of Yanina; he had read different accounts of his death, but the story seemed to acquire fresh meaning from the voice and expression of the young girl, and her sympathetic accent and the melancholy expression of her countenance at once charmed and horrified him. As to Haidee, these terrible reminiscences seemed to have overpowered her for a moment, for she ceased speaking, her head leaning on her hand like a beautiful flower bowing beneath the violence of the storm; and her eyes gazing on vacancy indicated that she was mentally contemplating the green summit of the Pindus and the blue waters of the lake of Yanina, which, like a magic mirror, seemed to reflect the sombre picture which she sketched. Monte Cristo looked at her with an indescribable expression of interest and pity.

"Go on," said the count in the Romaic language.

Haidee looked up abruptly, as if the sonorous tones of Monte Cristo's voice had awakened her from a dream; and she resumed her narrative. "It was about four o'clock in the afternoon, and although the day was brilliant out-of-doors, we were enveloped in the gloomy darkness of the cavern. One single, solitary light was burning there, and it appeared like a star set in a heaven of blackness; it was Selim's flaming lance. My mother was a Christian, and she prayed. Selim repeated from time to time the sacred words: 'God is great!' However, my mother had still some hope. As she was coming down, she thought she recognized the French officer who had been sent to Constantinople, and in whom my father placed so much confidence; for he knew that all the soldiers of the French emperor were naturally noble and generous. She advanced some steps towards the staircase, and listened. 'They are approaching,' said she; 'perhaps they bring us peace and liberty!'—'What do you fear, Vasiliki?' said Selim, in a voice at once so gentle and yet so proud. 'If they do not bring us peace, we will give them war; if they do not bring life, we will give them death.' And he renewed the flame of his lance with a gesture which made one think of Dionysus of Crete. [*] But I, being only a little child, was terrified by this undaunted courage, which appeared to me both ferocious and senseless, and I recoiled with horror from the idea of the frightful death amidst fire and flames which probably awaited us.

* The god of fruitfulness in Grecian mythology. In Crete he was supposed to be slain in winter with the decay of vegetation and to revive in the spring. Haidee's learned reference is to the behavior of an actor in the Dionysian festivals.—Ed.

"My mother experienced the same sensations, for I felt her tremble. 'Mamma, mamma,' said I, 'are we really to be killed?' And at the sound of my voice the slaves redoubled their cries and prayers and lamentations. 'My child,' said Vasiliki, 'may God preserve you from ever wishing for that death which to-day you so much dread!' Then, whispering to Selim, she asked what were her master's orders. 'If he send me his poniard, it will signify that the emperor's intentions are not favorable, and I am to set fire to the powder; if, on the contrary, he send me his ring, it will be a sign that the emperor pardons him, and I am to extinguish the match and leave the magazine untouched.'—'My friend,' said my mother, 'when your master's orders arrive, if it is the poniard which he sends, instead of despatching us by that horrible death which we both so much dread, you will mercifully kill us with this same poniard, will you not?'—'Yes, Vasiliki,' replied Selim tranquilly.

"Suddenly we heard loud cries; and, listening, discerned that they were cries of joy. The name of the French officer who had been sent to Constantinople resounded on all sides amongst our Palikares; it was evident that he brought the answer of the emperor, and that it was favorable."

"And do you not remember the Frenchman's name?" said Morcerf, quite ready to aid the memory of the narrator. Monte Cristo made a sign to him to be silent.

"I do not recollect it," said Haidee.

"The noise increased; steps were heard approaching nearer and nearer: they were descending the steps leading to the cavern. Selim made ready his lance. Soon a figure appeared in the gray twilight at the entrance of the cave, formed by the reflection of the few rays of daylight which had found their way into this gloomy retreat. 'Who are you?' cried Selim. 'But whoever you may be, I charge you not to advance another step.'—'Long live the emperor!' said the figure. 'He grants a full pardon to the Vizier Ali, and not only gives him his life, but restores to him his fortune and his possessions.' My mother uttered a cry of joy, and clasped me to her bosom. 'Stop,' said Selim, seeing that she was about to go out; 'you see I have not yet received the ring,'—'True,' said my mother. And she fell on her knees, at the same time holding me up towards heaven, as if she desired, while praying to God in my behalf, to raise me actually to his presence."

And for the second time Haidee stopped, overcome by such violent emotion that the perspiration stood upon her pale brow, and her stifled voice seemed hardly able to find utterance, so parched and dry were her throat and lips. Monte Cristo poured a little iced water into a glass, and presented it to her, saying with a mildness in which was also a shade of command,—"Courage."

Haidee dried her eyes, and continued: "By this time our eyes, habituated to the darkness, had recognized the messenger of the pasha,—it was a friend. Selim had also recognized him, but the brave young man only acknowledged one duty, which was to obey. 'In whose name do you come?' said he to him. 'I come in the name of our master, Ali Tepelini.'—'If you come from Ali himself,' said Selim, 'you know what you were charged to remit to me?'—'Yes,' said the messenger, 'and I bring you his ring.' At these words he raised his hand above his head, to show the token; but it was too far off, and there was not light enough to enable Selim, where he was standing, to distinguish and recognize the object presented to his view. 'I do not see what you have in your hand,' said Selim. 'Approach then,' said the messenger, 'or I will come nearer to you, if you prefer it.'—'I will agree to neither one nor the other,' replied the young soldier; 'place the object which I desire to see in the ray of light which shines there, and retire while I examine it.'—'Be it so,' said the envoy; and he retired, after having first deposited the token agreed on in the place pointed out to him by Selim.

"Oh, how our hearts palpitated; for it did, indeed, seem to be a ring which was placed there. But was it my father's ring? that was the question. Selim, still holding in his hand the lighted match, walked towards the opening in the cavern, and, aided by the faint light which streamed in through the mouth of the cave, picked up the token.

"'It is well,' said he, kissing it; 'it is my master's ring!' And throwing the match on the ground, he trampled on it and extinguished it. The messenger uttered a cry of joy and clapped his hands. At this signal four soldiers of the Serasker Koorshid suddenly appeared, and Selim fell, pierced by five blows. Each man had stabbed him separately, and, intoxicated by their crime, though still pale with fear, they sought all over the cavern to discover if there was any fear of fire, after which they amused themselves by rolling on the bags of gold. At this moment my mother seized me in her arms, and hurrying noiselessly along numerous turnings and windings known only to ourselves, she arrived at a private staircase of the kiosk, where was a scene of frightful tumult and confusion. The lower rooms were entirely filled with Koorshid's troops; that is to say, with our enemies. Just as my mother was on the point of pushing open a small door, we heard the voice of the pasha sounding in a loud and threatening tone. My mother applied her eye to the crack between the boards; I luckily found a small opening which afforded me a view of the apartment and what was passing within. 'What do you want?' said my father to some people who were holding a paper inscribed with characters of gold. 'What we want,' replied one, 'is to communicate to you the will of his highness. Do you see this firman?'—'I do,' said my father. 'Well, read it; he demands your head.'

"My father answered with a loud laugh, which was more frightful than even threats would have been, and he had not ceased when two reports of a pistol were heard; he had fired them himself, and had killed two men. The Palikares, who were prostrated at my father's feet, now sprang up and fired, and the room was filled with fire and smoke. At the same instant the firing began on the other side, and the balls penetrated the boards all round us. Oh, how noble did the grand vizier my father look at that moment, in the midst of the flying bullets, his scimitar in his hand, and his face blackened with the powder of his enemies! and how he terrified them, even then, and made them fly before him! 'Selim, Selim!' cried he, 'guardian of the fire, do your duty!'—'Selim is dead,' replied a voice which seemed to come from the depths of the earth, 'and you are lost, Ali!' At the same moment an explosion was heard, and the flooring of the room in which my father was sitting was suddenly torn up and shivered to atoms—the troops were firing from underneath. Three or four Palikares fell with their bodies literally ploughed with wounds.

"My father howled aloud, plunged his fingers into the holes which the balls had made, and tore up one of the planks entire. But immediately through this opening twenty more shots were fired, and the flame, rushing up like fire from the crater of a volcano, soon reached the tapestry, which it quickly devoured. In the midst of all this frightful tumult and these terrific cries, two reports, fearfully distinct, followed by two shrieks more heartrending than all, froze me with terror. These two shots had mortally wounded my father, and it was he who had given utterance to these frightful cries. However, he remained standing, clinging to a window. My mother tried to force the door, that she might go and die with him, but it was fastened on the inside. All around him were lying the Palikares, writhing in convulsive agonies, while two or three who were only slightly wounded were trying to escape by springing from the windows. At this crisis the whole flooring suddenly gave way, my father fell on one knee, and at the same moment twenty hands were thrust forth, armed with sabres, pistols, and poniards—

twenty blows were instantaneously directed against one man, and my father disappeared in a whirlwind of fire and smoke kindled by these demons, and which seemed like hell itself opening beneath his feet. I felt myself fall to the ground, my mother had fainted."

Haidee's arms fell by her side, and she uttered a deep groan, at the same time looking towards the count as if to ask if he were satisfied with her obedience to his commands. Monte Cristo arose and approached her, took her hand, and said to her in Romaic, "Calm yourself, my dear child, and take courage in remembering that there is a God who will punish traitors."

"It is a frightful story, count," said Albert, terrified at the paleness of Haidee's countenance, "and I reproach myself now for having been so cruel and thoughtless in my request."

"Oh, it is nothing," said Monte Cristo. Then, patting the young girl on the head, he continued, "Haidee is very courageous, and she sometimes even finds consolation in the recital of her misfortunes."

"Because, my lord," said Haidee eagerly, "my miseries recall to me the remembrance of your goodness."

Albert looked at her with curiosity, for she had not yet related what he most desired to know,—how she had become the slave of the count. Haidee saw at a glance the same expression pervading the countenances of her two auditors; she exclaimed, 'When my mother recovered her senses we were before the serasker. 'Kill,' said she, 'but spare the honor of the widow of Ali.'—'It is not to me to whom you must address yourself,' said Koorshid.

"'To whom, then?'—'To your new master.'

"'Who and where is he?'—'He is here.'

"And Koorshid pointed out one who had more than any contributed to the death of my father," said Haidee, in a tone of chastened anger. "Then," said Albert, "you became the property of this man?"

"No," replied Haidee, "he did not dare to keep us, so we were sold to some slave-merchants who were going to Constantinople. We traversed Greece, and arrived half dead at the imperial gates. They were surrounded by a crowd of people, who opened a way for us to pass, when suddenly my mother, having looked closely at an object which was attracting their attention, uttered a piercing cry and fell to the ground, pointing as she did so to a head which was placed over the gates, and beneath which were inscribed these words:

"'This is the head of Ali Tepelini Pasha of Yanina.' I cried bitterly, and tried to raise my mother from the earth, but she was dead! I was taken to the slave-market, and was purchased by a rich Armenian. He caused me to be instructed, gave me masters, and when I was thirteen years of age he sold me to the Sultan Mahmood."

"Of whom I bought her," said Monte Cristo, "as I told you, Albert, with the emerald which formed a match to the one I had made into a box for the purpose of holding my hashish pills."

"Oh, you are good, you are great, my lord!" said Haidee, kissing the count's hand, "and I am very fortunate in belonging to such a master!" Albert remained quite bewildered with all that he had seen and heard. "Come, finish your cup of coffee," said Monte Cristo; "the history is ended."

CHAPTER 78.
WE HEAR FROM YANINA.

If Valentine could have seen the trembling step and agitated countenance of Franz when he quitted the chamber of M. Noirtier, even she would have been constrained to pity him. Villefort had only just given utterance to a few incoherent sentences, and then retired to his study, where he received about two hours afterwards the following letter:—

"After all the disclosures which were made this morning, M. Noirtier de Villefort must see the utter impossibility of any alliance being formed between his family and that of M. Franz d'Epinay. M. d'Epinay must say that he is shocked and astonished that M. de Villefort, who appeared to be aware of all the circumstances detailed this morning, should not have anticipated him in this announcement."

No one who had seen the magistrate at this moment, so thoroughly unnerved by the recent inauspicious combination of circumstances, would have supposed for an instant that he had anticipated the annoyance; although it certainly never had occurred to him that his father would carry candor, or rather rudeness, so far as to relate such a history. And in justice to Villefort, it must be understood that M. Noirtier, who never cared for the opinion of his son on any subject, had always omitted to explain the affair to Villefort, so that he had all his life entertained the belief that General de Quesnel, or the Baron d'Epinay, as he was alternately styled, according as the speaker wished to identify him by his own family name, or by the title which had been conferred on him, fell the victim of assassination, and not that he was killed fairly in a duel. This harsh letter, coming as it did from a man generally so polite and respectful, struck a mortal blow at the pride of Villefort. Hardly had he read the letter, when his wife entered. The sudden departure of Franz, after being summoned by M. Noirtier, had so much astonished every one, that the position of Madame de Villefort, left alone with the notary and the witnesses, became every moment more embarrassing. Determined to bear it no longer, she arose and left the room; saying she would go and make some inquiries into the cause of his sudden disappearance.

M. de Villefort's communications on the subject were very limited and concise; he told her, in fact, that an explanation had taken place between M. Noirtier, M. d'Epinay, and himself, and that the marriage of Valentine and Franz would consequently be broken off. This was an awkward and unpleasant thing to have to report to those who were awaiting her return in the chamber of her father-in-law. She therefore contented herself with saying that M. Noirtier having at the commencement of the discussion been attacked by a sort of apoplectic fit, the affair would necessarily be deferred for some days longer. This news, false as it was following so singularly in the train of the two similar misfortunes which had so recently occurred, evidently astonished the auditors, and they retired without a word. During this time Valentine, at once terrified and happy, after having embraced and thanked the feeble old man for thus breaking with a single blow the chain which she had been accustomed to consider as irrefragable, asked leave to retire to her own room, in order to recover her composure. Noirtier looked the permission which she solicited. But instead of going to her own room, Valentine, having once gained her liberty, entered the gallery, and, opening a small door at the end of it, found herself at once in the garden.

In the midst of all the strange events which had crowded one on the other, an indefinable sentiment of dread had taken possession of Valentine's mind. She expected every moment that she should see Morrel appear, pale and trembling, to forbid the signing of the contract, like the Laird of Ravenswood in "The Bride of Lammermoor." It was high time for her to make her appearance at the gate, for Maximilian had long awaited her coming. He had half guessed what was going on when he saw Franz quit the cemetery with M. de Villefort. He followed M. d'Epinay, saw him enter, afterwards go out, and then re-enter with Albert and Chateau-Renaud. He had no longer any doubts as to the nature of the conference; he therefore quickly went to the gate in the clover-patch, prepared to hear the result of the proceedings, and very certain that Valentine would hasten to him the first moment she should be set at liberty. He was not mistaken; peering through the crevices of the wooden partition, he soon discovered the young girl, who cast aside all her usual precautions and walked at once to the barrier. The first glance which Maximilian directed towards her entirely reassured him, and the first words she spoke made his heart bound with delight.

"We are saved!" said Valentine. "Saved?" repeated Morrel, not being able to conceive such intense happiness; "by whom?"

"By my grandfather. Oh, Morrel, pray love him for all his goodness to us!" Morrel swore to love him with all his soul; and at that moment he could safely promise to do so, for he felt as though it were not enough to love him merely as a friend or even as a father. "But tell me, Valentine, how has it all been effected? What strange means has he used to compass this blessed end?"

Valentine was on the point of relating all that had passed, but she suddenly remembered that in doing so she must reveal a terrible secret which concerned others as well as her grandfather, and she said, "At some future time I will tell you all about it."

"But when will that be?"

"When I am your wife."

The conversation had now turned upon a topic so pleasing to Morrel, that he was ready to accede to anything that Valentine thought fit to propose, and he likewise felt that a piece of intelligence such as he just heard ought to be more than sufficient to content him for one day. However, he would not leave without the promise of seeing Valentine again the next night. Valentine promised all that Morrel required of her, and certainly it was less difficult now for her to believe that she should marry Maximilian than it was an hour ago to assure herself that she should not marry Franz.

During the time occupied by the interview we have just detailed, Madame de Villefort had gone to visit M. Noirtier. The old man looked at her with that stern and forbidding expression with which he was accustomed to receive her.

"Sir," said she, "it is superfluous for me to tell you that Valentine's marriage is broken off, since it was here that the affair was concluded." Noirtier's countenance remained immovable. "But one thing I can tell you, of which I do not think you are aware; that is, that I have always been opposed to this marriage, and that the contract was entered into entirely without my consent or approbation." Noirtier regarded his daughter-in-law with the look of a man desiring an explanation. "Now that this marriage, which I know you so much disliked, is done away with, I come to you on an errand which neither M. de Villefort nor Valentine could consistently undertake." Noirtier's eyes demanded the nature of her mission. "I come to entreat you, sir," continued Madame de Villefort, "as the only one who has the right of doing so, inasmuch as I am the only one who will receive no personal benefit from the transaction,—I come to entreat you to restore, not your love, for that she has always possessed, but to restore your fortune to your granddaughter."

There was a doubtful expression in Noirtier's eyes; he was evidently trying to discover the motive of this proceeding, and he could not succeed in doing so. "May I hope, sir," said Madame de Villefort, "that your intentions accord with my request?" Noirtier made a sign that they did. "In that case, sir," rejoined Madame de Villefort, "I will leave you overwhelmed with gratitude and happiness at your prompt acquiescence to my wishes." She then bowed to M. Noirtier and retired.

The next day M. Noirtier sent for the notary; the first will was torn up and a second made, in which he left the whole of his fortune to Valentine, on condition that she should never be separated from him. It was then generally reported that Mademoiselle de Villefort, the heiress of the marquis and marchioness of Saint-Meran, had regained the good graces of her grandfather, and that she would ultimately be in possession of an income of 300,000 livres.

While all the proceedings relative to the dissolution of the marriage-contract were being carried on at the house of M. de Villefort, Monte Cristo had paid his visit to the Count of Morcerf, who, in order to lose no time in responding to M. Danglars' wishes, and at the same time to pay all due deference to his position in society, donned his uniform of lieutenant-general, which he ornamented with all his crosses, and thus attired, ordered his finest horses and drove to the Rue de la Chausse d'Antin.

Danglars was balancing his monthly accounts, and it was perhaps not the most favorable moment for finding him in his best humor. At the first sight of his old friend, Danglars assumed his majestic air, and settled himself in his easy-chair. Morcerf, usually so stiff and formal, accosted the banker in an affable and smiling manner, and, feeling sure that the overture he was about to make would be well received, he did not consider it necessary to adopt any manoeuvres in order to gain his end, but went at once straight to the point.

"Well, baron," said he, "here I am at last; some time has elapsed since our plans were formed, and they are not yet executed." Morcerf paused at these words, quietly waiting till the cloud should have dispersed which had gathered on the brow of Danglars, and which he attributed to his silence; but, on the contrary, to his great surprise, it grew darker and darker. "To what do you allude, monsieur?" said Danglars;

as if he were trying in vain to guess at the possible meaning of the general's words.

"Ah," said Morcerf, "I see you are a stickler for forms, my dear sir, and you would remind me that the ceremonial rites should not be omitted. Ma foi, I beg your pardon, but as I have but one son, and it is the first time I have ever thought of marrying him, I am still serving my apprenticeship, you know; come, I will reform." And Morcerf with a forced smile arose, and, making a low bow to M. Danglars, said: "Baron, I have the honor of asking of you the hand of Mademoiselle Eugenie Danglars for my son, the Vicomte Albert de Morcerf."

But Danglars, instead of receiving this address in the favorable manner which Morcerf had expected, knit his brow, and without inviting the count, who was still standing, to take a seat, he said: "Monsieur, it will be necessary to reflect before I give you an answer."

"To reflect?" said Morcerf, more and more astonished; "have you not had enough time for reflection during the eight years which have elapsed since this marriage was first discussed between us?"

"Count," said the banker, "things are constantly occurring in the world to induce us to lay aside our most established opinions, or at all events to cause us to remodel them according to the change of circumstances, which may have placed affairs in a totally different light to that in which we at first viewed them."

"I do not understand you, baron," said Morcerf.

"What I mean to say is this, sir,—that during the last fortnight unforeseen circumstances have occurred"—

"Excuse me," said Morcerf, "but is it a play we are acting?"

"A play?"

"Yes, for it is like one; pray let us come more to the point, and endeavor thoroughly to understand each other."

"That is quite my desire."

"You have seen M. de Monte Cristo have you not?"

"I see him very often," said Danglars, drawing himself up; "he is a particular friend of mine."

"Well, in one of your late conversations with him, you said that I appeared to be forgetful and irresolute concerning this marriage, did you not?"

"I did say so."

"Well, here I am, proving at once that I am really neither the one nor the other, by entreating you to keep your promise on that score."

Danglars did not answer. "Have you so soon changed your mind," added Morcerf, "or have you only provoked my request that you may have the pleasure of seeing me humbled?" Danglars, seeing that if he continued the conversation in the same tone in which he had begun it, the whole thing might turn out to his own disadvantage, turned to Morcerf, and said: "Count, you must doubtless be surprised at my reserve, and I assure you it costs me much to act in such a manner towards you; but, believe me when I say that imperative necessity has imposed the painful task upon me."

"These are all so many empty words, my dear sir," said Morcerf: "they might satisfy a new acquaintance, but the Comte de Morcerf does not rank in that list; and when a man like him comes to another, recalls to him his plighted word, and this man fails to redeem the pledge, he has at least a right to exact from him a good reason for so doing." Danglars was a coward, but did not wish to appear so; he was piqued at the tone which Morcerf had just assumed. "I am not without a good reason for my conduct," replied the banker.

"What do you mean to say?"

"I mean to say that I have a good reason, but that it is difficult to explain."

"You must be aware, at all events, that it is impossible for me to understand motives before they are explained to me; but one thing at least is clear, which is, that you decline allying yourself with my family."

"No, sir," said Danglars; "I merely suspend my decision, that is all."

"And do you really flatter yourself that I shall yield to all your caprices, and quietly and humbly await the time of again being received into your good graces?"

"Then, count, if you will not wait, we must look upon these projects as if they had never been entertained." The count bit his lips till the blood almost started, to prevent the ebullition of anger which his proud and irritable temper scarcely allowed him to restrain; understanding, however, that in the present state of things the laugh would decidedly be against him, he turned from the door, towards which he had been directing his steps, and again confronted the banker. A cloud settled on his brow, evincing decided anxiety and uneasiness, instead of the expression of offended pride which had lately reigned there. "My dear Danglars," said Morcerf, "we have been acquainted for many years, and consequently we ought to make some allowance for each other's failings. You owe me an explanation, and really it is but fair that I should know what circumstance has occurred to deprive my son of your favor."

"It is from no personal ill-feeling towards the viscount, that is all I can say, sir," replied Danglars, who resumed his insolent manner as soon as he perceived that Morcerf was a little softened and calmed down. "And towards whom do you bear this personal ill-feeling, then?" said Morcerf, turning pale with anger. The expression of the count's face had not remained unperceived by the banker; he fixed on him a look of greater assurance than before, and said: "You may, perhaps, be better satisfied that I should not go farther into particulars."

A tremor of suppressed rage shook the whole frame of the count, and making a violent effort over himself, he said: "I have a right to insist on your giving me an explanation. Is it Madame de Morcerf who has displeased you? Is it my fortune which you find insufficient? Is it because my opinions differ from yours?"

"Nothing of the kind, sir," replied Danglars: "if such had been the case, I only should have been to blame, inasmuch as I was aware of all these things when I made the engagement. No, do not seek any longer to discover the reason. I really am quite ashamed to have been the cause of your undergoing such severe self-examination; let us drop the subject, and adopt the middle course of delay, which implies neither a rupture nor an engagement. Ma foi, there is no hurry. My daughter is only seventeen years old, and your son twenty-one. While we wait, time will be progressing, events will succeed each other; things which in the evening look dark and obscure, appear but too clearly in the light of morning, and sometimes the utterance of one word, or the lapse of a single day, will reveal the most cruel calumnies."

"Calumnies, did you say, sir?" cried Morcerf, turning livid with rage. "Does any one dare to slander me?"

"Monsieur, I told you that I considered it best to avoid all explanation."

"Then, sir, I am patiently to submit to your refusal?"

"Yes, sir, although I assure you the refusal is as painful for me to give as it is for you to receive, for I had reckoned on the honor of your alliance, and the breaking off of a marriage contract always injures the lady more than the gentleman."

"Enough, sir," said Morcerf, "we will speak no more on the subject." And clutching his gloves in anger, he left the apartment. Danglars observed that during the whole conversation Morcerf had never once dared to ask if it was on his own account that Danglars recalled his word. That evening he had a long conference with several friends; and M. Cavalcanti, who had remained in the drawing-room with the ladies, was the last to leave the banker's house.

The next morning, as soon as he awoke, Danglars asked for the newspapers; they were brought to him; he laid aside three or four, and at last fixed on the Impartial, the paper of which Beauchamp was the chief editor. He hastily tore off the cover, opened the journal with nervous precipitation, passed contemptuously over the Paris jottings, and arriving at the miscellaneous intelligence, stopped with a malicious smile, at a paragraph headed "We hear from Yanina." "Very good," observed Danglars, after having read the paragraph; "here is a little article on Colonel Fernand, which, if I am not mistaken, would render the explanation which the Comte de Morcerf required of me perfectly unnecessary."

At the same moment, that is, at nine o'clock in the morning, Albert de Morcerf, dressed in a black coat buttoned up to his chin, might have been seen walking with a quick and agitated step in the direction of Monte Cristo's house in the Champs Elysees. When he presented himself at the gate the porter informed him that the Count had gone out about half an hour previously. "Did he take Baptistin with him?"

"No, my lord."

"Call him, then; I wish to speak to him." The concierge went to seek the valet de chambre, and returned with him in an instant.

"My good friend," said Albert, "I beg pardon for my intrusion, but I was anxious to know from your own mouth if your master was really out or not."

"He is really out, sir," replied Baptistin.

"Out, even to me?"

"I know how happy my master always is to receive the vicomte," said Baptistin; "and I should therefore never think of including him in any general order."

"You are right; and now I wish to see him on an affair of great importance. Do you think it will be long before he comes in?"

"No, I think not, for he ordered his breakfast at ten o'clock."

"Well, I will go and take a turn in the Champs Elysees, and at ten o'clock I will return here; meanwhile, if the count should come in, will you beg him not to go out again without seeing me?"

"You may depend on my doing so, sir," said Baptistin.

Albert left the cab in which he had come at the count's door, intending to take a turn on foot. As he was passing the Allee des Veuves, he thought he saw the count's horses standing at Gosset's shooting-gallery; he approached, and soon recognized the coachman. "Is the count shooting in the gallery?" said Morcerf.

"Yes, sir," replied the coachman. While he was speaking, Albert had heard the report of two or three pistol-shots. He entered, and on his way met the waiter. "Excuse me, my lord," said the lad; "but will you have the kindness to wait a moment?"

"What for, Philip?" asked Albert, who, being a constant visitor there, did not understand this opposition to his entrance.

"Because the person who is now in the gallery prefers being alone, and never practices in the presence of any one."

"Not even before you, Philip? Then who loads his pistol?"

"His servant."

"A Nubian?"

"A negro."

"It is he, then."

"Do you know this gentleman?"

"Yes, and I am come to look for him; he is a friend of mine."

"Oh, that is quite another thing, then. I will go immediately and inform him of your arrival." And Philip, urged by his own curiosity, entered the gallery; a second afterwards, Monte Cristo appeared on the threshold. "I ask your pardon, my dear count," said Albert, "for following you here, and I must first tell you that it was not the fault of your servants that I did so; I alone am to blame for the indiscretion. I went to your house, and they told me you were out, but that they expected you home at ten o'clock to breakfast. I was walking about in order to pass away the time till ten o'clock, when I caught sight of your carriage and horses."

"What you have just said induces me to hope that you intend breakfasting with me."

"No, thank you, I am thinking of other things besides breakfast just now; perhaps we may take that meal at a later hour and in worse company."

"What on earth are you talking of?"

"I am to fight to-day."

"For what?"

"I am going to fight"—

"Yes, I understand that, but what is the quarrel? People fight for all sorts of reasons, you know."

"I fight in the cause of honor."

"Ah, that is something serious."

"So serious, that I come to beg you to render me a service."

"What is it?"

"To be my second."

"That is a serious matter, and we will not discuss it here; let us speak of nothing till we get home. Ali, bring me some water." The count turned up his sleeves, and passed into the little vestibule where the gentlemen were accustomed to wash their hands after shooting. "Come in, my lord," said Philip in a low tone, "and I will show you something droll." Morcerf entered, and in place of the usual target, he saw some playing-cards fixed against the wall. At a distance Albert thought it was a complete suit, for he counted from the ace to the ten. "Ah, ha," said Albert, "I see you were preparing for a game of cards."

"No," said the count, "I was making a suit."

"How?" said Albert.

"Those are really aces and twos which you see, but my shots have turned them into threes, fives, sevens, eights, nines, and tens." Albert approached. In fact, the bullets had actually pierced the cards in the exact places which the painted signs would otherwise have occupied, the lines and distances being as regularly kept as if they had been ruled with pencil. "Diable," said Morcerf.

"What would you have, my dear viscount?" said Monte Cristo, wiping his hands on the towel which Ali had brought him; "I must occupy my leisure moments in some way or other. But come, I am waiting for you." Both men entered Monte Cristo's carriage, which in the course of a few minutes deposited them safely at No. 30. Monte Cristo took Albert into his study, and pointing to a seat, placed another for himself. "Now let us talk the matter over quietly," said the count.

"You see I am perfectly composed," said Albert.

"With whom are you going to fight?"

"With Beauchamp."

"One of your friends!"

"Of course; it is always with friends that one fights."

"I suppose you have some cause of quarrel?"

"I have."

"What has he done to you?"

"There appeared in his journal last night—but wait, and read for yourself." And Albert handed over the paper to the count, who read as follows:—

"A correspondent at Yanina informs us of a fact of which until now we had remained in ignorance. The castle which formed the protection of the town was given up to the Turks by a French officer named Fernand, in whom the grand vizier, Ali Tepelini, had reposed the greatest confidence."

"Well," said Monte Cristo, "what do you see in that to annoy you?"

"What do I see in it?"

"Yes; what does it signify to you if the castle of Yanina was given up by a French officer?"

"It signifies to my father, the Count of Morcerf, whose Christian name is Fernand!"

"Did your father serve under Ali Pasha?"

"Yes; that is to say, he fought for the independence of the Greeks, and hence arises the calumny."

"Oh, my dear viscount, do talk reason!"

"I do not desire to do otherwise."

"Now, just tell me who the devil should know in France that the officer Fernand and the Count of Morcerf are one and the same person? and who cares now about Yanina, which was taken as long ago as the year 1822 or 1823?"

"That just shows the meanness of this slander. They have allowed all this time to elapse, and then all of a sudden rake up events which have been forgotten to furnish materials for scandal, in order to tarnish the lustre of our high position. I inherit my father's name, and I do not choose that the shadow of disgrace should darken it. I am going to Beauchamp, in whose journal this paragraph appears, and I shall insist on his retracting the assertion before two witnesses."

"Beauchamp will never retract."

"Then he must fight."

"No he will not, for he will tell you, what is very true, that perhaps there were fifty officers in the Greek army bearing the same name."

"We will fight, nevertheless. I will efface that blot on my father's character. My father, who was such a brave soldier, whose career was so brilliant"—

"Oh, well, he will add, 'We are warranted in believing that this Fernand is not the illustrious Count of Morcerf, who also bears the same Christian name.'"

"I am determined not to be content with anything short of an entire retractation."

"And you intend to make him do it in the presence of two witnesses, do you?"

"Yes."

"You do wrong."

"Which means, I suppose, that you refuse the service which I asked of you?"

"You know my theory regarding duels; I told you my opinion on that subject, if you remember, when we were at Rome."

"Nevertheless, my dear count, I found you this morning engaged in an occupation but little consistent with the notions you profess to entertain."

"Because, my dear fellow, you understand one must never be eccentric. If one's lot is cast among fools, it is necessary to study folly. I shall perhaps find myself one day called out by some harebrained scamp, who has no more real cause of quarrel with me than you have with Beauchamp; he may take me to task for some foolish trifle or other, he will bring his witnesses, or will insult me in some public place, and I am expected to kill him for all that."

"You admit that you would fight, then? Well, if so, why do you object to my doing so?"

"I do not say that you ought not to fight, I only say that a duel is a serious thing, and ought not to be undertaken without due reflection."

"Did he reflect before he insulted my father?"

"If he spoke hastily, and owns that he did so, you ought to be satisfied."

"Ah, my dear count, you are far too indulgent."

"And you are far too exacting. Supposing, for instance, and do not be angry at what I am going to say"—

"Well."

"Supposing the assertion to be really true?"

"A son ought not to submit to such a stain on his father's honor."

"Ma foi, we live in times when there is much to which we must submit."

"That is precisely the fault of the age."

"And do you undertake to reform it?"

"Yes, as far as I am personally concerned."

"Well, you are indeed exacting, my dear fellow!"

"Yes, I own it."

"Are you quite impervious to good advice?"

"Not when it comes from a friend."

"And do you account me that title?"

"Certainly I do."

"Well, then, before going to Beauchamp with your witnesses, seek further information on the subject."

"From whom?"

"From Haidee."

"Why, what can be the use of mixing a woman up in the affair?—what can she do in it?"

"She can declare to you, for example, that your father had no hand whatever in the defeat and death of the vizier; or if by chance he had, indeed, the misfortune to"—

"I have told you, my dear count, that I would not for one moment admit of such a proposition."

"You reject this means of information, then?"

"I do—most decidedly."

"Then let me offer one more word of advice."

"Do so, then, but let it be the last."

"You do not wish to hear it, perhaps?"

"On the contrary, I request it."

"Do not take any witnesses with you when you go to Beauchamp—visit him alone."

"That would be contrary to all custom."

"Your case is not an ordinary one."

"And what is your reason for advising me to go alone?"

"Because then the affair will rest between you and Beauchamp."

"Explain yourself."

"I will do so. If Beauchamp be disposed to retract, you ought at least to give him the opportunity of doing it of his own free will,—the satisfaction to you will be the same. If, on the contrary, he refuses to do so, it will then be quite time enough to admit two strangers into your secret."

"They will not be strangers, they will be friends."

"Ah, but the friends of to-day are the enemies of to-morrow; Beauchamp, for instance."

"So you recommend"—

"I recommend you to be prudent."

"Then you advise me to go alone to Beauchamp?"

"I do, and I will tell you why. When you wish to obtain some concession from a man's self-love, you must avoid even the appearance of wishing to wound it."

"I believe you are right."

"I am glad of it."

"Then I will go alone."

"Go; but you would do better still by not going at all."

"That is impossible."

"Do so, then; it will be a wiser plan than the first which you proposed."

"But if, in spite of all my precautions, I am at last obliged to fight, will you not be my second?"

"My dear viscount," said Monte Cristo gravely, "you must have seen before to-day that at all times and in all places I have been at your disposal, but the service which you have just demanded of me is one which it is out of my power to render you."

"Why?"

"Perhaps you may know at some future period, and in the mean time I request you to excuse my declining to put you in possession of my reasons."

"Well, I will have Franz and Chateau-Renaud; they will be the very men for it."

"Do so, then."

"But if I do fight, you will surely not object to giving me a lesson or two in shooting and fencing?"

"That, too, is impossible."

"What a singular being you are!—you will not interfere in anything."

"You are right—that is the principle on which I wish to act."

"We will say no more about it, then. Good-by, count." Morcerf took his hat, and left the room. He found his carriage at the door, and doing his utmost to restrain his anger he went at once to find Beauchamp, who was in his office. It was a gloomy, dusty-looking apartment, such as journalists' offices have always been from time immemorial. The servant announced M. Albert de Morcerf. Beauchamp repeated the name to himself, as though he could scarcely believe that he had heard aright, and then gave orders for him to be admitted. Albert entered. Beauchamp uttered an exclamation of surprise on seeing his friend leap over and trample under foot all the newspapers which were strewed about the room. "This way, this way, my dear Albert!" said he, holding out his hand to the young man. "Are you out of your senses, or do you come peaceably to take breakfast with me? Try and find a seat—there is one by that geranium, which is the only thing in the room to remind me that there are other leaves in the world besides leaves of paper."

"Beauchamp," said Albert, "it is of your journal that I come to speak."

"Indeed? What do you wish to say about it?"

"I desire that a statement contained in it should be rectified."

"To what do you refer? But pray sit down."

"Thank you," said Albert, with a cold and formal bow.

"Will you now have the kindness to explain the nature of the statement which has displeased you?"

"An announcement has been made which implicates the honor of a member of my family."

"What is it?" said Beauchamp, much surprised; "surely you must be mistaken."

"The story sent you from Yanina."

"Yanina?"

"Yes; really you appear to be totally ignorant of the cause which brings me here."

"Such is really the case, I assure you, upon my honor! Baptiste, give me yesterday's paper," cried Beauchamp.

"Here, I have brought mine with me," replied Albert.

Beauchamp took the paper, and read the article to which Albert pointed in an undertone. "You see it is a serious annoyance," said Morcerf, when Beauchamp had finished the perusal of the paragraph. "Is the officer referred to a relation of yours, then?" demanded the journalist.

"Yes," said Albert, blushing.

"Well, what do you wish me to do for you?" said Beauchamp mildly.

"My dear Beauchamp, I wish you to contradict this statement." Beauchamp looked at Albert with a benevolent expression.

"Come," said he, "this matter will want a good deal of talking over; a retractation is always a serious thing, you know. Sit down, and I will read it again." Albert resumed his seat, and Beauchamp read, with more attention than at first, the lines denounced by his friend. "Well," said Albert in a determined tone, "you see that your paper his insulted a member of my family, and I insist on a retractation being made."

"You insist?"

"Yes, I insist."

"Permit me to remind you that you are not in the Chamber, my dear Viscount."

"Nor do I wish to be there," replied the young man, rising. "I repeat that I am determined to have the announcement of yesterday contradicted. You have known me long enough," continued Albert, biting his lips convulsively, for he saw that Beauchamp's anger was beginning to rise,—"you have been my friend, and therefore sufficiently intimate with me to be aware that I am likely to maintain my resolution on this point."

"If I have been your friend, Morcerf, your present manner of speaking would almost lead me to forget that I ever bore that title. But wait a moment, do not let us get angry, or at least not yet. You are irritated and vexed—tell me how this Fernand is related to you?"

"He is merely my father," said Albert—"M. Fernand Mondego, Count of Morcerf, an old soldier who has fought in twenty battles and whose honorable scars they would denounce as badges of disgrace."

"Is it your father?" said Beauchamp; "that is quite another thing. Then I can well understand your indignation, my dear Albert. I will look at it again;" and he read the paragraph for the third time, laying a stress on each word as he proceeded. "But the paper nowhere identifies this Fernand with your father."

"No; but the connection will be seen by others, and therefore I will have the article contradicted." At the words "I will," Beauchamp steadily raised his eyes to Albert's countenance, and then as gradually lowering them, he remained thoughtful for a few moments. "You will retract this assertion, will you not, Beauchamp?" said Albert with increased though stifled anger.

"Yes," replied Beauchamp.

"Immediately?" said Albert.

"When I am convinced that the statement is false."

"What?"

"The thing is worth looking into, and I will take pains to investigate the matter thoroughly."

"But what is there to investigate, sir?" said Albert, enraged beyond measure at Beauchamp's last remark. "If you do not believe that it is my father, say so immediately;

and if, on the contrary, you believe it to be him, state your reasons for doing so." Beauchamp looked at Albert with the smile which was so peculiar to him, and which in its numerous modifications served to express every varied emotion of his mind. "Sir," replied he, "if you came to me with the idea of demanding satisfaction, you should have gone at once to the point, and not have entertained me with the idle conversation to which I have been patiently listening for the last half hour. Am I to put this construction on your visit?"

"Yes, if you will not consent to retract that infamous calumny."

"Wait a moment—no threats, if you please, M. Fernand Mondego, Vicomte de Morcerf; I never allow them from my enemies, and therefore shall not put up with them from my friends. You insist on my contradicting the article relating to General Fernand, an article with which, I assure you on my word of honor, I had nothing whatever to do?"

"Yes, I insist on it," said Albert, whose mind was beginning to get bewildered with the excitement of his feelings.

"And if I refuse to retract, you wish to fight, do you?" said Beauchamp in a calm tone.

"Yes," replied Albert, raising his voice.

"Well," said Beauchamp, "here is my answer, my dear sir. The article was not inserted by me—I was not even aware of it; but you have, by the step you have taken, called my attention to the paragraph in question, and it will remain until it shall be either contradicted or confirmed by some one who has a right to do so."

"Sir," said Albert, rising, "I will do myself the honor of sending my seconds to you, and you will be kind enough to arrange with them the place of meeting and the weapons."

"Certainly, my dear sir."

"And this evening, if you please, or to-morrow at the latest, we will meet."

"No, no, I will be on the ground at the proper time; but in my opinion (and I have a right to dictate the preliminaries, as it is I who have received the provocation)—in my opinion the time ought not to be yet. I know you to be well skilled in the management of the sword, while I am only moderately so; I know, too, that you are a good marksman—there we are about equal. I know that a duel between us two would be a serious affair, because you are brave, and I am brave also. I do not therefore wish either to kill you, or to be killed myself without a cause. Now, I am going to put a question to you, and one very much to the purpose too. Do you insist on this retraction so far as to kill me if I do not make it, although I have repeated more than once, and affirmed on my honor, that I was ignorant of the thing with which you charge me, and although I still declare that it is impossible for any one but you to recognize the Count of Morcerf under the name of Fernand?"

"I maintain my original resolution."

"Very well, my dear sir; then I consent to cut throats with you. But I require three weeks' preparation; at the end of that time I shall come and say to you, 'The assertion is false, and I retract it,' or 'The assertion is true,' when I shall immediately draw the sword from its sheath, or the pistols from the case, whichever you please."

"Three weeks!" cried Albert; "they will pass as slowly as three centuries when I am all the time suffering dishonor."

"Had you continued to remain on amicable terms with me, I should have said, 'Patience, my friend;' but you have constituted yourself my enemy, therefore I say, 'What does that signify to me, sir?'"

"Well, let it be three weeks then," said Morcerf; "but remember, at the expiration of that time no delay or subterfuge will justify you in"—

"M. Albert de Morcerf," said Beauchamp, rising in his turn, "I cannot throw you out of window for three weeks— that is to say, for twenty-four days to come—nor have you any right to split my skull open till that time has elapsed. To-day is the 29th of August; the 21st of September will, therefore, be the conclusion of the term agreed on, and till that time arrives—and it is the advice of a gentleman which I am about to give you—till then we will refrain from growling and barking like two dogs chained within sight of each other." When he had concluded his speech, Beauchamp bowed coldly to Albert, turned his back upon him, and went to the press-room.

Albert vented his anger on a pile of newspapers, which he sent flying all over the office by switching them violently with his stick; after which ebullition he departed—not, however, without walking several times to the door of the press-room, as if he had half a mind to enter. While Albert was lashing the front of his carriage in the same manner that he had the newspapers which were the innocent agents of his discomfiture, as he was crossing the barrier he perceived Morrel, who was walking with a quick step and a bright eye. He was passing the Chinese Baths, and appeared to have come from the direction of the Porte Saint-Martin, and to be going towards the Madeleine. "Ah," said Morcerf, "there goes a happy man!" And it so happened Albert was not mistaken in his opinion.

CHAPTER 79.
THE LEMONADE.

Morrel was, in fact, very happy. M. Noirtier had just sent for him, and he was in such haste to know the reason of his doing so that he had not stopped to take a cab, placing infinitely more dependence on his own two legs than on the four legs of a cab-horse. He had therefore set off at a furious rate from the Rue Meslay, and was hastening with rapid strides in the direction of the Faubourg Saint-Honore. Morrel advanced with a firm, manly tread, and poor Barrois followed him as he best might. Morrel was only thirty-one, Barrois was sixty years of age; Morrel was deeply in love, and Barrois was dying with heat and exertion. These two men, thus opposed in age and interests, resembled two parts of a triangle, presenting the extremes of separation, yet nevertheless possessing their point of union. This point of union was Noirtier, and it was he who had just sent for Morrel, with the request that the latter would lose no time in coming to him—a command which Morrel obeyed to the letter, to the great discomfiture of Barrois. On arriving at the house, Morrel was not even out of breath, for love lends wings to our desires; but Barrois, who had long forgotten what it was to love, was sorely fatigued by the expedition he had been constrained to use.

The old servant introduced Morrel by a private entrance, closed the door of the study, and soon the rustling of a dress announced the arrival of Valentine. She looked marvellously beautiful in her deep mourning dress, and Morrel experienced such intense delight in gazing upon her that he felt as if he could almost have dispensed with the conversation of her grandfather. But the easy-chair of the old man was heard rolling along the floor, and he soon made his appearance in the room. Noirtier acknowledged by a look of extreme kindness and benevolence the thanks which Morrel lavished on him for his timely intervention on behalf of Valentine and himself—an intervention which had saved them from despair. Morrel then cast on the invalid an interrogative look as to the new favor which he designed to bestow on him. Valentine was sitting at a little distance from them, timidly awaiting the moment when she should be obliged to speak. Noirtier fixed his eyes on her. "Am I to say what you told me?" asked Valentine. Noirtier made a sign that she was to do so.

"Monsieur Morrel," said Valentine to the young man, who was regarding her with the most intense interest, "my grandfather, M. Noirtier, had a thousand things to say, which he told me three days ago; and now, he has sent for you, that I may repeat them to you. I will repeat them, then; and since he has chosen me as his interpreter, I will be faithful to the trust, and will not alter a word of his intentions."

"Oh, I am listening with the greatest impatience," replied the young man; "speak, I beg of you." Valentine cast down her eyes; this was a good omen for Morrel, for he knew that nothing but happiness could have the power of thus overcoming Valentine. "My grandfather intends leaving this house," said she, "and Barrois is looking out suitable apartments for him in another."

"But you, Mademoiselle de Villefort,—you, who are necessary to M. Noirtier's happiness"—

"I?" interrupted Valentine; "I shall not leave my grandfather,—that is an understood thing between us. My apartment will be close to his. Now, M. de Villefort must either give his consent to this plan or his refusal; in the first case, I shall leave directly, and in the second, I shall wait till I am of age, which will be in about ten months. Then I shall be free, I shall have an independent fortune, and"—

"And what?" demanded Morrel.

"And with my grandfather's consent I shall fulfil the promise which I have made you." Valentine pronounced these last few words in such a low tone, that nothing but Morrel's intense interest in what she was saying could have enabled him to hear them. "Have I not explained your wishes, grandpapa?" said Valentine, addressing Noirtier. "Yes," looked the old man.—"Once under my grandfather's roof, M. Morrel can visit me in the presence of my good and worthy protector, if we still feel that the union we contemplated will be likely to insure our future comfort and happiness; in that case I shall expect M. Morrel to come and claim me at my own hands. But, alas, I have heard it said that hearts inflamed by obstacles to their desire grew cold in time of security; I trust we shall never find it so in our experience!"

"Oh," cried Morrel, almost tempted to throw himself on his knees before Noirtier and Valentine, and to adore them as two superior beings, "what have I ever done in my life to merit such unbounded happiness?"

"Until that time," continued the young girl in a calm and self-possessed tone of voice, "we will conform to circumstances, and be guided by the wishes of our friends, so long as those wishes do not tend finally to separate us; in a word, and I repeat it, because it expresses all I wish to convey,—we will wait."

"And I swear to make all the sacrifices which this word imposes, sir," said Morrel, "not only with resignation, but with cheerfulness."

"Therefore," continued Valentine, looking playfully at Maximilian, "no more inconsiderate actions—no more rash projects; for you surely would not wish to compromise one who from this day regards herself as destined, honorably and happily, to bear your name?"

Morrel looked obedience to her commands. Noirtier regarded the lovers with a look of ineffable tenderness, while

Barrois, who had remained in the room in the character of a man privileged to know everything that passed, smiled on the youthful couple as he wiped the perspiration from his bald forehead. "How hot you look, my good Barrois," said Valentine.

"Ah, I have been running very fast, mademoiselle, but I must do M. Morrel the justice to say that he ran still faster." Noirtier directed their attention to a waiter, on which was placed a decanter containing lemonade and a glass. The decanter was nearly full, with the exception of a little, which had been already drunk by M. Noirtier.

"Come, Barrois," said the young girl, "take some of this lemonade; I see you are coveting a good draught of it."

"The fact is, mademoiselle," said Barrois, "I am dying with thirst, and since you are so kind as to offer it me, I cannot say I should at all object to drinking your health in a glass of it."

"Take some, then, and come back immediately." Barrois took away the waiter, and hardly was he outside the door, which in his haste he forgot to shut, than they saw him throw back his head and empty to the very dregs the glass which Valentine had filled. Valentine and Morrel were exchanging their adieux in the presence of Noirtier when a ring was heard at the door-bell. It was the signal of a visit. Valentine looked at her watch.

"It is past noon," said she, "and to-day is Saturday; I dare say it is the doctor, grandpapa." Noirtier looked his conviction that she was right in her supposition. "He will come in here, and M. Morrel had better go,—do you not think so, grandpapa?"

"Yes," signed the old man.

"Barrois," cried Valentine, "Barrois!"

"I am coming, mademoiselle," replied he. "Barrois will open the door for you," said Valentine, addressing Morrel. "And now remember one thing, Monsieur Officer, that my grandfather commands you not to take any rash or ill-advised step which would be likely to compromise our happiness."

"I promised him to wait," replied Morrel; "and I will wait."

At this moment Barrois entered. "Who rang?" asked Valentine.

"Doctor d'Avrigny," said Barrois, staggering as if he would fall.

"What is the matter, Barrois?" said Valentine. The old man did not answer, but looked at his master with wild staring eyes, while with his cramped hand he grasped a piece of furniture to enable him to stand upright. "He is going to fall!" cried Morrel. The rigors which had attacked Barrois gradually increased, the features of the face became quite altered, and the convulsive movement of the muscles appeared to indicate the approach of a most serious nervous disorder. Noirtier, seeing Barrois in this pitiable condition, showed by his looks all the various emotions of sorrow and sympathy which can animate the heart of man. Barrois made some steps towards his master.

"Ah, sir," said he, "tell me what is the matter with me. I am suffering—I cannot see. A thousand fiery darts are piercing my brain. Ah, don't touch me, pray don't." By this time his haggard eyes had the appearance of being ready to start from their sockets; his head fell back, and the lower extremities of the body began to stiffen. Valentine uttered a cry of horror; Morrel took her in his arms, as if to defend her from some unknown danger. "M. d'Avrigny, M. d'Avrigny," cried she, in a stifled voice. "Help, help!" Barrois turned round and with a great effort stumbled a few steps, then fell at the feet of Noirtier, and resting his hand on the knee of the invalid, exclaimed, "My master, my good master!" At this moment M. de Villefort, attracted by the noise, appeared on the threshold. Morrel relaxed his hold of Valentine, and retreating to a distant corner of the room remained half hidden behind a curtain. Pale as if he had been gazing on a serpent, he fixed his terrified eye on the agonized sufferer.

Noirtier, burning with impatience and terror, was in despair at his utter inability to help his old domestic, whom he regarded more in the light of a friend than a servant. One might by the fearful swelling of the veins of his forehead and the contraction of the muscles round the eye, trace the terrible conflict which was going on between the living energetic mind and the inanimate and helpless body. Barrois, his features convulsed, his eyes suffused with blood, and his head thrown back, was lying at full length, beating the floor with his hands, while his legs had become so stiff, that they looked as if they would break rather than bend. A slight appearance of foam was visible around the mouth, and he breathed painfully, and with extreme difficulty.

Villefort seemed stupefied with astonishment, and remained gazing intently on the scene before him without uttering a word. He had not seen Morrel. After a moment of dumb contemplation, during which his face became pale and his hair seemed to stand on end, he sprang towards the door, crying out, "Doctor, doctor! come instantly, pray come!"

"Madame, madame!" cried Valentine, calling her step-mother, and running up-stairs to meet her; "come quick, quick!—and bring your bottle of smelling-salts with you."

"What is the matter?" said Madame de Villefort in a harsh and constrained tone.

"Oh, come, come!"

"But where is the doctor?" exclaimed Villefort; "where is he?" Madame de Villefort now deliberately descended the staircase. In one hand she held her handkerchief, with which she appeared to be wiping her face, and in the other a bottle of English smelling-salts. Her first look on entering the room was at Noirtier, whose face, independent of the emotion which such a scene could not fail of producing, proclaimed him to be in possession of his usual health; her second glance was at the dying man. She turned pale, and her eye passed quickly from the servant and rested on the master.

"In the name of heaven, madame," said Villefort, "where is the doctor? He was with you just now. You see this is a fit of apoplexy, and he might be saved if he could but be bled!"

"Has he eaten anything lately?" asked Madame de Villefort, eluding her husband's question. "Madame," replied Valentine, "he has not even breakfasted. He has been running very fast on an errand with which my grandfather charged him, and when he returned, took nothing but a glass of lemonade."

"Ah," said Madame de Villefort, "why did he not take wine? Lemonade was a very bad thing for him."

"Grandpapa's bottle of lemonade was standing just by his side; poor Barrois was very thirsty, and was thankful to drink anything he could find." Madame de Villefort started. Noirtier looked at her with a glance of the most profound scrutiny. "He has such a short neck," said she. "Madame," said Villefort, "I ask where is M. d'Avrigny? In God's name answer me!"

"He is with Edward, who is not quite well," replied Madame de Villefort, no longer being able to avoid answering.

Villefort rushed up-stairs to fetch him. "Take this," said Madame de Villefort, giving her smelling-bottle to Valentine. "They will, no doubt, bleed him; therefore I will retire, for I cannot endure the sight of blood;" and she followed her husband up-stairs. Morrel now emerged from his hiding-place, where he had remained quite unperceived, so great had been the general confusion. "Go away as quick as you can, Maximilian," said Valentine, "and stay till I send for you. Go."

Morrel looked towards Noirtier for permission to retire. The old man, who had preserved all his usual coolness, made a sign to him to do so. The young man pressed Valentine's hand to his lips, and then left the house by a back staircase. At the same moment that he quitted the room, Villefort and the doctor entered by an opposite door. Barrois was now showing signs of returning consciousness. The crisis seemed past, a low moaning was heard, and he raised himself on one knee. D'Avrigny and Villefort laid him on a couch. "What do you prescribe, doctor?" demanded Villefort. "Give me some water and ether. You have some in the house, have you not?"

"Yes."

"Send for some oil of turpentine and tartar emetic."

Villefort immediately despatched a messenger. "And now let every one retire."

"Must I go too?" asked Valentine timidly.

"Yes, mademoiselle, you especially," replied the doctor abruptly.

Valentine looked at M. d'Avrigny with astonishment, kissed her grandfather on the forehead, and left the room. The doctor closed the door after her with a gloomy air. "Look, look, doctor," said Villefort, "he is quite coming round again; I really do not think, after all, it is anything of consequence." M. d'Avrigny answered by a melancholy smile. "How do you feel, Barrois?" asked he. "A little better, sir."

"Will you drink some of this ether and water?"

"I will try; but don't touch me."

"Why not?"

"Because I feel that if you were only to touch me with the tip of your finger the fit would return."

"Drink."

Barrois took the glass, and, raising it to his purple lips, took about half of the liquid offered him. "Where do you suffer?" asked the doctor.

"Everywhere. I feel cramps over my whole body."

"Do you find any dazzling sensation before the eyes?"

"Yes."

"Any noise in the ears?"

"Frightful."

"When did you first feel that?"

"Just now."

"Suddenly?"

"Yes, like a clap of thunder."

"Did you feel nothing of it yesterday or the day before?"

"Nothing."

"No drowsiness?"

"None."

"What have you eaten to-day?"

"I have eaten nothing; I only drank a glass of my master's lemonade—that's all;" and Barrois turned towards Noirtier, who, immovably fixed in his arm-chair, was contemplating this terrible scene without allowing a word or a movement to escape him.

"Where is this lemonade?" asked the doctor eagerly.

"Down-stairs in the decanter."

"Whereabouts downstairs?"

"In the kitchen."

"Shall I go and fetch it, doctor?" inquired Villefort.

"No, stay here and try to make Barrois drink the rest of this glass of ether and water. I will go myself and fetch the lemonade." D'Avrigny bounded towards the door, flew down the back staircase, and almost knocked down Madame de Villefort, in his haste, who was herself going down to the kitchen. She cried out, but d'Avrigny paid no attention to her; possessed with but one idea, he cleared the last four steps with a bound, and rushed into the kitchen, where he saw the decanter about three parts empty still standing on the waiter, where it had been left. He darted upon it as an eagle would seize upon its prey. Panting with loss of breath, he returned to the room he had just left. Madame de Villefort was slowly ascending the steps which led to her room. "Is this the decanter you spoke of?" asked d'Avrigny.

"Yes, doctor."

"Is this the same lemonade of which you partook?"

"I believe so."

"What did it taste like?"

"It had a bitter taste."

The doctor poured some drops of the lemonade into the palm of his hand, put his lips to it, and after having rinsed his mouth as a man does when he is tasting wine, he spat the liquor into the fireplace.

"It is no doubt the same," said he. "Did you drink some too, M. Noirtier?"

"Yes."

"And did you also discover a bitter taste?"

"Yes."

"Oh, doctor," cried Barrois, "the fit is coming on again. Oh, do something for me." The doctor flew to his patient. "That emetic, Villefort—see if it is coming." Villefort sprang into the passage, exclaiming, "The emetic! the emetic!—is it come yet?" No one answered. The most profound terror reigned throughout the house. "If I had anything by means of which I could inflate the lungs," said d'Avrigny, looking around him, "perhaps I might prevent suffocation. But there is nothing which would do—nothing!" "Oh, sir," cried Barrois, "are you going to let me die without help? Oh, I am dying! Oh, save me!"

"A pen, a pen!" said the doctor. There was one lying on the table; he endeavored to introduce it into the mouth of the patient, who, in the midst of his convulsions, was making vain attempts to vomit; but the jaws were so clinched that the pen could not pass them. This second attack was much more violent than the first, and he had slipped from the couch to the ground, where he was writhing in agony. The doctor left him in this paroxysm, knowing that he could do nothing to alleviate it, and, going up to Noirtier, said abruptly, "How do you find yourself?—well?"

"Yes."

"Have you any weight on the chest; or does your stomach feel light and comfortable—eh?"

"Yes."

"Then you feel pretty much as you generally do after you have had the dose which I am accustomed to give you every Sunday?"

"Yes."

"Did Barrois make your lemonade?"

"Yes."

"Was it you who asked him to drink some of it?"

"No."

"Was it M. de Villefort?"

"No."

"Madame?"

"No."

"It was your granddaughter, then, was it not?"

"Yes." A groan from Barrois, accompanied by a yawn which seemed to crack the very jawbones, attracted the attention of M. d'Avrigny; he left M. Noirtier, and returned to the sick man. "Barrois," said the doctor, "can you speak?" Barrois muttered a few unintelligible words. "Try and make an effort to do so, my good man." said d'Avrigny. Barrois reopened his bloodshot eyes. "Who made the lemonade?"

"I did."

"Did you bring it to your master directly it was made?"

"No."

"You left it somewhere, then, in the meantime?"

"Yes; I left it in the pantry, because I was called away."

"Who brought it into this room, then?"

"Mademoiselle Valentine." D'Avrigny struck his forehead with his hand. "Gracious heaven," exclaimed he. "Doctor, doctor!" cried Barrois, who felt another fit coming.

"Will they never bring that emetic?" asked the doctor.

"Here is a glass with one already prepared," said Villefort, entering the room.

"Who prepared it?"

"The chemist who came here with me."

"Drink it," said the doctor to Barrois. "Impossible, doctor; it is too late; my throat is closing up. I am choking! Oh, my heart! Ah, my head!—Oh, what agony!—Shall I suffer like this long?"

"No, no, friend," replied the doctor, "you will soon cease to suffer."

"Ah, I understand you," said the unhappy man. "My God, have mercy upon me!" and, uttering a fearful cry, Barrois fell back as if he had been struck by lightning. D'Avrigny put his hand to his heart, and placed a glass before his lips.

"Well?" said Villefort. "Go to the kitchen and get me some syrup of violets." Villefort went immediately. "Do not be alarmed, M. Noirtier," said d'Avrigny; "I am going to take my patient into the next room to bleed him; this sort of attack is very frightful to witness."

And taking Barrois under the arms, he dragged him into an adjoining room; but almost immediately he returned to fetch the lemonade. Noirtier closed his right eye. "You want Valentine, do you not? I will tell them to send her to you." Villefort returned, and d'Avrigny met him in the passage. "Well, how is he now?" asked he. "Come in here," said d'Avrigny, and he took him into the chamber where the sick man lay. "Is he still in a fit?" said the procureur.

"He is dead."

Villefort drew back a few steps, and, clasping his hands, exclaimed, with real amazement and sympathy, "Dead?— and so soon too!"

"Yes, it is very soon," said the doctor, looking at the corpse before him; "but that ought not to astonish you; Monsieur and Madame de Saint-Meran died as soon. People die very suddenly in your house, M. de Villefort."

"What?" cried the magistrate, with an accent of horror and consternation, "are you still harping on that terrible idea?"

"Still, sir; and I shall always do so," replied d'Avrigny, "for it has never for one instant ceased to retain possession of my mind; and that you may be quite sure I am not mistaken this time, listen well to what I am going to say, M. de Villefort." The magistrate trembled convulsively. "There is a poison which destroys life almost without leaving any perceptible traces. I know it well; I have studied it in all its forms and in the effects which it produces. I recognized the presence of this poison in the case of poor Barrois as well as in that of Madame de Saint-Meran. There is a way of detecting its presence. It restores the blue color of litmus-paper reddened by an acid, and it turns syrup of violets green. We have no litmus-paper, but, see, here they come with the syrup of violets."

The doctor was right; steps were heard in the passage. M. d'Avrigny opened the door, and took from the hands of the chambermaid a cup which contained two or three spoonfuls of the syrup, he then carefully closed the door. "Look," said he to the procureur, whose heart beat so loudly that it might almost be heard, "here is in this cup some syrup of violets, and this decanter contains the remainder of the lemonade of which M. Noirtier and Barrois partook. If the lemonade be pure and inoffensive, the syrup will retain its color; if, on the contrary, the lemonade be drugged with poison, the syrup will become green. Look closely!"

The doctor then slowly poured some drops of the lemonade from the decanter into the cup, and in an instant a light cloudy sediment began to form at the bottom of the cup; this sediment first took a blue shade, then from the color of sapphire it passed to that of opal, and from opal to emerald. Arrived at this last hue, it changed no more. The result of the experiment left no doubt whatever on the mind.

"The unfortunate Barrois has been poisoned," said d'Avrigny, "and I will maintain this assertion before God and man." Villefort said nothing, but he clasped his hands, opened his haggard eyes, and, overcome with his emotion, sank into a chair.

CHAPTER 80.
THE ACCUSATION.

M. D'Avrigny soon restored the magistrate to consciousness, who had looked like a second corpse in that chamber of death. "Oh, death is in my house!" cried Villefort.

"Say, rather, crime!" replied the doctor.

"M. d'Avrigny," cried Villefort, "I cannot tell you all I feel at this moment,—terror, grief, madness."

"Yes," said M. d'Avrigny, with an imposing calmness, "but I think it is now time to act. I think it is time to stop this torrent of mortality. I can no longer bear to be in possession of these secrets without the hope of seeing the victims and society generally revenged." Villefort cast a gloomy look around him. "In my house," murmured he, "in my house!"

"Come, magistrate," said M. d'Avrigny, "show yourself a man; as an interpreter of the law, do honor to your profession by sacrificing your selfish interests to it."

"You make me shudder, doctor. Do you talk of a sacrifice?"

"I do."

"Do you then suspect any one?"

"I suspect no one; death raps at your door—it enters— it goes, not blindfolded, but circumspectly, from room to room. Well, I follow its course, I track its passage; I adopt the wisdom of the ancients, and feel my way, for my friendship for your family and my respect for you are as a twofold bandage over my eyes; well"—

"Oh, speak, speak, doctor; I shall have courage."

"Well, sir, you have in your establishment, or in your family, perhaps, one of the frightful monstrosities of which each century produces only one. Locusta and Agrippina, living at the same time, were an exception, and proved the determination of providence to effect the entire ruin of the Roman empire, sullied by so many crimes. Brunehilde and Fredegonde were the results of the painful struggle of civilization in its infancy, when man was learning to control mind, were it even by an emissary from the realms of darkness. All these women had been, or were, beautiful. The same flower of innocence had flourished, or was still flourishing, on their brow, that is seen on the brow of the culprit in your house." Villefort shrieked, clasped his hands, and looked at the doctor with a supplicating air. But the latter went on without pity:—

"'Seek whom the crime will profit,' says an axiom of jurisprudence."

"Doctor," cried Villefort, "alas, doctor, how often has man's justice been deceived by those fatal words. I know not why, but I feel that this crime"—

"You acknowledge, then, the existence of the crime?"

"Yes, I see too plainly that it does exist. But it seems that it is intended to affect me personally. I fear an attack myself, after all these disasters."

"Oh, man," murmured d'Avrigny, "the most selfish of all animals, the most personal of all creatures, who believes the earth turns, the sun shines, and death strikes for him alone,—an ant cursing God from the top of a blade of grass! And have those who have lost their lives lost nothing?—M. de Saint-Meran, Madame de Saint-Meran, M. Noirtier"—

"How? M. Noirtier?"

"Yes; think you it was the poor servant's life was coveted? No, no; like Shakespeare's 'Polonius,' he died for another. It was Noirtier the lemonade was intended for—it is Noirtier, logically speaking, who drank it. The other drank it only by accident, and, although Barrois is dead, it was Noirtier whose death was wished for."

"But why did it not kill my father?"

"I told you one evening in the garden after Madame de Saint-Meran's death—because his system is accustomed to that very poison, and the dose was trifling to him, which would be fatal to another; because no one knows, not even the assassin, that, for the last twelve months, I have given M. Noirtier brucine for his paralytic affection, while the assassin is not ignorant, for he has proved that brucine is a violent poison."

"Oh, have pity—have pity!" murmured Villefort, wringing his hands.

"Follow the culprit's steps; he first kills M. de Saint-Meran"—

"O doctor!"

"I would swear to it; what I heard of his symptoms agrees too well with what I have seen in the other cases." Villefort ceased to contend; he only groaned. "He first kills M. de Saint-Meran," repeated the doctor, "then Madame de Saint-Meran,—a double fortune to inherit." Villefort wiped the perspiration from his forehead. "Listen attentively."

"Alas," stammered Villefort, "I do not lose a single word."

"M. Noirtier," resumed M. d'Avrigny in the same pitiless tone,—"M. Noirtier had once made a will against you—against your family—in favor of the poor, in fact; M. Noirtier is spared, because nothing is expected from him. But he has no sooner destroyed his first will and made a second, than, for fear he should make a third, he is struck down. The will was made the day before yesterday, I believe; you see there has been no time lost."

"Oh, mercy, M. d'Avrigny!"

"No mercy, sir! The physician has a sacred mission on earth; and to fulfil it he begins at the source of life, and goes down to the mysterious darkness of the tomb. When crime has been committed, and God, doubtless in anger, turns away his face, it is for the physician to bring the culprit to justice."

"Have mercy on my child, sir," murmured Villefort.

"You see it is yourself who have first named her—you, her father."

"Have pity on Valentine! Listen—it is impossible! I would as willingly accuse myself! Valentine, whose heart is pure as a diamond or a lily."

"No pity, procureur; the crime is fragrant. Mademoiselle herself packed all the medicines which were sent to M. de Saint-Meran; and M. de Saint-Meran is dead. Mademoiselle de Villefort prepared all the cooling draughts which Madame de Saint-Meran took, and Madame de Saint-Meran is dead. Mademoiselle de Villefort took from the hands of Barrois, who was sent out, the lemonade which M. Noirtier had every morning, and he has escaped by a miracle. Mademoiselle de Villefort is the culprit—she is the poisoner! To you, as the king's attorney, I denounce Mademoiselle de Villefort, do your duty."

"Doctor, I resist no longer—I can no longer defend myself—I believe you; but, for pity's sake, spare my life, my honor!"

"M. de Villefort," replied the doctor, with increased vehemence, "there are occasions when I dispense with all foolish human circumspection. If your daughter had committed only one crime, and I saw her meditating another,

I would say 'Warn her, punish her, let her pass the remainder of her life in a convent, weeping and praying.' If she had committed two crimes, I would say, 'Here, M. de Villefort, is a poison that the prisoner is not acquainted with,—one that has no known antidote, quick as thought, rapid as lightning, mortal as the thunderbolt; give her that poison, recommending her soul to God, and save your honor and your life, for it is yours she aims at; and I can picture her approaching your pillow with her hypocritical smiles and her sweet exhortations. Woe to you, M. de Villefort, if you do not strike first!' This is what I would say had she only killed two persons but she has seen three deaths,—has contemplated three murdered persons,—has knelt by three corpses! To the scaffold with the poisoner—to the scaffold! Do you talk of your honor? Do what I tell you, and immortality awaits you!"

Villefort fell on his knees. "Listen," said he; "I have not the strength of mind you have, or rather that which you would not have, if instead of my daughter Valentine your daughter Madeleine were concerned." The doctor turned pale. "Doctor, every son of woman is born to suffer and to die; I am content to suffer and to await death."

"Beware," said M. d'Avrigny, "it may come slowly; you will see it approach after having struck your father, your wife, perhaps your son."

Villefort, suffocating, pressed the doctor's arm. "Listen," cried he; "pity me—help me! No, my daughter is not guilty. If you drag us both before a tribunal I will still say, 'No, my daughter is not guilty;—there is no crime in my house. I will not acknowledge a crime in my house; for when crime enters a dwelling, it is like death—it does not come alone.' Listen. What does it signify to you if I am murdered? Are you my friend? Are you a man? Have you a heart? No, you are a physician! Well, I tell you I will not drag my daughter before a tribunal, and give her up to the executioner! The bare idea would kill me—would drive me like a madman to dig my heart out with my finger-nails! And if you were mistaken, doctor—if it were not my daughter— if I should come one day, pale as a spectre, and say to you, 'Assassin, you have killed my child!'—hold—if that should happen, although I am a Christian, M. d'Avrigny, I should kill myself."

"Well," said the doctor, after a moment's silence, "I will wait." Villefort looked at him as if he had doubted his words. "Only," continued M. d'Avrigny, with a slow and solemn tone, "if any one falls ill in your house, if you feel yourself attacked, do not send for me, for I will come no more. I will consent to share this dreadful secret with you, but I will not allow shame and remorse to grow and increase in my conscience, as crime and misery will in your house."

"Then you abandon me, doctor?"

"Yes, for I can follow you no farther, and I only stop at the foot of the scaffold. Some further discovery will be made, which will bring this dreadful tragedy to a close. Adieu."

"I entreat you, doctor!"

"All the horrors that disturb my thoughts make your house odious and fatal. Adieu, sir."

"One word—one single word more, doctor! You go, leaving me in all the horror of my situation, after increasing it by what you have revealed to me. But what will be reported of the sudden death of the poor old servant?"

"True," said M. d'Avrigny; "we will return." The doctor went out first, followed by M. de Villefort. The terrified servants were on the stairs and in the passage where the doctor would pass. "Sir," said d'Avrigny to Villefort, so loud that all might hear, "poor Barrois has led too sedentary a life of late; accustomed formerly to ride on horseback, or in the carriage, to the four corners of Europe, the monotonous walk around that arm-chair has killed him—his blood has thickened. He was stout, had a short, thick neck; he was attacked with apoplexy, and I was called in too late. By the way," added he in a low tone, "take care to throw away that cup of syrup of violets in the ashes."

The doctor, without shaking hands with Villefort, without adding a word to what he had said, went out, amid the tears and lamentations of the whole household. The same evening all Villefort's servants, who had assembled in the kitchen, and had a long consultation, came to tell Madame de Villefort that they wished to leave. No entreaty, no proposition of increased wages, could induce them to remain; to every argument they replied, "We must go, for death is in this house." They all left, in spite of prayers and entreaties, testifying their regret at leaving so good a master and mistress, and especially Mademoiselle Valentine, so good, so kind, and so gentle. Villefort looked at Valentine as they said this. She was in tears, and, strange as it was, in spite of the emotions he felt at the sight of these tears, he looked also at Madame de Villefort, and it appeared to him as if a slight gloomy smile had passed over her thin lips, like a meteor seen passing inauspiciously between two clouds in a stormy sky.

CHAPTER 81.
THE ROOM OF THE RETIRED BAKER.

The evening of the day on which the Count of Morcerf had left Danglars' house with feelings of shame and anger at the rejection of the projected alliance, M. Andrea Cavalcanti, with curled hair, mustaches in perfect order, and white gloves which fitted admirably, had entered the courtyard of the banker's house in La Chaussee d'Antin. He had not been more than ten minutes in the drawing-room before he drew Danglars aside into the recess of a bow-window, and, after an ingenious preamble, related to him all his anxieties and cares since his noble father's departure. He acknowledged the extreme kindness which had been shown him by the banker's family, in which he had been received as a son, and where, besides, his warmest affections had found an object on which to centre in Mademoiselle Danglars. Danglars listened with the most profound attention; he had expected this declaration for the last two or three days, and when at last it came his eyes glistened as much as they had lowered on listening to Morcerf. He would not, however, yield immediately to the young man's request, but made a few conscientious objections. "Are you not rather young, M. Andrea, to think of marrying?"

"I think not, sir," replied M. Cavalcanti; "in Italy the nobility generally marry young. Life is so uncertain, that we ought to secure happiness while it is within our reach."

"Well, sir," said Danglars, "in case your proposals, which do me honor, are accepted by my wife and daughter, by whom shall the preliminary arrangements be settled? So important a negotiation should, I think, be conducted by the respective fathers of the young people."

"Sir, my father is a man of great foresight and prudence. Thinking that I might wish to settle in France, he left me at his departure, together with the papers establishing my identity, a letter promising, if he approved of my choice, 150,000 livres per annum from the day I was married. So far as I can judge, I suppose this to be a quarter of my father's revenue."

"I," said Danglars, "have always intended giving my daughter 500,000 francs as her dowry; she is, besides, my sole heiress."

"All would then be easily arranged if the baroness and her daughter are willing. We should command an annuity of 175,000 livres. Supposing, also, I should persuade the marquis to give me my capital, which is not likely, but still is possible, we would place these two or three millions in your hands, whose talent might make it realize ten per cent."

"I never give more than four per cent, and generally only three and a half; but to my son-in-law I would give five, and we would share the profit."

"Very good, father-in-law," said Cavalcanti, yielding to his low-born nature, which would escape sometimes through the aristocratic gloss with which he sought to conceal it. Correcting himself immediately, he said, "Excuse me, sir; hope alone makes me almost mad,—what will not reality do?"

"But," said Danglars,—who, on his part, did not perceive how soon the conversation, which was at first disinterested, was turning to a business transaction,—"there is, doubtless, a part of your fortune your father could not refuse you?"

"Which?" asked the young man.

"That you inherit from your mother."

"Truly, from my mother, Leonora Corsinari."

"How much may it amount to?"

"Indeed, sir," said Andrea, "I assure you I have never given the subject a thought, but I suppose it must have been at least two millions." Danglars felt as much overcome with joy as the miser who finds a lost treasure, or as the shipwrecked mariner who feels himself on solid ground instead of in the abyss which he expected would swallow him up.

"Well, sir," said Andrea, bowing to the banker respectfully, "may I hope?"

"You may not only hope," said Danglars, "but consider it a settled thing, if no obstacle arises on your part."

"I am, indeed, rejoiced," said Andrea.

"But," said Danglars thoughtfully, "how is it that your patron, M. de Monte Cristo, did not make his proposal for you?" Andrea blushed imperceptibly. "I have just left the count, sir," said he; "he is, doubtless, a delightful man but inconceivably peculiar in his ideas. He esteems me highly. He even told me he had not the slightest doubt that my father would give me the capital instead of the interest of my property. He has promised to use his influence to obtain it for me; but he also declared that he never had taken on himself the responsibility of making proposals for another, and he never would. I must, however, do him the justice to add that he assured me if ever he had regretted the repugnance he felt to such a step it was on this occasion, because he thought the projected union would be a happy and suitable one. Besides, if he will do nothing officially, he will answer any questions you propose to him. And now," continued he, with one of his most charming smiles, "having finished talking to the father-in-law, I must address myself to the banker."

"And what may you have to say to him?" said Danglars, laughing in his turn.

"That the day after to-morrow I shall have to draw upon you for about four thousand francs; but the count, expecting my bachelor's revenue could not suffice for the coming month's outlay, has offered me a draft for twenty thousand francs. It bears his signature, as you see, which is all-sufficient."

"Bring me a million such as that," said Danglars, "I shall be well pleased," putting the draft in his pocket. "Fix your own hour for to-morrow, and my cashier shall call on you with a check for eighty thousand francs."

"At ten o'clock then, if you please; I should like it early, as I am going into the country to-morrow."

"Very well, at ten o'clock; you are still at the Hotel des Princes?"

"Yes."

The following morning, with the banker's usual punctuality, the eighty thousand francs were placed in the young man's hands as he was on the point of starting, after having left two hundred francs for Caderousse. He went out chiefly to avoid this dangerous enemy, and returned as late as possible in the evening. But scarcely had he stepped out of his carriage when the porter met him with a parcel in his hand. "Sir," said he, "that man has been here."

"What man?" said Andrea carelessly, apparently forgetting him whom he but too well recollected.

"Him to whom your excellency pays that little annuity."

"Oh," said Andrea, "my father's old servant. Well, you gave him the two hundred francs I had left for him?"

"Yes, your excellency." Andrea had expressed a wish to be thus addressed. "But," continued the porter, "he would not take them." Andrea turned pale, but as it was dark his pallor was not perceptible. "What? he would not take them?" said he with slight emotion.

"No, he wished to speak to your excellency; I told him you were gone out, and after some dispute he believed me and gave me this letter, which he had brought with him already sealed."

"Give it me," said Andrea, and he read by the light of his carriage-lamp,—"You know where I live; I expect you tomorrow morning at nine o'clock."

Andrea examined it carefully, to ascertain if the letter had been opened, or if any indiscreet eyes had seen its contents; but it was so carefully folded, that no one could have read it, and the seal was perfect. "Very well," said he. "Poor man, he is a worthy creature." He left the porter to ponder on these words, not knowing which most to admire, the master or the servant. "Take out the horses quickly, and come up to me," said Andrea to his groom. In two seconds the young man had reached his room and burnt Caderousse's letter. The servant entered just as he had finished. "You are about my height, Pierre," said he.

"I have that honor, your excellency."

"You had a new livery yesterday?"

"Yes, sir."

"I have an engagement with a pretty little girl for this evening, and do not wish to be known; lend me your livery till to-morrow. I may sleep, perhaps, at an inn." Pierre obeyed. Five minutes after, Andrea left the hotel, completely disguised, took a cabriolet, and ordered the driver to take him to the Cheval Rouge, at Picpus. The next morning he left that inn as he had left the Hotel des Princes, without being noticed, walked down the Faubourg St. Antoine, along the boulevard to Rue Menilmontant, and stopping at the door of the third house on the left looked for some one of whom to make inquiry in the porter's absence. "For whom are you looking, my fine fellow?" asked the fruiteress on the opposite side.

"Monsieur Pailletin, if you please, my good woman," replied Andrea.

"A retired baker?" asked the fruiteress.

"Exactly."

"He lives at the end of the yard, on the left, on the third story." Andrea went as she directed him, and on the third floor he found a hare's paw, which, by the hasty ringing of the bell, it was evident he pulled with considerable ill-temper. A moment after Caderousse's face appeared at the grating in the door. "Ah, you are punctual," said he, as he drew back the door.

"Confound you and your punctuality!" said Andrea, throwing himself into a chair in a manner which implied that he would rather have flung it at the head of his host.

"Come, come, my little fellow, don't be angry. See, I have thought about you—look at the good breakfast we are going to have; nothing but what you are fond of." Andrea, indeed, inhaled the scent of something cooking which was not unwelcome to him, hungry as he was; it was that mixture of fat and garlic peculiar to provincial kitchens of an inferior order, added to that of dried fish, and above all, the pungent smell of musk and cloves. These odors escaped from two deep dishes which were covered and placed on a stove, and from a copper pan placed in an old iron pot. In an adjoining room Andrea saw also a tolerably clean table prepared for two, two bottles of wine sealed, the one with green, the other with yellow, a supply of brandy in a decanter, and a measure of fruit in a cabbage-leaf, cleverly arranged on an earthenware plate.

"What do you think of it, my little fellow?" said Caderousse. "Ay, that smells good! You know I used to be a famous cook; do you recollect how you used to lick your fingers? You were among the first who tasted any of my dishes, and I think you relished them tolerably." While speaking, Caderousse went on peeling a fresh supply of onions.

"But," said Andrea, ill-temperedly, "by my faith, if it was only to breakfast with you, that you disturbed me, I wish the devil had taken you!"

"My boy," said Caderousse sententiously, "one can talk while eating. And then, you ungrateful being, you are not pleased to see an old friend? I am weeping with joy." He was truly crying, but it would have been difficult to say whether joy or the onions produced the greatest effect on the lachrymal glands of the old inn-keeper of the Pont-du-Gard. "Hold your tongue, hypocrite," said Andrea; "you love me!"

"Yes, I do, or may the devil take me. I know it is a weakness," said Caderousse, "but it overpowers me."

"And yet it has not prevented your sending for me to play me some trick."

"Come," said Caderousse, wiping his large knife on his apron, "if I did not like you, do you think I should endure the wretched life you lead me? Think for a moment. You have your servant's clothes on—you therefore keep a servant; I have none, and am obliged to prepare my own meals. You abuse my cookery because you dine at the table d'hote of the Hotel des Princes, or the Cafe de Paris. Well, I too could keep a servant; I too could have a tilbury; I too could dine where I like; but why do I not? Because I would not annoy my little Benedetto. Come, just acknowledge that I could, eh?" This address was accompanied by a look which was by no means difficult to understand. "Well," said Andrea, "admitting your love, why do you want me to breakfast with you?"

"That I may have the pleasure of seeing you, my little fellow."

"What is the use of seeing me after we have made all our arrangements?"

"Eh, dear friend," said Caderousse, "are wills ever made without codicils? But you first came to breakfast, did you not? Well, sit down, and let us begin with these pilchards, and this fresh butter; which I have put on some vine-leaves to please you, wicked one. Ah, yes; you look at my room, my four straw chairs, my images, three francs each. But what do you expect? This is not the Hotel des Princes."

"Come, you are growing discontented, you are no longer happy; you, who only wish to live like a retired baker." Caderousse sighed. "Well, what have you to say? you have seen your dream realized."

"I can still say it is a dream; a retired baker, my poor Benedetto, is rich—he has an annuity."

"Well, you have an annuity."

"I have?"

"Yes, since I bring you your two hundred francs." Caderousse shrugged his shoulders. "It is humiliating," said he, "thus to receive money given grudgingly,—an uncertain supply which may soon fail. You see I am obliged to economize, in case your prosperity should cease. Well, my friend, fortune is inconstant, as the chaplain of the regiment said. I know your prosperity is great, you rascal; you are to marry the daughter of Danglars."

"What? of Danglars?"

"Yes, to be sure; must I say Baron Danglars? I might as well say Count Benedetto. He was an old friend of mine and if he had not so bad a memory he ought to invite me to your wedding, seeing he came to mine. Yes, yes, to mine; gad, he was not so proud then,—he was an under-clerk to the good M. Morrel. I have dined many times with him and the Count of Morcerf, so you see I have some high connections and were I to cultivate them a little, we might meet in the same drawing-rooms."

"Come, your jealousy represents everything to you in the wrong light."

"That is all very fine, Benedetto mio, but I know what I am saying. Perhaps I may one day put on my best coat, and presenting myself at the great gate, introduce myself. Meanwhile let us sit down and eat." Caderousse set the example and attacked the breakfast with good appetite, praising each dish he set before his visitor. The latter seemed to have resigned himself; he drew the corks, and partook largely of the fish with the garlic and fat. "Ah, mate," said Caderousse, "you are getting on better terms with your old landlord!"

"Faith, yes," replied Andrea, whose hunger prevailed over every other feeling.

"So you like it, you rogue?"

"So much that I wonder how a man who can cook thus can complain of hard living."

"Do you see," said Caderousse, "all my happiness is marred by one thought?"

"What is that?"

"That I am dependent on another, I who have always gained my own livelihood honestly."

"Do not let that disturb you, I have enough for two."

"No, truly; you may believe me if you will; at the end of every month I am tormented by remorse."

"Good Caderousse!"

"So much so, that yesterday I would not take the two hundred francs."

"Yes, you wished to speak to me; but was it indeed remorse, tell me?"

"True remorse; and, besides, an idea had struck me." Andrea shuddered; he always did so at Caderousse's ideas. "It is miserable—do you see?—always to wait till the end of the month."—"Oh," said Andrea philosophically, determined to watch his companion narrowly, "does not life pass in waiting? Do I, for instance, fare better? Well, I wait patiently, do I not?"

"Yes; because instead of expecting two hundred wretched francs, you expect five or six thousand, perhaps ten, perhaps even twelve, for you take care not to let any one know the utmost. Down there, you always had little presents and Christmas-boxes which you tried to hide from your poor friend Caderousse. Fortunately he is a cunning fellow, that friend Caderousse."

"There you are beginning again to ramble, to talk again and again of the past! But what is the use of teasing me with going all over that again?"

"Ah, you are only one and twenty, and can forget the past; I am fifty, and am obliged to recollect it. But let us return to business."

"Yes."

"I was going to say, if I were in your place"—

"Well."

"I would realize"—

"How would you realize?"

"I would ask for six months' in advance, under pretence of being able to purchase a farm, then with my six months I would decamp."

"Well, well," said Andrea, "that isn't a bad idea."

"My dear friend," said Caderousse, "eat of my bread, and take my advice; you will be none the worse off, physically or morally."

"But," said Andrea, "why do you not act on the advice you gave me? Why do you not realize a six months', a year's advance even, and retire to Brussels? Instead of living the retired baker, you might live as a bankrupt, using his privileges; that would be very good."

"But how the devil would you have me retire on twelve hundred francs?"

"Ah, Caderousse," said Andrea, "how covetous you are! Two months ago you were dying with hunger."

"The appetite grows by what it feeds on," said Caderousse, grinning and showing his teeth, like a monkey laughing or a tiger growling. "And," added he, biting off with his large white teeth an enormous mouthful of bread, "I have formed a plan." Caderousse's plans alarmed Andrea still more than his ideas; ideas were but the germ, the plan was reality. "Let me see your plan; I dare say it is a pretty one."

"Why not? Who formed the plan by which we left the establishment of M——! eh? was it not I? and it was no bad one I believe, since here we are!"

"I do not say," replied Andrea, "that you never make a good one; but let us see your plan."

"Well," pursued Caderousse, "can you without expending one sou, put me in the way of getting fifteen thousand francs? No, fifteen thousand are not enough,—I cannot again become an honest man with less than thirty thousand francs."

"No," replied Andrea, dryly, "no, I cannot."

"I do not think you understand me," replied Caderousse, calmly; "I said without your laying out a sou."

"Do you want me to commit a robbery, to spoil all my good fortune—and yours with mine—and both of us to be dragged down there again?"

"It would make very little difference to me," said Caderousse, "if I were retaken, I am a poor creature to live alone, and sometimes pine for my old comrades; not like you, heartless creature, who would be glad never to see them again." Andrea did more than tremble this time, he turned pale.

"Come, Caderousse, no nonsense!" said he.

"Don't alarm yourself, my little Benedetto, but just point out to me some means of gaining those thirty thousand francs without your assistance, and I will contrive it."

"Well, I'll see—I'll try to contrive some way," said Andrea.

"Meanwhile you will raise my monthly allowance to five hundred francs, my little fellow? I have a fancy, and mean to get a housekeeper."

"Well, you shall have your five hundred francs," said Andrea; "but it is very hard for me, my poor Caderousse— you take advantage"—

"Bah," said Caderousse, "when you have access to countless stores." One would have said Andrea anticipated his companion's words, so did his eye flash like lightning, but it was but for a moment. "True," he replied, "and my protector is very kind."

"That dear protector," said Caderousse; "and how much does he give you monthly?"

"Five thousand francs."

"As many thousands as you give me hundreds! Truly, it is only bastards who are thus fortunate. Five thousand francs per month! What the devil can you do with all that?"

"Oh, it is no trouble to spend that; and I am like you, I want capital."

"Capital?—yes—I understand—every one would like capital."

"Well, and I shall get it."

"Who will give it to you—your prince?"

"Yes, my prince. But unfortunately I must wait."

"You must wait for what?" asked Caderousse.

"For his death."

"The death of your prince?"

"Yes."

"How so?"

"Because he has made his will in my favor."

"Indeed?"

"On my honor."

"For how much?"

"For five hundred thousand."

"Only that? It's little enough."

"But so it is."

"No it cannot be!"

"Are you my friend, Caderousse?"

"Yes, in life or death."

"Well, I will tell you a secret."

"What is it?"

"But remember"—

"Ah, pardieu, mute as a carp."

"Well, I think"—Andrea stopped and looked around.

"You think? Do not fear; pardieu, we are alone."

"I think I have discovered my father."

"Your true father?"

"Yes."

"Not old Cavalcanti?"

"No, for he has gone again; the true one, as you say."

"And that father is"—

"Well, Caderousse, it is Monte Cristo."

"Bah!"

"Yes, you understand, that explains all. He cannot acknowledge me openly, it appears, but he does it through M. Cavalcanti, and gives him fifty thousand francs for it."

"Fifty thousand francs for being your father? I would have done it for half that, for twenty thousand, for fifteen thousand; why did you not think of me, ungrateful man?"

"Did I know anything about it, when it was all done when I was down there?"

"Ah, truly? And you say that by his will"—

"He leaves me five hundred thousand livres."

"Are you sure of it?"

"He showed it me; but that is not all—there is a codicil, as I said just now."

"Probably."

"And in that codicil he acknowledges me."

"Oh, the good father, the brave father, the very honest father!" said Caderousse, twirling a plate in the air between his two hands.

"Now say if I conceal anything from you?"

"No, and your confidence makes you honorable in my opinion; and your princely father, is he rich, very rich?"

"Yes, he is that; he does not himself know the amount of his fortune."

"Is it possible?"

"It is evident enough to me, who am always at his house. The other day a banker's clerk brought him fifty thousand francs in a portfolio about the size of your plate; yesterday his banker brought him a hundred thousand francs in gold." Caderousse was filled with wonder; the young man's words sounded to him like metal, and he thought he could hear the rushing of cascades of louis. "And you go into that house?" cried he briskly.

"When I like."

Caderousse was thoughtful for a moment. It was easy to perceive he was revolving some unfortunate idea in his mind. Then suddenly,—"How I should like to see all that," cried he; "how beautiful it must be!"

"It is, in fact, magnificent," said Andrea.

"And does he not live in the Champs-Elysees?"

"Yes, No. 30."

"Ah," said Caderousse, "No. 30."

"Yes, a fine house standing alone, between a court-yard and a garden,—you must know it."

"Possibly; but it is not the exterior I care for, it is the interior. What beautiful furniture there must be in it!"

"Have you ever seen the Tuileries?"

"No."

"Well, it surpasses that."

"It must be worth one's while to stoop, Andrea, when that good M. Monte Cristo lets fall his purse."

"It is not worth while to wait for that," said Andrea; "money is as plentiful in that house as fruit in an orchard."

"But you should take me there one day with you."

"How can I? On what plea?"

"You are right; but you have made my mouth water. I must absolutely see it; I shall find a way."

"No nonsense, Caderousse!"

"I will offer myself as floor-polisher."

"The rooms are all carpeted."

"Well, then, I must be contented to imagine it."

"That is the best plan, believe me."

"Try, at least, to give me an idea of what it is."

"How can I?"

"Nothing is easier. Is it large?"

"Middling."

"How is it arranged?"

"Faith, I should require pen, ink, and paper to make a plan."

"They are all here," said Caderousse, briskly. He fetched from an old secretary a sheet of white paper and pen and ink. "Here," said Caderousse, "draw me all that on the paper, my boy." Andrea took the pen with an imperceptible smile and began. "The house, as I said, is between the court and the garden; in this way, do you see?" Andrea drew the garden, the court and the house.

"High walls?"

"Not more than eight or ten feet."

"That is not prudent," said Caderousse.

"In the court are orange-trees in pots, turf, and clumps of flowers."

"And no steel-traps?"

"No."

"The stables?"

"Are on either side of the gate, which you see there." And Andrea continued his plan.

"Let us see the ground floor," said Caderousse.

"On the ground-floor, dining-room, two drawing-rooms, billiard-room, staircase in the hall, and a little back staircase."

"Windows?"

"Magnificent windows, so beautiful, so large, that I believe a man of your size should pass through each frame."

"Why the devil have they any stairs with such windows?"

"Luxury has everything."

"But shutters?"

"Yes, but they are never used. That Count of Monte Cristo is an original, who loves to look at the sky even at night."

"And where do the servants sleep?"

"Oh, they have a house to themselves. Picture to yourself a pretty coach-house at the right-hand side where the ladders are kept. Well, over that coach-house are the servants' rooms, with bells corresponding with the different apartments."

"Ah, diable—bells did you say?"

"What do you mean?"

"Oh, nothing! I only say they cost a load of money to hang, and what is the use of them, I should like to know?"

"There used to be a dog let loose in the yard at night, but it has been taken to the house at Auteuil, to that you went to, you know."

"Yes."

"I was saying to him only yesterday, 'You are imprudent, Monsieur Count; for when you go to Auteuil and take your servants the house is left unprotected.' 'Well,' said he, 'what next?' 'Well, next, some day you will be robbed.'"

"What did he answer?"

"He quietly said, 'What do I care if I am?'"

"Andrea, he has some secretary with a spring."

"How do you know?"

"Yes, which catches the thief in a trap and plays a tune. I was told there were such at the last exhibition."

"He has simply a mahogany secretary, in which the key is always kept."

"And he is not robbed?"

"No; his servants are all devoted to him."

"There ought to be some money in that secretary?"

"There may be. No one knows what there is."

"And where is it?"

"On the first floor."

"Sketch me the plan of that floor, as you have done of the ground floor, my boy."

"That is very simple." Andrea took the pen. "On the first story, do you see, there is the anteroom and the drawing-room; to the right of the drawing-room, a library and a study; to the left, a bedroom and a dressing-room. The famous secretary is in the dressing-room."

"Is there a window in the dressing-room?"

"Two,—one here and one there." Andrea sketched two windows in the room, which formed an angle on the plan, and appeared as a small square added to the rectangle of the bedroom. Caderousse became thoughtful. "Does he often go to Auteuil?" added he.

"Two or three times a week. To-morrow, for instance, he is going to spend the day and night there."

"Are you sure of it?"

"He has invited me to dine there."

"There's a life for you," said Caderousse; "a town house and a country house."

"That is what it is to be rich."

"And shall you dine there?"

"Probably."

"When you dine there, do you sleep there?"

"If I like; I am at home there." Caderousse looked at the young man, as if to get at the truth from the bottom of his heart. But Andrea drew a cigar-case from his pocket, took a Havana, quietly lit it, and began smoking. "When do you want your twelve hundred francs?" said he to Caderousse.

"Now, if you have them." Andrea took five and twenty louis from his pocket.

"Yellow boys?" said Caderousse; "no, I thank you."

"Oh, you despise them."

"On the contrary, I esteem them, but will not have them."

"You can change them, idiot; gold is worth five sous."

"Exactly; and he who changes them will follow friend Caderousse, lay hands on him, and demand what farmers pay him their rent in gold. No nonsense, my good fellow; silver simply, round coins with the head of some monarch or other on them. Anybody may possess a five-franc piece."

"But do you suppose I carry five hundred francs about with me? I should want a porter."

"Well, leave them with your porter; he is to be trusted. I will call for them."

"To-day?"

"No, to-morrow; I shall not have time to day."

"Well, to-morrow I will leave them when I go to Auteuil."

"May I depend on it?"

"Certainly."

"Because I shall secure my housekeeper on the strength of it."

"Now see here, will that be all? Eh? And will you not torment me any more?"

"Never." Caderousse had become so gloomy that Andrea feared he should be obliged to notice the change. He redoubled his gayety and carelessness. "How sprightly you are," said Caderousse; "One would say you were already in possession of your property."

"No, unfortunately; but when I do obtain it"—

"Well?"

"I shall remember old friends, I can tell you that."

"Yes, since you have such a good memory."

"What do you want? It looks as if you were trying to fleece me?"

"I? What an idea! I, who am going to give you another piece of good advice."

"What is it?"

"To leave behind you the diamond you have on your finger. We shall both get into trouble. You will ruin both yourself and me by your folly."

"How so?" said Andrea.

"How? You put on a livery, you disguise yourself as a servant, and yet keep a diamond on your finger worth four or five thousand francs."

"You guess well."

"I know something of diamonds; I have had some."

"You do well to boast of it," said Andrea, who, without becoming angry, as Caderousse feared, at this new extortion, quietly resigned the ring. Caderousse looked so closely at it that Andrea well knew that he was examining to see if all the edges were perfect.

"It is a false diamond," said Caderousse.

"You are joking now," replied Andrea.

"Do not be angry, we can try it." Caderousse went to the window, touched the glass with it, and found it would cut.

"Confiteor," said Caderousse, putting the diamond on his little finger; "I was mistaken; but those thieves of jewellers imitate so well that it is no longer worth while to rob a jeweller's shop—it is another branch of industry paralyzed."

"Have you finished?" said Andrea,—"do you want anything more?—will you have my waistcoat or my hat? Make free, now you have begun."

"No; you are, after all, a good companion; I will not detain you, and will try to cure myself of my ambition."

"But take care the same thing does not happen to you in selling the diamond you feared with the gold."

"I shall not sell it—do not fear."

"Not at least till the day after to-morrow," thought the young man.

"Happy rogue," said Caderousse; "you are going to find your servants, your horses, your carriage, and your betrothed!"

"Yes," said Andrea.

"Well, I hope you will make a handsome wedding-present the day you marry Mademoiselle Danglars."

"I have already told you it is a fancy you have taken in your head."

"What fortune has she?"

"But I tell you"—

"A million?" Andrea shrugged his shoulders.

"Let it be a million," said Caderousse; "you can never have so much as I wish you."

"Thank you," said the young man.

"Oh, I wish it you with all my heart!" added Caderousse with his hoarse laugh. "Stop, let me show you the way."

"It is not worth while."

"Yes, it is."

"Why?"

"Because there is a little secret, a precaution I thought it desirable to take, one of Huret & Fitchet's locks, revised and improved by Gaspard Caderousse; I will manufacture you a similar one when you are a capitalist."

"Thank you," said Andrea; "I will let you know a week beforehand." They parted. Caderousse remained on the landing until he had not only seen Andrea go down the three stories, but also cross the court. Then he returned hastily, shut his door carefully, and began to study, like a clever architect, the plan Andrea had left him.

"Dear Benedetto," said he, "I think he will not be sorry to inherit his fortune, and he who hastens the day when he can touch his five hundred thousand will not be his worst friend."

CHAPTER 82.
THE BURGLARY.

The day following that on which the conversation we have related took place, the Count of Monte Cristo set out for Auteuil, accompanied by Ali and several attendants, and also taking with him some horses whose qualities he was desirous of ascertaining. He was induced to undertake this journey, of which the day before he had not even thought and which had not occurred to Andrea either, by the arrival of Bertuccio from Normandy with intelligence respecting the house and sloop. The house was ready, and the sloop which had arrived a week before lay at anchor in a small creek with her crew of six men, who had observed all the requisite formalities and were ready again to put to sea.

The count praised Bertuccio's zeal, and ordered him to prepare for a speedy departure, as his stay in France would not be prolonged more than a month. "Now," said he, "I may require to go in one night from Paris to Treport; let eight fresh horses be in readiness on the road, which will enable me to go fifty leagues in ten hours."

"Your highness had already expressed that wish," said Bertuccio, "and the horses are ready. I have bought them, and stationed them myself at the most desirable posts, that is, in villages, where no one generally stops."

"That's well," said Monte Cristo; "I remain here a day or two—arrange accordingly." As Bertuccio was leaving the room to give the requisite orders, Baptistin opened the door: he held a letter on a silver waiter.

"What are you doing here?" asked the count, seeing him covered with dust; "I did not send for you, I think?"

Baptistin, without answering, approached the count, and presented the letter. "Important and urgent," said he. The count opened the letter, and read:—

"M. de Monte Cristo is apprised that this night a man will enter his house in the Champs-Elysees with the intention of carrying off some papers supposed to be in the secretary in the dressing-room. The count's well-known courage will render unnecessary the aid of the police, whose interference might seriously affect him who sends this advice. The count, by any opening from the bedroom, or by concealing himself in the dressing-room, would be able to defend his property himself. Many attendants or apparent precautions would prevent the villain from the attempt, and M. de Monte Cristo would lose the opportunity of discovering an enemy whom chance has revealed to him who now sends this warning to the count,—a warning he might not be able to send another time, if this first attempt should fail and another be made."

The count's first idea was that this was an artifice—a gross deception, to draw his attention from a minor danger in order to expose him to a greater. He was on the point of sending the letter to the commissary of police, notwithstanding the advice of his anonymous friend, or perhaps because of that advice, when suddenly the idea occurred to him that it might be some personal enemy, whom he alone should recognize and over whom, if such were the case, he alone would gain any advantage, as Fiesco [*] had done over the Moor who would have killed him. We know the Count's vigorous and daring mind, denying anything to be impossible, with that energy which marks the great man. From his past life, from his resolution to shrink from nothing, the count had acquired an inconceivable relish for the contests in which he had engaged, sometimes against nature, that is to say, against God, and sometimes against the world, that is, against the devil.

* The Genoese conspirator.

"They do not want my papers," said Monte Cristo, "they want to kill me; they are no robbers, but assassins. I will not allow the prefect of police to interfere with my private affairs. I am rich enough, forsooth, to distribute his authority on this occasion." The count recalled Baptistin, who had left the room after delivering the letter. "Return to Paris," said he; "assemble the servants who remain there. I want all my household at Auteuil."

"But will no one remain in the house, my lord?" asked Baptistin.

"Yes, the porter."

"My lord will remember that the lodge is at a distance from the house."

"Well?"

"The house might be stripped without his hearing the least noise."

"By whom?"

"By thieves."

"You are a fool, M. Baptistin. Thieves might strip the house—it would annoy me less than to be disobeyed." Baptistin bowed.

"You understand me?" said the count. "Bring your comrades here, one and all; but let everything remain as usual, only close the shutters of the ground floor."

"And those of the second floor?"

"You know they are never closed. Go!"

The count signified his intention of dining alone, and that no one but Ali should attend him. Having dined with his usual tranquillity and moderation, the count, making a signal to Ali to follow him, went out by the side-gate and on reaching the Bois de Boulogne turned, apparently without design towards Paris and at twilight; found himself opposite his house in the Champs-Elysees. All was dark; one solitary, feeble light was burning in the porter's lodge, about forty paces distant from the house, as Baptistin had said. Monte Cristo leaned against a tree, and with that scrutinizing glance which was so rarely deceived, looked up and down the avenue, examined the passers-by, and carefully looked down the neighboring streets, to see that no one was concealed. Ten minutes passed thus, and he was convinced that no one was watching him. He hastened to the side-door with Ali, entered hurriedly, and by the servants' staircase, of which he had the key, gained his bedroom without opening or disarranging a single curtain, without even the porter having the slightest suspicion that the house, which he supposed empty, contained its chief occupant.

Arrived in his bedroom, the count motioned to Ali to stop; then he passed into the dressing-room, which he examined. Everything appeared as usual—the precious secretary in its place, and the key in the secretary. He double locked it, took the key, returned to the bedroom door, removed the double staple of the bolt, and went in. Meanwhile Ali had procured the arms the count required—namely, a short carbine and a pair of double-barrelled pistols, with which as sure an aim might be taken as with a single-barrelled one. Thus armed, the count held the lives of five men in his hands. It was about half-past nine. The count and Ali ate in haste a crust of bread and drank a glass of Spanish wine; then Monte Cristo slipped aside one of the movable panels, which enabled him to see into the adjoining room. He had within his reach his pistols and carbine, and Ali, standing near him, held one of the small Arabian hatchets, whose form has not varied since the Crusades. Through one of the windows of the bedroom, on a line with that in the dressing-room, the count could see into the street.

Two hours passed thus. It was intensely dark; still Ali, thanks to his wild nature, and the count, thanks doubtless to his long confinement, could distinguish in the darkness the slightest movement of the trees. The little light in the lodge had long been extinct. It might be expected that the attack, if indeed an attack was projected, would be made from the staircase of the ground floor, and not from a window; in Monte Cristo's opinion, the villains sought his life, not his money. It would be his bedroom they would attack, and they must reach it by the back staircase, or by the window in the dressing-room. The clock of the Invalides struck a quarter to twelve; the west wind bore on its moistened gusts the doleful vibration of the three strokes.

As the last stroke died away, the count thought he heard a slight noise in the dressing-room; this first sound, or rather this first grinding, was followed by a second, then a third; at the fourth, the count knew what to expect. A firm and well-practised hand was engaged in cutting the four sides of a pane of glass with a diamond. The count felt his heart beat more rapidly. Inured as men may be to danger, forewarned as they may be of peril, they understand, by the fluttering of the heart and the shuddering of the frame, the enormous difference between a dream and a reality, between the project and the execution. However, Monte Cristo only made a sign to apprise Ali, who, understanding that danger was approaching from the other side, drew nearer to his master. Monte Cristo was eager to ascertain the strength and number of his enemies.

The window whence the noise proceeded was opposite the opening by which the count could see into the dressing-room. He fixed his eyes on that window—he distinguished a shadow in the darkness; then one of the panes became quite opaque, as if a sheet of paper were stuck on the outside, then the square cracked without falling. Through the opening an arm was passed to find the fastening, then a second; the window turned on its hinges, and a man entered. He was alone.

"That's a daring rascal," whispered the count.

At that moment Ali touched him slightly on the shoulder. He turned; Ali pointed to the window of the room in which they were, facing the street. "I see!" said he, "there are two of them; one does the work while the other stands guard." He made a sign to Ali not to lose sight of the man in the street, and turned to the one in the dressing-room.

The glass-cutter had entered, and was feeling his way, his arms stretched out before him. At last he appeared to have made himself familiar with his surroundings. There were two doors; he bolted them both.

When he drew near to the bedroom door, Monte Cristo expected that he was coming in, and raised one of his pistols;

but he simply heard the sound of the bolts sliding in their copper rings. It was only a precaution. The nocturnal visitor, ignorant of the fact that the count had removed the staples, might now think himself at home, and pursue his purpose with full security. Alone and free to act as he wished, the man then drew from his pocket something which the count could not discern, placed it on a stand, then went straight to the secretary, felt the lock, and contrary to his expectation found that the key was missing. But the glass-cutter was a prudent man who had provided for all emergencies. The count soon heard the rattling of a bunch of skeleton keys, such as the locksmith brings when called to force a lock, and which thieves call nightingales, doubtless from the music of their nightly song when they grind against the bolt. "Ah, ha," whispered Monte Cristo with a smile of disappointment, "he is only a thief."

But the man in the dark could not find the right key. He reached the instrument he had placed on the stand, touched a spring, and immediately a pale light, just bright enough to render objects distinct, was reflected on his hands and countenance. "By heavens," exclaimed Monte Cristo, starting back, "it is"—

Ali raised his hatchet. "Don't stir," whispered Monte Cristo, "and put down your hatchet; we shall require no arms." Then he added some words in a low tone, for the exclamation which surprise had drawn from the count, faint as it had been, had startled the man who remained in the pose of the old knife-grinder. It was an order the count had just given, for immediately Ali went noiselessly, and returned, bearing a black dress and a three-cornered hat. Meanwhile Monte Cristo had rapidly taken off his great-coat, waistcoat, and shirt, and one might distinguish by the glimmering through the open panel that he wore a pliant tunic of steel mail, of which the last in France, where daggers are no longer dreaded, was worn by King Louis XVI., who feared the dagger at his breast, and whose head was cleft with a hatchet. The tunic soon disappeared under a long cassock, as did his hair under a priest's wig; the three-cornered hat over this effectually transformed the count into an abbe.

The man, hearing nothing more, stood erect, and while Monte Cristo was completing his disguise had advanced straight to the secretary, whose lock was beginning to crack under his nightingale.

"Try again," whispered the count, who depended on the secret spring, which was unknown to the picklock, clever as he might be—"try again, you have a few minutes' work there." And he advanced to the window. The man whom he had seen seated on a fence had got down, and was still pacing the street; but, strange as it appeared, he cared not for those who might pass from the avenue of the Champs-Elysees or by the Faubourg St. Honore; his attention was engrossed with what was passing at the count's, and his only aim appeared to be to discern every movement in the dressing-room.

Monte Cristo suddenly struck his finger on his forehead and a smile passed over his lips; then drawing near to Ali, he whispered,—

"Remain here, concealed in the dark, and whatever noise you hear, whatever passes, only come in or show yourself if I call you." Ali bowed in token of strict obedience. Monte Cristo then drew a lighted taper from a closet, and when the thief was deeply engaged with his lock, silently opened the door, taking care that the light should shine directly on his face. The door opened so quietly that the thief heard no sound; but, to his astonishment, the room was suddenly illuminated. He turned.

"Ah, good-evening, my dear M. Caderousse," said Monte Cristo; "what are you doing here, at such an hour?"

"The Abbe Busoni!" exclaimed Caderousse; and, not knowing how this strange apparition could have entered when he had bolted the doors, he let fall his bunch of keys, and remained motionless and stupefied. The count placed himself between Caderousse and the window, thus cutting off from the thief his only chance of retreat. "The Abbe Busoni!" repeated Caderousse, fixing his haggard gaze on the count.

"Yes, undoubtedly, the Abbe Busoni himself," replied Monte Cristo. "And I am very glad you recognize me, dear

M. Caderousse; it proves you have a good memory, for it must be about ten years since we last met." This calmness of Busoni, combined with his irony and boldness, staggered Caderousse.

"The abbe, the abbe!" murmured he, clinching his fists, and his teeth chattering.

"So you would rob the Count of Monte Cristo?" continued the false abbe.

"Reverend sir," murmured Caderousse, seeking to regain the window, which the count pitilessly blocked—"reverend sir, I don't know—believe me—I take my oath"—

"A pane of glass out," continued the count, "a dark lantern, a bunch of false keys, a secretary half forced—it is tolerably evident"—

Caderousse was choking; he looked around for some corner to hide in, some way of escape.

"Come, come," continued the count, "I see you are still the same,—an assassin."

"Reverend sir, since you know everything, you know it was not I—it was La Carconte; that was proved at the trial, since I was only condemned to the galleys."

"Is your time, then, expired, since I find you in a fair way to return there?"

"No, reverend sir; I have been liberated by some one."

"That some one has done society a great kindness."

"Ah," said Caderousse, "I had promised"—

183

"And you are breaking your promise!" interrupted Monte Cristo.

"Alas, yes!" said Caderousse very uneasily.

"A bad relapse, that will lead you, if I mistake not, to the Place de Greve. So much the worse, so much the worse—diavolo, as they say in my country."

"Reverend sir, I am impelled"—

"Every criminal says the same thing."

"Poverty"—

"Pshaw!" said Busoni disdainfully; "poverty may make a man beg, steal a loaf of bread at a baker's door, but not cause him to open a secretary in a house supposed to be inhabited. And when the jeweller Johannes had just paid you 40,000. francs for the diamond I had given you, and you killed him to get the diamond and the money both, was that also poverty?"

"Pardon, reverend sir," said Caderousse; "you have saved my life once, save me again!"

"That is but poor encouragement."

"Are you alone, reverend sir, or have you there soldiers ready to seize me?"

"I am alone," said the abbe, "and I will again have pity on you, and will let you escape, at the risk of the fresh miseries my weakness may lead to, if you tell me the truth."

"Ah, reverend sir," cried Caderousse, clasping his hands, and drawing nearer to Monte Cristo, "I may indeed say you are my deliverer!"

"You mean to say you have been freed from confinement?"

"Yes, that is true, reverend sir."

"Who was your liberator?"

"An Englishman."

"What was his name?"

"Lord Wilmore."

"I know him; I shall know if you lie."

"Ah, reverend sir, I tell you the simple truth."

"Was this Englishman protecting you?"

"No, not me, but a young Corsican, my companion."

"What was this young Corsican's name?"

"Benedetto."

"Is that his Christian name?"

"He had no other; he was a foundling."

"Then this young man escaped with you?"

"He did."

"In what way?"

"We were working at St. Mandrier, near Toulon. Do you know St. Mandrier?"

"I do."

"In the hour of rest, between noon and one o'clock"—

"Galley-slaves having a nap after dinner! We may well pity the poor fellows!" said the abbe.

"Nay," said Caderousse, "one can't always work—one is not a dog."

"So much the better for the dogs," said Monte Cristo.

"While the rest slept, then, we went away a short distance; we severed our fetters with a file the Englishman had given us, and swam away."

"And what is become of this Benedetto?"

"I don't know."

"You ought to know."

"No, in truth; we parted at Hyeres." And, to give more weight to his protestation, Caderousse advanced another step towards the abbe, who remained motionless in his place, as calm as ever, and pursuing his interrogation. "You lie," said the Abbe Busoni, with a tone of irresistible authority.

"Reverend sir!"

"You lie! This man is still your friend, and you, perhaps, make use of him as your accomplice."

"Oh, reverend sir!"

"Since you left Toulon what have you lived on? Answer me!"

"On what I could get."

"You lie," repeated the abbe a third time, with a still more imperative tone. Caderousse, terrified, looked at the count. "You have lived on the money he has given you."

"True," said Caderousse; "Benedetto has become the son of a great lord."

"How can he be the son of a great lord?"

"A natural son."

"And what is that great lord's name?"

"The Count of Monte Cristo, the very same in whose house we are."

"Benedetto the count's son?" replied Monte Cristo, astonished in his turn.

"Well, I should think so, since the count has found him a false father—since the count gives him four thousand francs a month, and leaves him 500,000 francs in his will."

"Ah, yes," said the factitious abbe, who began to understand; "and what name does the young man bear meanwhile?"

"Andrea Cavalcanti."

"Is it, then, that young man whom my friend the Count of Monte Cristo has received into his house, and who is going to marry Mademoiselle Danglars?"

"Exactly."

"And you suffer that, you wretch—you, who know his life and his crime?"

"Why should I stand in a comrade's way?" said Caderousse.

"You are right; it is not you who should apprise M. Danglars, it is I."

"Do not do so, reverend sir."

"Why not?"

"Because you would bring us to ruin."

"And you think that to save such villains as you I will become an abettor of their plot, an accomplice in their crimes?"

"Reverend sir," said Caderousse, drawing still nearer.

"I will expose all."

"To whom?"

"To M. Danglars."

"By heaven!" cried Caderousse, drawing from his waistcoat an open knife, and striking the count in the breast, "you shall disclose nothing, reverend sir!" To Caderousse's great astonishment, the knife, instead of piercing the count's breast, flew back blunted. At the same moment the count seized with his left hand the assassin's wrist, and wrung it with such strength that the knife fell from his stiffened fingers, and Caderousse uttered a cry of pain. But the count, disregarding his cry, continued to wring the bandit's wrist, until, his arm being dislocated, he fell first on his knees, then flat on the floor. The count then placed his foot on his head, saying, "I know not what restrains me from crushing thy skull, rascal."

"Ah, mercy—mercy!" cried Caderousse. The count withdrew his foot. "Rise!" said he. Caderousse rose.

"What a wrist you have, reverend sir!" said Caderousse, stroking his arm, all bruised by the fleshy pincers which had held it; "what a wrist!"

"Silence! God gives me strength to overcome a wild beast like you; in the name of that God I act,—remember that, wretch,—and to spare thee at this moment is still serving him."

"Oh!" said Caderousse, groaning with pain.

"Take this pen and paper, and write what I dictate."

"I don't know how to write, reverend sir."

"You lie! Take this pen, and write!" Caderousse, awed by the superior power of the abbe, sat down and wrote:—

Sir,—The man whom you are receiving at your house, and to whom you intend to marry your daughter, is a felon who escaped with me from confinement at Toulon. He was No. 59, and I No. 58. He was called Benedetto, but he is ignorant of his real name, having never known his parents.

"Sign it!" continued the count.

"But would you ruin me?"

"If I sought your ruin, fool, I should drag you to the first guard-house; besides, when that note is delivered, in all probability you will have no more to fear. Sign it, then!"

Caderousse signed it. "The address, 'To monsieur the Baron Danglars, banker, Rue de la Chaussee d'Antin.'" Caderousse wrote the address. The abbe took the note. "Now," said he, "that suffices—begone!"

"Which way?"

"The way you came."

"You wish me to get out at that window?"

"You got in very well."

"Oh, you have some design against me, reverend sir."

"Idiot! what design can I have?"

"Why, then, not let me out by the door?"

"What would be the advantage of waking the porter?"—

"Ah, reverend sir, tell me, do you wish me dead?"

"I wish what God wills."

"But swear that you will not strike me as I go down."

"Cowardly fool!"

"What do you intend doing with me?"

"I ask you what can I do? I have tried to make you a happy man, and you have turned out a murderer."

"Oh, monsieur," said Caderousse, "make one more attempt—try me once more!"

"I will," said the count. "Listen—you know if I may be relied on."

"Yes," said Caderousse.

"If you arrive safely at home"—

"What have I to fear, except from you?"

"If you reach your home safely, leave Paris, leave France, and wherever you may be, so long as you conduct yourself well, I will send you a small annuity; for, if you return home safely, then"—

"Then?" asked Caderousse, shuddering.

"Then I shall believe God has forgiven you, and I will forgive you too."

"As true as I am a Christian," stammered Caderousse, "you will make me die of fright!"

"Now begone," said the count, pointing to the window.

Caderousse, scarcely yet relying on this promise, put his legs out of the window and stood on the ladder. "Now go down," said the abbe, folding his arms. Understanding he had nothing more to fear from him, Caderousse began to go down. Then the count brought the taper to the window, that it might be seen in the Champs-Elysees that a man was getting out of the window while another held a light.

"What are you doing, reverend sir? Suppose a watchman should pass?" And he blew out the light. He then descended, but it was only when he felt his foot touch the ground that he was satisfied of his safety.

Monte Cristo returned to his bedroom, and, glancing rapidly from the garden to the street, he saw first Caderousse, who after walking to the end of the garden, fixed his ladder against the wall at a different part from where he came in. The count then looking over into the street, saw the man who appeared to be waiting run in the same direction, and place himself against the angle of the wall where Caderousse would come over. Caderousse climbed the ladder slowly, and looked over the coping to see if the street was quiet. No one could be seen or heard. The clock of the Invalides struck one. Then Caderousse sat astride the coping, and drawing up his ladder passed it over the wall; then he began to descend, or rather to slide down by the two stanchions, which he did with an ease which proved how accustomed he was to the exercise. But, once started, he could not stop. In vain did he see a man start from the shadow when he was halfway down—in vain did he see an arm raised as he touched the ground. Before he could defend himself that arm struck him so violently in the back that he let go the ladder, crying, "Help!" A second blow struck him almost immediately in the side, and he fell, calling, "Help, murder!" Then, as he rolled on the ground, his adversary seized him by the hair, and struck him a third blow in the chest. This time Caderousse endeavored to call again, but he could only utter a groan, and he shuddered as the blood flowed from his three wounds. The assassin, finding that he no longer cried out, lifted his head up by the hair; his eyes were closed, and the mouth was distorted. The murderer, supposing him dead, let fall his head and disappeared. Then Caderousse, feeling that he was leaving him, raised himself on his elbow, and with a dying voice cried with great effort, "Murder! I am dying! Help, reverend sir,—help!"

This mournful appeal pierced the darkness. The door of the back-staircase opened, then the side-gate of the garden, and Ali and his master were on the spot with lights.

CHAPTER 83.
THE HAND OF GOD.

Caderousse continued to call piteously, "Help, reverend sir, help!"

"What is the matter?" asked Monte Cristo.

"Help," cried Caderousse; "I am murdered!"

"We are here;—take courage."

"Ah, it's all over! You are come too late—you are come to see me die. What blows, what blood!" He fainted. Ali and his master conveyed the wounded man into a room. Monte Cristo motioned to Ali to undress him, and he then examined his dreadful wounds. "My God!" he exclaimed, "thy vengeance is sometimes delayed, but only that it may fall the more effectually." Ali looked at his master for further instructions. "Bring here immediately the king's attorney, M. de Villefort, who lives in the Faubourg St. Honore. As you pass the lodge, wake the porter, and send him for a surgeon." Ali obeyed, leaving the abbe alone with Caderousse, who had not yet revived.

When the wretched man again opened his eyes, the count looked at him with a mournful expression of pity, and his lips moved as if in prayer. "A surgeon, reverend sir—a surgeon!" said Caderousse.

"I have sent for one," replied the abbe.

"I know he cannot save my life, but he may strengthen me to give my evidence."

"Against whom?"

"Against my murderer."

"Did you recognize him?"

"Yes; it was Benedetto."

"The young Corsican?"

"Himself."

"Your comrade?"

"Yes. After giving me the plan of this house, doubtless hoping I should kill the count and he thus become his heir, or that the count would kill me and I should be out of his way, he waylaid me, and has murdered me."

"I have also sent for the procureur."

"He will not come in time; I feel my life fast ebbing."

"Wait a moment," said Monte Cristo. He left the room, and returned in five minutes with a phial. The dying man's eyes were all the time riveted on the door, through which he hoped succor would arrive. "Hasten, reverend sir, hasten! I shall faint again!" Monte Cristo approached, and dropped on his purple lips three or four drops of the contents of the phial. Caderousse drew a deep breath. "Oh," said he, "that is life to me; more, more!"

"Two drops more would kill you," replied the abbe.

"Oh, send for some one to whom I can denounce the wretch!"

"Shall I write your deposition? You can sign it."

"Yes, yes," said Caderousse; and his eyes glistened at the thought of this posthumous revenge. Monte Cristo wrote:—

"I die, murdered by the Corsican Benedetto, my comrade in the galleys at Toulouse, No. 59."

"Quick, quick!" said Caderousse, "or I shall be unable to sign it."

Monte Cristo gave the pen to Caderousse, who collected all his strength, signed it, and fell back on his bed, saying: "You will relate all the rest, reverend sir; you will say he calls himself Andrea Cavalcanti. He lodges at the Hotel des Princes. Oh, I am dying!" He again fainted. The abbe made him smell the contents of the phial, and he again opened his eyes. His desire for revenge had not forsaken him.

"Ah, you will tell all I have said, will you not, reverend sir?"

"Yes, and much more."

"What more will you say?"

"I will say he had doubtless given you the plan of this house, in the hope the count would kill you. I will say, likewise, he had apprised the count, by a note, of your intention, and, the count being absent, I read the note and sat up to await you."

"And he will be guillotined, will be not?" said Caderousse. "Promise me that, and I will die with that hope."

"I will say," continued the count, "that he followed and watched you the whole time, and when he saw you leave the house, ran to the angle of the wall to conceal himself."

"Did you see all that?"

"Remember my words: 'If you return home safely, I shall believe God has forgiven you, and I will forgive you also.'"

"And you did not warn me!" cried Caderousse, raising himself on his elbows. "You knew I should be killed on leaving this house, and did not warn me!"

"No; for I saw God's justice placed in the hands of Benedetto, and should have thought it sacrilege to oppose the designs of providence."

"God's justice! Speak not of it, reverend sir. If God were just, you know how many would be punished who now escape."

"Patience," said the abbe, in a tone which made the dying man shudder; "have patience!" Caderousse looked at him with amazement. "Besides," said the abbe, "God is merciful to all, as he has been to you; he is first a father, then a judge."

"Do you then believe in God?" said Caderousse.

"Had I been so unhappy as not to believe in him until now," said Monte Cristo, "I must believe on seeing you." Caderousse raised his clinched hands towards heaven.

"Listen," said the abbe, extending his hand over the wounded man, as if to command him to believe; "this is what the God in whom, on your death-bed, you refuse to believe, has done for you—he gave you health, strength, regular employment, even friends—a life, in fact, which a man might enjoy with a calm conscience. Instead of improving these gifts, rarely granted so abundantly, this has been your course—you have given yourself up to sloth and drunkenness, and in a fit of intoxication have ruined your best friend."

"Help!" cried Caderousse; "I require a surgeon, not a priest; perhaps I am not mortally wounded—I may not die; perhaps they can yet save my life."

"Your wounds are so far mortal that, without the three drops I gave you, you would now be dead. Listen, then."

"Ah," murmured Caderousse, "what a strange priest you are; you drive the dying to despair, instead of consoling them."

"Listen," continued the abbe. "When you had betrayed your friend God began not to strike, but to warn you. Poverty overtook you. You had already passed half your life in coveting that which you might have honorably acquired; and already you contemplated crime under the excuse of want, when God worked a miracle in your behalf, sending you, by my hands, a fortune—brilliant, indeed, for you, who had never possessed any. But this unexpected, unhoped-for, unheard-of fortune sufficed you no longer when you once possessed it; you wished to double it, and how?—by a murder! You succeeded, and then God snatched it from you, and brought you to justice."

"It was not I who wished to kill the Jew," said Caderousse; "it was La Carconte."

"Yes," said Monte Cristo, "and God,—I cannot say in justice, for his justice would have slain you,—but God, in his mercy, spared your life."

"Pardieu, to transport me for life, how merciful!"

"You thought it a mercy then, miserable wretch! The coward who feared death rejoiced at perpetual disgrace; for like all galley-slaves, you said, 'I may escape from prison, I cannot from the grave.' And you said truly; the way was opened for you unexpectedly. An Englishman visited Toulon, who had vowed to rescue two men from infamy, and his choice fell on you and your companion. You received a second fortune, money and tranquillity were restored to you, and you, who had been condemned to a felon's life, might live as other men. Then, wretched creature, then you tempted God a third time. 'I have not enough,' you said, when you had more than you before possessed, and you committed a third crime, without reason, without excuse. God is wearied; he has punished you." Caderousse was fast sinking. "Give me drink," said he: "I thirst—I burn!" Monte Cristo gave him a glass of water. "And yet that villain, Benedetto, will escape!"

"No one, I tell you, will escape; Benedetto will be punished."

"Then, you, too, will be punished, for you did not do your duty as a priest—you should have prevented Benedetto from killing me."

"I?" said the count, with a smile which petrified the dying man, "when you had just broken your knife against the coat of mail which protected my breast! Yet perhaps if I had found you humble and penitent, I might have prevented Benedetto from killing you; but I found you proud and blood-thirsty, and I left you in the hands of God."

"I do not believe there is a God," howled Caderousse; "you do not believe it; you lie—you lie!"

"Silence," said the abbe; "you will force the last drop of blood from your veins. What! you do not believe in God when he is striking you dead? you will not believe in him, who requires but a prayer, a word, a tear, and he will forgive? God, who might have directed the assassin's dagger so as to end your career in a moment, has given you this quarter of an hour for repentance. Reflect, then, wretched man, and repent."

"No," said Caderousse, "no; I will not repent. There is no God; there is no providence—all comes by chance."—

"There is a providence; there is a God," said Monte Cristo, "of whom you are a striking proof, as you lie in utter despair, denying him, while I stand before you, rich, happy, safe and entreating that God in whom you endeavor not to believe, while in your heart you still believe in him."

"But who are you, then?" asked Caderousse, fixing his dying eyes on the count. "Look well at me!" said Monte Cristo, putting the light near his face. "Well, the abbe— the Abbe Busoni." Monte Cristo took off the wig which disfigured him, and let fall his black hair, which added so much to the beauty of his pallid features. "Oh?" said Caderousse, thunderstruck, "but for that black hair, I should say you were the Englishman, Lord Wilmore."

"I am neither the Abbe Busoni nor Lord Wilmore," said Monte Cristo; "think again,—do you not recollect me?" Those was a magic effect in the count's words, which once more revived the exhausted powers of the miserable man. "Yes, indeed," said he; "I think I have seen you and known you formerly."

"Yes, Caderousse, you have seen me; you knew me once."

"Who, then, are you? and why, if you knew me, do you let me die?"

"Because nothing can save you; your wounds are mortal. Had it been possible to save you, I should have considered it another proof of God's mercy, and I would again have endeavored to restore you, I swear by my father's tomb."

"By your father's tomb!" said Caderousse, supported by a supernatural power, and half-raising himself to see more distinctly the man who had just taken the oath which all men hold sacred; "who, then, are you?" The count had watched the approach of death. He knew this was the last struggle. He approached the dying man, and, leaning over him with a calm and melancholy look, he whispered, "I am—I am"— And his almost closed lips uttered a name so low that the count himself appeared afraid to hear it. Caderousse, who had raised himself on his knees, and stretched out his arm, tried to draw back, then clasping his hands, and raising them with a desperate effort, "O my God, my God!" said he, "pardon me for having denied thee; thou dost exist, thou art indeed man's father in heaven, and his judge on earth. My God, my Lord, I have long despised thee! Pardon me, my God; receive me, O my Lord!" Caderousse sighed deeply, and fell back with a groan. The blood no longer flowed from his wounds. He was dead.

"One!" said the count mysteriously, his eyes fixed on the corpse, disfigured by so awful a death. Ten minutes afterwards the surgeon and the procureur arrived, the one accompanied by the porter, the other by Ali, and were received by the Abbe Busoni, who was praying by the side of the corpse.

CHAPTER 84.
BEAUCHAMP.

The daring attempt to rob the count was the topic of conversation throughout Paris for the next fortnight. The dying man had signed a deposition declaring Benedetto to be the assassin. The police had orders to make the strictest search for the murderer. Caderousse's knife, dark lantern, bunch of keys, and clothing, excepting the waistcoat, which could not be found, were deposited at the registry; the corpse was conveyed to the morgue. The count told every one that this adventure had happened during his absence at Auteuil, and that he only knew what was related by the Abbe Busoni, who that evening, by mere chance, had requested to pass the night in his house, to examine some valuable books in his library. Bertuccio alone turned pale whenever Benedetto's name was mentioned in his presence, but there was no reason why any one should notice his doing so. Villefort, being called on to prove the crime, was preparing his brief with the same ardor that he was accustomed to exercise when required to speak in criminal cases.

But three weeks had already passed, and the most diligent search had been unsuccessful; the attempted robbery and the murder of the robber by his comrade were almost forgotten in anticipation of the approaching marriage of Mademoiselle

Danglars to the Count Andrea Cavalcanti. It was expected that this wedding would shortly take place, as the young man was received at the banker's as the betrothed. Letters had been despatched to M. Cavalcanti, as the count's father, who highly approved of the union, regretted his inability to leave Parma at that time, and promised a wedding gift of a hundred and fifty thousand livres. It was agreed that the three millions should be intrusted to Danglars to invest; some persons had warned the young man of the circumstances of his future father-in-law, who had of late sustained repeated losses; but with sublime disinterestedness and confidence the young man refused to listen, or to express a single doubt to the baron. The baron adored Count Andrea Cavalcanti: not so Mademoiselle Eugenie Danglars. With an instinctive hatred of matrimony, she suffered Andrea's attentions in order to get rid of Morcerf; but when Andrea urged his suit, she betrayed an entire dislike to him. The baron might possibly have perceived it, but, attributing it to a caprice, feigned ignorance.

The delay demanded by Beauchamp had nearly expired. Morcerf appreciated the advice of Monte Cristo to let things die away of their own accord. No one had taken up the remark about the general, and no one had recognized in the officer who betrayed the castle of Yanina the noble count in the House of Peers. Albert, however felt no less insulted; the few lines which had irritated him were certainly intended as an insult. Besides, the manner in which Beauchamp had closed the conference left a bitter recollection in his heart. He cherished the thought of the duel, hoping to conceal its true cause even from his seconds. Beauchamp had not been seen since the day he visited Albert, and those of whom the latter inquired always told him he was out on a journey which would detain him some days. Where he was no one knew.

One morning Albert was awakened by his valet de chambre, who announced Beauchamp. Albert rubbed his eyes, ordered his servant to introduce him into the small smoking-room on the ground-floor, dressed himself quickly, and went down. He found Beauchamp pacing the room; on perceiving him Beauchamp stopped. "Your arrival here, without waiting my visit at your house to-day, looks well, sir," said Albert. "Tell me, may I shake hands with you, saying, 'Beauchamp, acknowledge you have injured me, and retain my friendship,' or must I simply propose to you a choice of arms?"

"Albert," said Beauchamp, with a look of sorrow which stupefied the young man, "let us first sit down and talk."

"Rather, sir, before we sit down, I must demand your answer."

"Albert," said the journalist, "these are questions which it is difficult to answer."

"I will facilitate it by repeating the question, 'Will you, or will you not, retract?'"

"Morcerf, it is not enough to answer 'yes' or 'no' to questions which concern the honor, the social interest, and the life of such a man as Lieutenant-general the Count of Morcerf, peer of France."

"What must then be done?"

"What I have done, Albert. I reasoned thus—money, time, and fatigue are nothing compared with the reputation and interests of a whole family; probabilities will not suffice, only facts will justify a deadly combat with a friend. If I strike with the sword, or discharge the contents of a pistol at man with whom, for three years, I have been on terms of intimacy, I must, at least, know why I do so; I must meet him with a heart at ease, and that quiet conscience which a man needs when his own arm must save his life."

"Well," said Morcerf, impatiently, "what does all this mean?"

"It means that I have just returned from Yanina."

"From Yanina?"

"Yes."

"Impossible!"

"Here is my passport; examine the visa—Geneva, Milan, Venice, Trieste, Delvino, Yanina. Will you believe the government of a republic, a kingdom, and an empire?" Albert cast his eyes on the passport, then raised them in astonishment to Beauchamp. "You have been to Yanina?" said he.

"Albert, had you been a stranger, a foreigner, a simple lord, like that Englishman who came to demand satisfaction three or four months since, and whom I killed to get rid of, I should not have taken this trouble; but I thought this mark of consideration due to you. I took a week to go, another to return, four days of quarantine, and forty-eight hours to stay there; that makes three weeks. I returned last night, and here I am."

"What circumlocution! How long you are before you tell me what I most wish to know?"

"Because, in truth, Albert"—

"You hesitate?"

"Yes,—I fear."

"You fear to acknowledge that your correspondent his deceived you? Oh, no self-love, Beauchamp. Acknowledge it, Beauchamp; your courage cannot be doubted."

"Not so," murmured the journalist; "on the contrary"—

Albert turned frightfully pale; he endeavored to speak, but the words died on his lips. "My friend," said Beauchamp, in the most affectionate tone, "I should gladly make an apology; but, alas,"—

"But what?"

"The paragraph was correct, my friend."

"What? That French officer"—

"Yes."

"Fernand?"

"Yes."

"The traitor who surrendered the castle of the man in whose service he was"—

"Pardon me, my friend, that man was your father!" Albert advanced furiously towards Beauchamp, but the latter restrained him more by a mild look than by his extended hand.

"My friend," said he, "here is a proof of it."

Albert opened the paper, it was an attestation of four notable inhabitants of Yanina, proving that Colonel Fernand Mondego, in the service of Ali Tepelini, had surrendered the castle for two million crowns. The signatures were perfectly legal. Albert tottered and fell overpowered in a chair. It could no longer be doubted; the family name was fully given. After a moment's mournful silence, his heart overflowed, and he gave way to a flood of tears. Beauchamp, who had watched with sincere pity the young man's paroxysm of grief, approached him. "Now, Albert," said he, "you understand me—do you not? I wished to see all, and to judge of everything for myself, hoping the explanation would be in your father's favor, and that I might do him justice. But, on the contrary, the particulars which are given prove that Fernand Mondego, raised by Ali Pasha to the rank of governor-general, is no other than Count Fernand of Morcerf; then, recollecting the honor you had done me, in admitting me to your friendship, I hastened to you."

Albert, still extended on the chair, covered his face with both hands, as if to prevent the light from reaching him. "I hastened to you," continued Beauchamp, "to tell you, Albert, that in this changing age, the faults of a father cannot revert upon his children. Few have passed through this revolutionary period, in the midst of which we were born, without some stain of infamy or blood to soil the uniform of the soldier, or the gown of the magistrate. Now I have these proofs, Albert, and I am in your confidence, no human power can force me to a duel which your own conscience would reproach you with as criminal, but I come to offer you what you can no longer demand of me. Do you wish these proofs, these attestations, which I alone possess, to be destroyed? Do you wish this frightful secret to remain with us? Confided to me, it shall never escape my lips; say, Albert, my friend, do you wish it?"

Albert threw himself on Beauchamp's neck. "Ah, noble fellow!" cried he.

"Take these," said Beauchamp, presenting the papers to Albert.

Albert seized them with a convulsive hand, tore them in pieces, and trembling lest the least vestige should escape and one day appear to confront him, he approached the wax-light, always kept burning for cigars, and burned every fragment. "Dear, excellent friend," murmured Albert, still burning the papers.

"Let all be forgotten as a sorrowful dream," said Beauchamp; "let it vanish as the last sparks from the blackened paper, and disappear as the smoke from those silent ashes."

"Yes, yes," said Albert, "and may there remain only the eternal friendship which I promised to my deliverer, which shall be transmitted to our children's children, and shall always remind me that I owe my life and the honor of my name to you,—for had this been known, oh, Beauchamp, I should have destroyed myself; or,—no, my poor mother! I could not have killed her by the same blow,—I should have fled from my country."

"Dear Albert," said Beauchamp. But this sudden and factitious joy soon forsook the young man, and was succeeded by a still greater grief.

"Well," said Beauchamp, "what still oppresses you, my friend?"

"I am broken-hearted," said Albert. "Listen, Beauchamp! I cannot thus, in a moment relinquish the respect, the confidence, and pride with which a father's untarnished name inspires a son. Oh, Beauchamp, Beauchamp, how shall I now approach mine? Shall I draw back my forehead from his embrace, or withhold my hand from his? I am the most wretched of men. Ah, my mother, my poor mother!" said Albert, gazing through his tears at his mother's portrait; "if you know this, how much must you suffer!"

"Come," said Beauchamp, taking both his hands, "take courage, my friend."

"But how came that first note to be inserted in your journal? Some unknown enemy—an invisible foe—has done this."

"The more must you fortify yourself, Albert. Let no trace of emotion be visible on your countenance, bear your grief as the cloud bears within it ruin and death—a fatal secret, known only when the storm bursts. Go, my friend, reserve your strength for the moment when the crash shall come."

"You think, then, all is not over yet?" said Albert, horror-stricken.

"I think nothing, my friend; but all things are possible. By the way"—

"What?" said Albert, seeing that Beauchamp hesitated.

"Are you going to marry Mademoiselle Danglars?"

"Why do you ask me now?"

"Because the rupture or fulfilment of this engagement is connected with the person of whom we were speaking."

"How?" said Albert, whose brow reddened; "you think M. Danglars"—

"I ask you only how your engagement stands? Pray put no construction on my words I do not mean they should convey, and give them no undue weight."

"No." said Albert, "the engagement is broken off."

"Well," said Beauchamp. Then, seeing the young man was about to relapse into melancholy, "Let us go out, Albert," said he; "a ride in the wood in the phaeton, or on horseback, will refresh you; we will then return to breakfast, and you shall attend to your affairs, and I to mine."

"Willingly," said Albert; "but let us walk. I think a little exertion would do me good." The two friends walked out on the fortress. When arrived at the Madeleine,—"Since we are out," said Beauchamp, "let us call on M. de Monte Cristo; he is admirably adapted to revive one's spirits, because he never interrogates, and in my opinion those who ask no questions are the best comforters."

"Gladly," said Albert; "I love him—let us call."

CHAPTER 85.
THE JOURNEY.

Monte Cristo uttered a joyful exclamation on seeing the young men together. "Ah, ha!" said he, "I hope all is over, explained and settled."

"Yes," said Beauchamp; "the absurd reports have died away, and should they be renewed, I would be the first to oppose them; so let us speak no more of it."

"Albert will tell you," replied the count "that I gave him the same advice. Look," added he. "I am finishing the most execrable morning's work."

"What is it?" said Albert; "arranging your papers, apparently."

"My papers, thank God, no,—my papers are all in capital order, because I have none; but M. Cavalcanti's."

"M. Cavalcanti's?" asked Beauchamp.

"Yes; do you not know that this is a young man whom the count is introducing?" said Morcerf.

"Let us not misunderstand each other," replied Monte Cristo; "I introduce no one, and certainly not M. Cavalcanti."

"And who," said Albert with a forced smile, "is to marry Mademoiselle Danglars instead of me, which grieves me cruelly."

"What? Cavalcanti is going to marry Mademoiselle Danglars?" asked Beauchamp.

"Certainly; do you come from the end of the world?" said Monte Cristo; "you, a journalist, the husband of renown? It is the talk of all Paris."

"And you, count, have made this match?" asked Beauchamp.

"I? Silence, purveyor of gossip, do not spread that report. I make a match? No, you do not know me; I have done all in my power to oppose it."

"Ah, I understand," said Beauchamp, "on our friend Albert's account."

"On my account?" said the young man; "oh, no, indeed, the count will do me the justice to assert that I have, on the contrary, always entreated him to break off my engagement, and happily it is ended. The count pretends I have not him to thank;—so be it—I will erect an altar Deo ignoto."

"Listen," said Monte Cristo; "I have had little to do with it, for I am at variance both with the father-in-law and the young man; there is only Mademoiselle Eugenie, who appears but little charmed with the thoughts of matrimony, and who, seeing how little I was disposed to persuade her to renounce her dear liberty, retains any affection for me."

"And do you say this wedding is at hand?"

"Oh, yes, in spite of all I could say. I do not know the young man; he is said to be of good family and rich, but I never trust to vague assertions. I have warned M. Danglars of it till I am tired, but he is fascinated with his Luccanese. I have even informed him of a circumstance I consider very serious; the young man was either charmed by his nurse, stolen by gypsies, or lost by his tutor, I scarcely know which. But I do know his father lost sight of him for more than ten years; what he did during these ten years, God only knows. Well, all that was useless. They have commissioned me to write to the major to demand papers, and here they are. I send them, but like Pilate—washing my hands."

"And what does Mademoiselle d'Armilly say to you for robbing her of her pupil?"

"Oh, well, I don't know; but I understand that she is going to Italy. Madame Danglars asked me for letters of recommendation for the impresari; I gave her a few lines for the director of the Valle Theatre, who is under some obligation to me. But what is the matter, Albert? you look dull; are you, after all, unconsciously in love with Mademoiselle Eugenie?"

"I am not aware of it," said Albert, smiling sorrowfully. Beauchamp turned to look at some paintings. "But," continued Monte Cristo, "you are not in your usual spirits?"

"I have a dreadful headache," said Albert.

"Well, my dear viscount," said Monte Cristo, "I have an infallible remedy to propose to you."

"What is that?" asked the young man.

"A change."

"Indeed?" said Albert.

"Yes; and as I am just now excessively annoyed, I shall go from home. Shall we go together?"

"You annoyed, count?" said Beauchamp; "and by what?"

"Ah, you think very lightly of it; I should like to see you with a brief preparing in your house."

"What brief?"

"The one M. de Villefort is preparing against my amiable assassin—some brigand escaped from the gallows apparently."

"True," said Beauchamp; "I saw it in the paper. Who is this Caderousse?"

"Some provincial, it appears. M. de Villefort heard of him at Marseilles, and M. Danglars recollects having seen him. Consequently, the procureur is very active in the affair, and the prefect of police very much interested; and, thanks to that interest, for which I am very grateful, they send me all the robbers of Paris and the neighborhood, under pretence of their being Caderousse's murderers, so that in three months, if this continues, every robber and assassin in France will have the plan of my house at his fingers' end. I am resolved to desert them and go to some remote corner of the earth, and shall be happy if you will accompany me, viscount."

"Willingly."

"Then it is settled?"

"Yes, but where?"

"I have told you, where the air is pure, where every sound soothes, where one is sure to be humbled, however proud may be his nature. I love that humiliation, I, who am master of the universe, as was Augustus."

"But where are you really going?"

"To sea, viscount; you know I am a sailor. I was rocked when an infant in the arms of old ocean, and on the bosom of the beautiful Amphitrite; I have sported with the green mantle of the one and the azure robe of the other; I love the sea as a mistress, and pine if I do not often see her."

"Let us go, count."

"To sea?"

"Yes."

"You accept my proposal?"

"I do."

"Well, Viscount, there will be in my court-yard this evening a good travelling britzka, with four post-horses, in which one may rest as in a bed. M. Beauchamp, it holds four very well, will you accompany us?"

"Thank you, I have just returned from sea."

"What? you have been to sea?"

"Yes; I have just made a little excursion to the Borromean Islands." [*]

* Lake Maggiore.

"What of that? come with us," said Albert.

"No, dear Morcerf; you know I only refuse when the thing is impossible. Besides, it is important," added he in a low tone, "that I should remain in Paris just now to watch the paper."

"Ah, you are a good and an excellent friend," said Albert; "yes, you are right; watch, watch, Beauchamp, and try to discover the enemy who made this disclosure." Albert and Beauchamp parted, the last pressure of their hands expressing what their tongues could not before a stranger.

"Beauchamp is a worthy fellow," said Monte Cristo, when the journalist was gone; "is he not, Albert?"

"Yes, and a sincere friend; I love him devotedly. But now we are alone,—although it is immaterial to me,—where are we going?"

"Into Normandy, if you like."

"Delightful; shall we be quite retired? have no society, no neighbors?"

"Our companions will be riding-horses, dogs to hunt with, and a fishing-boat."

"Exactly what I wish for; I will apprise my mother of my intention, and return to you."

"But shall you be allowed to go into Normandy?"

"I may go where I please."

"Yes, I am aware you may go alone, since I once met you in Italy—but to accompany the mysterious Monte Cristo?"

"You forget, count, that I have often told you of the deep interest my mother takes in you."

"'Woman is fickle.' said Francis I.; 'woman is like a wave of the sea,' said Shakespeare; both the great king and the great poet ought to have known woman's nature well."

"Woman's, yes; my mother is not woman, but a woman."

"As I am only a humble foreigner, you must pardon me if I do not understand all the subtle refinements of your language."

"What I mean to say is, that my mother is not quick to give her confidence, but when she does she never changes."

"Ah, yes, indeed," said Monte Cristo with a sigh; "and do you think she is in the least interested in me?"

"I repeat it, you must really be a very strange and superior man, for my mother is so absorbed by the interest you have excited, that when I am with her she speaks of no one else."

"And does she try to make you dislike me?"

"On the contrary, she often says, 'Morcerf, I believe the count has a noble nature; try to gain his esteem.'"

"Indeed?" said Monte Cristo, sighing.

"You see, then," said Albert, "that instead of opposing, she will encourage me."

"Adieu, then, until five o'clock; be punctual, and we shall arrive at twelve or one."

"At Treport?"

"Yes; or in the neighborhood."

"But can we travel forty-eight leagues in eight hours?"

"Easily," said Monte Cristo.

"You are certainly a prodigy; you will soon not only surpass the railway, which would not be very difficult in France, but even the telegraph."

"But, viscount, since we cannot perform the journey in less than seven or eight hours, do not keep me waiting."

"Do not fear, I have little to prepare." Monte Cristo smiled as he nodded to Albert, then remained a moment absorbed in deep meditation. But passing his hand across his forehead as if to dispel his revery, he rang the bell twice and Bertuccio entered. "Bertuccio," said he, "I intend going this evening to Normandy, instead of to-morrow or the next day. You will have sufficient time before five o'clock; despatch a messenger to apprise the grooms at the first station. M. de Morcerf will accompany me." Bertuccio obeyed and despatched a courier to Pontoise to say the travelling-carriage would arrive at six o'clock. From Pontoise another express was sent to the next stage, and in six hours all the horses stationed on the road were ready. Before his departure, the count went to Haidee's apartments, told her his intention, and resigned everything to her care. Albert was punctual. The journey soon became interesting from its rapidity, of which Morcerf had formed no previous idea. "Truly," said Monte Cristo, "with your posthorses going at the rate of two leagues an hour, and that absurd law that one traveller shall not pass another without permission, so that an invalid or ill-tempered traveller may detain those who are well and active, it is impossible to move; I escape this annoyance by travelling with my own postilion and horses; do I not, Ali?"

The count put his head out of the window and whistled, and the horses appeared to fly. The carriage rolled with a thundering noise over the pavement, and every one turned to notice the dazzling meteor. Ali, smiling, repeated the sound, grasped the reins with a firm hand, and spurred his horses, whose beautiful manes floated in the breeze. This child of the desert was in his element, and with his black face and sparkling eyes appeared, in the cloud of dust he raised, like the genius of the simoom and the god of the hurricane. "I never knew till now the delight of speed," said Morcerf, and the last cloud disappeared from his brow; "but where the devil do you get such horses? Are they made to order?"

"Precisely," said the count; "six years since I bought a horse in Hungary remarkable for its swiftness. The thirty-two that we shall use to-night are its progeny; they are all entirely black, with the exception of a star upon the forehead."

"That is perfectly admirable; but what do you do, count, with all these horses?"

"You see, I travel with them."

"But you are not always travelling."

"When I no longer require them, Bertuccio will sell them, and he expects to realize thirty or forty thousand francs by the sale."

"But no monarch in Europe will be wealthy enough to purchase them."

"Then he will sell them to some Eastern vizier, who will empty his coffers to purchase them, and refill them by applying the bastinado to his subjects."

"Count, may I suggest one idea to you?"

"Certainly."

"It is that, next to you, Bertuccio must be the richest gentleman in Europe."

"You are mistaken, viscount; I believe he has not a franc in his possession."

"Then he must be a wonder. My dear count, if you tell me many more marvellous things, I warn you I shall not believe them."

"I countenance nothing that is marvellous, M. Albert. Tell me, why does a steward rob his master?"

"Because, I suppose, it is his nature to do so, for the love of robbing."

"You are mistaken; it is because he has a wife and family, and ambitious desires for himself and them. Also because he is not sure of always retaining his situation, and wishes to provide for the future. Now, M. Bertuccio is alone in the world; he uses my property without accounting for the use he makes of it; he is sure never to leave my service."

"Why?"

"Because I should never get a better."

"Probabilities are deceptive."

"But I deal in certainties; he is the best servant over whom one has the power of life and death."

"Do you possess that right over Bertuccio?"

"Yes."

There are words which close a conversation with an iron door; such was the count's "yes." The whole journey was performed with equal rapidity; the thirty-two horses, dispersed over seven stages, brought them to their destination in eight hours. At midnight they arrived at the gate of a beautiful park. The porter was in attendance; he had been apprised by the groom of the last stage of the count's approach. At half past two in the morning Morcerf was conducted to his apartments, where a bath and supper were prepared. The servant who had travelled at the back of the carriage waited on him; Baptistin, who rode in front, attended the count. Albert bathed, took his supper, and went to bed. All night he was lulled by the melancholy noise of the surf. On rising, he went to his window, which opened on a terrace, having the sea in front, and at the back a pretty park bounded by a small forest. In a creek lay a little sloop, with a narrow keel and high masts, bearing on its flag the Monte Cristo arms which were a mountain on a sea azure, with a cross gules on the shield. Around the schooner lay a number of small fishing-boats belonging to the fishermen of the neighboring village, like humble subjects awaiting orders from their queen. There, as in every spot where Monte Cristo stopped, if but for two days, luxury abounded and life went on with the utmost ease.

Albert found in his anteroom two guns, with all the accoutrements for hunting; a lofty room on the ground-floor containing all the ingenious instruments the English— eminent in piscatory pursuits, since they are patient and sluggish—have invented for fishing. The day passed in pursuing those exercises in which Monte Cristo excelled. They killed a dozen pheasants in the park, as many trout in the stream, dined in a summer-house overlooking the ocean, and took tea in the library.

Towards the evening of the third day. Albert, completely exhausted with the exercise which invigorated Monte Cristo, was sleeping in an arm-chair near the window, while the count was designing with his architect the plan of a conservatory in his house, when the sound of a horse at full speed on the high road made Albert look up. He was disagreeably surprised to see his own valet de chambre, whom he had not brought, that he might not inconvenience Monte Cristo.

"Florentin here!" cried he, starting up; "is my mother ill?" And he hastened to the door. Monte Cristo watched and saw him approach the valet, who drew a small sealed parcel from his pocket, containing a newspaper and a letter. "From whom is this?" said he eagerly. "From M. Beauchamp," replied Florentin.

"Did he send you?"

"Yes, sir; he sent for me to his house, gave me money for my journey, procured a horse, and made me promise not to stop till I had reached you, I have come in fifteen hours."

Albert opened the letter with fear, uttered a shriek on reading the first line, and seized the paper. His sight was dimmed, his legs sank under him, and he would have fallen had not Florentin supported him.

"Poor young man," said Monte Cristo in a low voice; "it is then true that the sin of the father shall fall on the children to the third and fourth generation." Meanwhile Albert had revived, and, continuing to read, he threw back his head, saying, "Florentin, is your horse fit to return immediately?"

"It is a poor lame post-horse."

"In what state was the house when you left?"

"All was quiet, but on returning from M. Beauchamp's, I found madame in tears: she had sent for me to know when you would return. I told her my orders from M. Beauchamp; she first extended her arms to prevent me, but after a moment's reflection, 'Yes, go, Florentin,' said she, 'and may he come quickly.'"

"Yes, my mother," said Albert, "I will return, and woe to the infamous wretch! But first of all I must get there."

He went back to the room where he had left Monte Cristo. Five minutes had sufficed to make a complete transformation in his appearance. His voice had become rough and hoarse; his face was furrowed with wrinkles; his eyes burned under the blue-veined lids, and he tottered like a drunken man. "Count," said he, "I thank you for your hospitality, which I would gladly have enjoyed longer; but I must return to Paris."

"What has happened?"

"A great misfortune, more important to me than life. Don't question me, I beg of you, but lend me a horse."

"My stables are at your command, viscount; but you will kill yourself by riding on horseback. Take a post-chaise or a carriage."

"No, it would delay me, and I need the fatigue you warn me of; it will do me good." Albert reeled as if he had been shot, and fell on a chair near the door. Monte Cristo did not see this second manifestation of physical exhaustion; he was at the window, calling, "Ali, a horse for M. de Morcerf—quick! he is in a hurry!" These words restored Albert; he darted from the room, followed by the count. "Thank you!" cried he, throwing himself on his horse. "Return as soon as you can, Florentin. Must I use any password to procure a horse?"

"Only dismount; another will be immediately saddled." Albert hesitated a moment. "You may think my departure strange and foolish," said the young man; "you do not know how a paragraph in a newspaper may exasperate one. Read that," said he, "when I am gone, that you may not be witness of my anger."

While the count picked up the paper he put spurs to his horse, which leaped in astonishment at such an unusual stimulus, and shot away with the rapidity of an arrow. The count watched him with a feeling of compassion, and when he had completely disappeared, read as follows:—

"The French officer in the service of Ali Pasha of Yanina alluded to three weeks since in the Impartial, who not only surrendered the castle of Yanina, but sold his benefactor to the Turks, styled himself truly at that time Fernand, as our esteemed contemporary states; but he has since added to his Christian name a title of nobility and a family name. He now calls himself the Count of Morcerf, and ranks among the peers."

Thus the terrible secret, which Beauchamp had so generously destroyed, appeared again like an armed phantom; and another paper, deriving its information from some malicious source, had published two days after Albert's departure for Normandy the few lines which had rendered the unfortunate young man almost crazy.

CHAPTER 86.
THE TRIAL.

At eight o'clock in the morning Albert had arrived at Beauchamp's door. The valet de chambre had received orders to usher him in at once. Beauchamp was in his bath. "Here I am," said Albert.

"Well, my poor friend," replied Beauchamp, "I expected you."

"I need not say I think you are too faithful and too kind to have spoken of that painful circumstance. Your having sent for me is another proof of your affection. So, without losing time, tell me, have you the slightest idea whence this terrible blow proceeds?"

"I think I have some clew."

"But first tell me all the particulars of this shameful plot." Beauchamp proceeded to relate to the young man, who was overwhelmed with shame and grief, the following facts. Two days previously, the article had appeared in another paper besides the Impartial, and, what was more serious, one that was well known as a government paper. Beauchamp was breakfasting when he read the paragraph. He sent immediately for a cabriolet, and hastened to the publisher's office. Although professing diametrically opposite principles from those of the editor of the other paper, Beauchamp—as it sometimes, we may say often, happens—was his intimate friend. The editor was reading, with apparent delight, a leading article in the same paper on beet-sugar, probably a composition of his own.

"Ah, pardieu," said Beauchamp, "with the paper in your hand, my friend, I need not tell you the cause of my visit."

"Are you interested in the sugar question?" asked the editor of the ministerial paper.

"No," replied Beauchamp, "I have not considered the question; a totally different subject interests me."

"What is it?"

"The article relative to Morcerf."

"Indeed? Is it not a curious affair?"

"So curious, that I think you are running a great risk of a prosecution for defamation of character."

"Not at all; we have received with the information all the requisite proofs, and we are quite sure M. de Morcerf will not raise his voice against us; besides, it is rendering a service to one's country to denounce these wretched criminals who are unworthy of the honor bestowed on them." Beauchamp was thunderstruck. "Who, then, has so correctly informed you?" asked he; "for my paper, which gave the first information on the subject, has been obliged to stop for want of proof; and yet we are more interested than you in exposing M. de Morcerf, as he is a peer of France, and we are of the opposition."

"Oh, that is very simple; we have not sought to scandalize. This news was brought to us. A man arrived yesterday from Yanina, bringing a formidable array of documents; and when we hesitated to publish the accusatory article, he told us it should be inserted in some other paper."

Beauchamp understood that nothing remained but to submit, and left the office to despatch a courier to Morcerf. But he had been unable to send to Albert the following particulars, as the events had transpired after the messenger's departure; namely, that the same day a great agitation was manifest in the House of Peers among the usually calm members of that dignified assembly. Every one had arrived almost before the usual hour, and was conversing on the melancholy event which was to attract the attention of the public towards one of their most illustrious colleagues. Some were perusing the article, others making comments and recalling circumstances which substantiated the charges still more. The Count of Morcerf was no favorite with his colleagues. Like all upstarts, he had had recourse to a great deal of haughtiness to maintain his position. The true nobility laughed at him, the talented repelled him, and the honorable instinctively despised him. He was, in fact, in the unhappy position of the victim marked for sacrifice; the finger of God once pointed at him, every one was prepared to raise the hue and cry.

The Count of Morcerf alone was ignorant of the news. He did not take in the paper containing the defamatory article, and had passed the morning in writing letters and in trying a horse. He arrived at his usual hour, with a proud look and insolent demeanor; he alighted, passed through the corridors, and entered the house without observing the hesitation of the door-keepers or the coolness of his colleagues. Business had already been going on for half an hour when he entered. Every one held the accusing paper, but, as usual, no one liked to take upon himself the responsibility of the attack. At length an honorable peer, Morcerf's acknowledged enemy, ascended the tribune with that solemnity which announced that the expected moment had arrived. There was an impressive silence; Morcerf alone knew not why such profound attention was given to an orator who was not always listened to with so much complacency. The count did not notice the introduction, in which the speaker announced that his communication would be of that vital importance that it demanded the undivided attention of the House; but at the mention of Yanina and Colonel Fernand, he turned so frightfully pale that every member shuddered and fixed his eyes upon him. Moral wounds have this peculiarity,—they may be hidden, but they never close; always painful, always ready to bleed when touched, they remain fresh and open in the heart.

The article having been read during the painful hush that followed, a universal shudder pervaded the assembly, and immediately the closest attention was given to the orator as he resumed his remarks. He stated his scruples and the difficulties of the case; it was the honor of M. de Morcerf, and that of the whole House, he proposed to defend, by provoking a debate on personal questions, which are always such painful themes of discussion. He concluded by calling for an investigation, which might dispose of the calumnious report before it had time to spread, and restore M. de Morcerf to the position he had long held in public opinion. Morcerf was so completely overwhelmed by this great and unexpected calamity that he could scarcely stammer a few words as he looked around on the assembly. This timidity, which might proceed from the astonishment of innocence as well as the shame of guilt, conciliated some in his favor; for men who are truly generous are always ready to compassionate when the misfortune of their enemy surpasses the limits of their hatred.

The president put it to the vote, and it was decided that the investigation should take place. The count was asked what time he required to prepare his defence. Morcerf's courage had revived when he found himself alive after this horrible blow. "My lords," answered he, "it is not by time I could repel the attack made on me by enemies unknown to me, and, doubtless, hidden in obscurity; it is immediately, and by a thunderbolt, that I must repel the flash of lightning which, for a moment, startled me. Oh, that I could, instead of taking up this defence, shed my last drop of blood to prove to my noble colleagues that I am their equal in worth." These words made a favorable impression on behalf of the accused. "I demand, then, that the examination shall take place as soon as possible, and I will furnish the house with all necessary information."

"What day do you fix?" asked the president.

"To-day I am at your service," replied the count. The president rang the bell. "Does the House approve that the examination should take place to-day?"

"Yes," was the unanimous answer.

A committee of twelve members was chosen to examine the proofs brought forward by Morcerf. The investigation would begin at eight o'clock that evening in the committee-room, and if postponement were necessary, the proceedings would be resumed each evening at the same hour. Morcerf asked leave to retire; he had to collect the documents he had long been preparing against this storm, which his sagacity had foreseen.

Albert listened, trembling now with hope, then with anger, and then again with shame, for from Beauchamp's confidence he knew his father was guilty, and he asked himself how, since he was guilty, he could prove his innocence. Beauchamp hesitated to continue his narrative. "What next?" asked Albert.

"What next? My friend, you impose a painful task on me. Must you know all?"

"Absolutely; and rather from your lips than another's."

"Muster up all your courage, then, for never have you required it more." Albert passed his hand over his forehead, as if to try his strength, as a man who is preparing to defend his life proves his shield and bends his sword. He thought himself strong enough, for he mistook fever for energy. "Go on," said he.

"The evening arrived; all Paris was in expectation. Many said your father had only to show himself to crush the charge against him; many others said he would not appear; while some asserted that they had seen him start for Brussels; and others went to the police-office to inquire if he had taken out a passport. I used all my influence with one of the committee, a young peer of my acquaintance, to get admission to one of the galleries. He called for me at seven o'clock, and, before any one had arrived, asked one of the door-keepers to place me in a box. I was concealed by a column, and might witness the whole of the terrible scene which was about to take place. At eight o'clock all were in their places, and M. de Morcerf entered at the last stroke. He held some papers in his hand; his countenance was calm, and his step firm, and he was dressed with great care in his military uniform, which was buttoned completely up to the chin. His presence produced a good effect. The committee was made up of Liberals, several of whom came forward to shake hands with him."

Albert felt his heart bursting at these particulars, but gratitude mingled with his sorrow: he would gladly have embraced those who had given his father this proof of esteem at a moment when his honor was so powerfully attacked. "At this moment one of the door-keepers brought in a letter for the president. 'You are at liberty to speak, M. de Morcerf,' said the president, as he unsealed the letter; and the count began his defence, I assure you, Albert, in a most eloquent and skilful manner. He produced documents proving that the Vizier of Yanina had up to the last moment honored him with his entire confidence, since he had interested him with a negotiation of life and death with the emperor. He produced the ring, his mark of authority, with which Ali Pasha generally sealed his letters, and which the latter had given him, that he might, on his return at any hour of the day or night, gain access to the presence, even in the harem. Unfortunately, the negotiation failed, and when he returned to defend his benefactor, he was dead. 'But,' said the count, 'so great was Ali Pasha's confidence, that on his death-bed he resigned his favorite mistress and her daughter to my care.'" Albert started on hearing these words; the history of Haidee recurred to him, and he remembered what she had said of that message and the ring, and the manner in which she had been sold and made a slave. "And what effect did this discourse produce?" anxiously inquired Albert. "I acknowledge it affected me, and, indeed, all the committee also," said Beauchamp.

"Meanwhile, the president carelessly opened the letter which had been brought to him; but the first lines aroused his attention; he read them again and again, and fixing his eyes on M. de Morcerf, 'Count,' said he, 'you have said that the Vizier of Yanina confided his wife and daughter to your care?'—'Yes, sir,' replied Morcerf; 'but in that, like all the rest, misfortune pursued me. On my return, Vasiliki and her daughter Haidee had disappeared.'—'Did you know them?'—'My intimacy with the pasha and his unlimited confidence had gained me an introduction to them, and I had seen them above twenty times.'

"'Have you any idea what became of them?'—'Yes, sir; I heard they had fallen victims to their sorrow, and, perhaps, to their poverty. I was not rich; my life was in constant danger; I could not seek them, to my great regret.' The president frowned imperceptibly. 'Gentlemen,' said he, 'you have heard the Comte de Morcerf's defence. Can you, sir, produce any witnesses to the truth of what you have asserted?'—'Alas, no, monsieur,' replied the count; 'all those who surrounded the vizier, or who knew me at his court, are either dead or gone away, I know not where. I believe that

I alone, of all my countrymen, survived that dreadful war. I have only the letters of Ali Tepelini, which I have placed before you; the ring, a token of his good-will, which is here; and, lastly, the most convincing proof I can offer, after an anonymous attack, and that is the absence of any witness against my veracity and the purity of my military life.' A murmur of approbation ran through the assembly; and at this moment, Albert, had nothing more transpired, your father's cause had been gained. It only remained to put it to the vote, when the president resumed: 'Gentlemen and you, monsieur,—you will not be displeased, I presume, to listen to one who calls himself a very important witness, and who has just presented himself. He is, doubtless, come to prove the perfect innocence of our colleague. Here is a letter I have just received on the subject; shall it be read, or shall it be passed over? and shall we take no notice of this incident?' M. de Morcerf turned pale, and clinched his hands on the papers he held. The committee decided to hear the letter; the count was thoughtful and silent. The president read:—

"'Mr. President,—I can furnish the committee of inquiry into the conduct of the Lieutenant-General the Count of Morcerf in Epirus and in Macedonia with important particulars.'

"The president paused, and the count turned pale. The president looked at his auditors. 'Proceed,' was heard on all sides. The president resumed:—

"'I was on the spot at the death of Ali Pasha. I was present during his last moments. I know what is become of Vasiliki and Haidee. I am at the command of the committee, and even claim the honor of being heard. I shall be in the lobby when this note is delivered to you.'

"'And who is this witness, or rather this enemy?' asked the count, in a tone in which there was a visible alteration. 'We shall know, sir,' replied the president. 'Is the committee willing to hear this witness?'—'Yes, yes,' they all said at once. The door-keeper was called. 'Is there any one in the lobby?' said the president.

"'Yes, sir.'—'Who is it?'—'A woman, accompanied by a servant.' Every one looked at his neighbor. 'Bring her in,' said the president. Five minutes after the door-keeper again appeared; all eyes were fixed on the door, and I," said Beauchamp, "shared the general expectation and anxiety. Behind the door-keeper walked a woman enveloped in a large veil, which completely concealed her. It was evident, from her figure and the perfumes she had about her, that she was young and fastidious in her tastes, but that was all. The president requested her to throw aside her veil, and it was then seen that she was dressed in the Grecian costume, and was remarkably beautiful."

"Ah," said Albert, "it was she."

"Who?"

"Haidee."

"Who told you that?"

"Alas, I guess it. But go on, Beauchamp. You see I am calm and strong. And yet we must be drawing near the disclosure."

"M. de Morcerf," continued Beauchamp, "looked at this woman with surprise and terror. Her lips were about to pass his sentence of life or death. To the committee the adventure was so extraordinary and curious, that the interest they had felt for the count's safety became now quite a secondary matter. The president himself advanced to place a seat for the young lady; but she declined availing herself of it. As for the count, he had fallen on his chair; it was evident that his legs refused to support him.

"'Madame,' said the president, 'you have engaged to furnish the committee with some important particulars respecting the affair at Yanina, and you have stated that you were an eyewitness of the event.'—'I was, indeed,' said the stranger, with a tone of sweet melancholy, and with the sonorous voice peculiar to the East.

"'But allow me to say that you must have been very young then.'—'I was four years old; but as those events deeply concerned me, not a single detail has escaped my memory.'—'In what manner could these events concern you? and who are you, that they should have made so deep an impression on you?'—'On them depended my father's life,' replied she. 'I am Haidee, the daughter of Ali Tepelini, pasha of Yanina, and of Vasiliki, his beloved wife.'

"The blush of mingled pride and modesty which suddenly suffused the cheeks of the young woman, the brilliancy of her eye, and her highly important communication, produced an indescribable effect on the assembly. As for the count, he could not have been more overwhelmed if a thunderbolt had fallen at his feet and opened an immense gulf before him. 'Madame,' replied the president, bowing with profound respect, 'allow me to ask one question; it shall be the last: Can you prove the authenticity of what you have now stated?'—'I can, sir,' said Haidee, drawing from under her veil a satin satchel highly perfumed; 'for here is the register of my birth, signed by my father and his principal officers, and that of my baptism, my father having consented to my being brought up in my mother's faith,—this latter has been sealed by the grand primate of Macedonia and Epirus; and lastly (and perhaps the most important), the record of the sale of my person and that of my mother to the Armenian merchant El-Kobbir, by the French officer, who, in his infamous bargain with the Porte, had reserved as his part of the booty the wife and daughter of his benefactor, whom he sold for the sum of four hundred thousand francs.' A greenish pallor spread over the count's cheeks, and his eyes became bloodshot at these terrible imputations, which were listened to by the assembly with ominous silence.

"Haidee, still calm, but with a calmness more dreadful than the anger of another would have been, handed to the president the record of her sale, written in Arabic. It had been supposed some of the papers might be in the Arabian, Romaic, or Turkish language, and the interpreter of the House was in attendance. One of the noble peers, who was familiar with the Arabic language, having studied it during the famous Egyptian campaign, followed with his eye as the translator read aloud:—

"'I, El-Kobbir, a slave-merchant, and purveyor of the harem of his highness, acknowledge having received for transmission to the sublime emperor, from the French lord, the Count of Monte Cristo, an emerald valued at eight hundred thousand francs; as the ransom of a young Christian slave of eleven years of age, named Haidee, the acknowledged daughter of the late lord Ali Tepelini, pasha of Yanina, and of Vasiliki, his favorite; she having been sold to me seven years previously, with her mother, who had died on arriving at Constantinople, by a French colonel in the service of the Vizier Ali Tepelini, named Fernand Mondego. The above-mentioned purchase was made on his highness's account, whose mandate I had, for the sum of four hundred thousand francs.

"'Given at Constantinople, by authority of his highness, in the year 1247 of the Hegira.

"'Signed El-Kobbir.'

"'That this record should have all due authority, it shall bear the imperial seal, which the vendor is bound to have affixed to it.'

"Near the merchant's signature there was, indeed, the seal of the sublime emperor. A dreadful silence followed the reading of this document; the count could only stare, and his gaze, fixed as if unconsciously on Haidee, seemed one of fire and blood. 'Madame,' said the president, 'may reference be made to the Count of Monte Cristo, who is now, I believe, in Paris?'—'Sir,' replied Haidee, 'the Count of Monte Cristo, my foster-father, has been in Normandy the last three days.'

"'Who, then, has counselled you to take this step, one for which the court is deeply indebted to you, and which is perfectly natural, considering your birth and your misfortunes?'—'Sir,' replied Haidee, 'I have been led to take this step from a feeling of respect and grief. Although a Christian, may God forgive me, I have always sought to revenge my illustrious father. Since I set my foot in France, and knew the traitor lived in Paris, I have watched carefully. I live retired in the house of my noble protector, but I do it from choice. I love retirement and silence, because I can live with my thoughts and recollections of past days. But the Count of Monte Cristo surrounds me with every paternal care, and I am ignorant of nothing which passes in the world. I learn all in the silence of my apartments,—for instance, I see all the newspapers, every periodical, as well as every new piece of music; and by thus watching the course of the life of others, I learned what had transpired this morning in the House of Peers, and what was to take place this evening; then I wrote.'

"'Then,' remarked the president, 'the Count of Monte Cristo knows nothing of your present proceedings?'—'He is quite unaware of them, and I have but one fear, which is that he should disapprove of what I have done. But it is a glorious day for me,' continued the young girl, raising her ardent gaze to heaven, 'that on which I find at last an opportunity of avenging my father!'

"The count had not uttered one word the whole of this time. His colleagues looked at him, and doubtless pitied his prospects, blighted under the perfumed breath of a woman. His misery was depicted in sinister lines on his countenance. 'M. de Morcerf,' said the president, 'do you recognize this lady as the daughter of Ali Tepelini, pasha of Yanina?'—'No,' said Morcerf, attempting to rise, 'it is a base plot, contrived by my enemies.' Haidee, whose eyes had been fixed on the door, as if expecting some one, turned hastily, and, seeing the count standing, shrieked, 'You do not know me?' said she. 'Well, I fortunately recognize you! You are Fernand Mondego, the French officer who led the troops of my noble father! It is you who surrendered the castle of Yanina! It is you who, sent by him to Constantinople, to treat with the emperor for the life or death of your benefactor, brought back a false mandate granting full pardon! It is you who, with that mandate, obtained the pasha's ring, which gave you authority over Selim, the fire-keeper! It is you who stabbed Selim. It is you who sold us, my mother and me, to the merchant, El-Kobbir! Assassin, assassin, assassin, you have still on your brow your master's blood! Look, gentlemen, all!'

"These words had been pronounced with such enthusiasm and evident truth, that every eye was fixed on the count's forehead, and he himself passed his hand across it, as if he felt Ali's blood still lingering there. 'You positively recognize M. de Morcerf as the officer, Fernand Mondego?'—'Indeed I do!' cried Haidee. 'Oh, my mother, it was you who said, "You were free, you had a beloved father, you were destined to be almost a queen. Look well at that man; it is he who raised your father's head on the point of a spear; it is he who sold us; it is he who forsook us! Look well at his right hand, on which he has a large wound; if you forgot his features, you would know him by that hand, into which fell, one by one, the gold pieces of the merchant El-Kobbir!" I know him! Ah, let him say now if he does not recognize me!' Each word fell like a dagger on Morcerf, and deprived him of a portion of his energy; as she uttered the last, he hid his mutilated hand hastily in his bosom, and fell back on his seat, overwhelmed by wretchedness and despair.

This scene completely changed the opinion of the assembly respecting the accused count.

"'Count of Morcerf,' said the president, 'do not allow yourself to be cast down; answer. The justice of the court is supreme and impartial as that of God; it will not suffer you to be trampled on by your enemies without giving you an opportunity of defending yourself. Shall further inquiries be made? Shall two members of the House be sent to Yanina? Speak!' Morcerf did not reply. Then all the members looked at each other with terror. They knew the count's energetic and violent temper; it must be, indeed, a dreadful blow which would deprive him of courage to defend himself. They expected that his stupefied silence would be followed by a fiery outburst. 'Well,' asked the president, 'what is your decision?'

"'I have no reply to make,' said the count in a low tone.

"'Has the daughter of Ali Tepelini spoken the truth?' said the president. 'Is she, then, the terrible witness to whose charge you dare not plead "Not guilty"? Have you really committed the crimes of which you are accused?' The count looked around him with an expression which might have softened tigers, but which could not disarm his judges. Then he raised his eyes towards the ceiling, but withdrew then, immediately, as if he feared the roof would open and reveal to his distressed view that second tribunal called heaven, and that other judge named God. Then, with a hasty movement, he tore open his coat, which seemed to stifle him, and flew from the room like a madman; his footstep was heard one moment in the corridor, then the rattling of his carriage-wheels as he was driven rapidly away. 'Gentlemen,' said the president, when silence was restored, 'is the Count of Morcerf convicted of felony, treason, and conduct unbecoming a member of this House?'—'Yes,' replied all the members of the committee of inquiry with a unanimous voice.

"Haidee had remained until the close of the meeting. She heard the count's sentence pronounced without betraying an expression of joy or pity; then drawing her veil over her face she bowed majestically to the councillors, and left with that dignified step which Virgil attributes to his goddesses."

CHAPTER 87.
THE CHALLENGE.

"Then," continued Beauchamp, "I took advantage of the silence and the darkness to leave the house without being seen. The usher who had introduced me was waiting for me at the door, and he conducted me through the corridors to a private entrance opening into the Rue de Vaugirard. I left with mingled feelings of sorrow and delight. Excuse me, Albert,—sorrow on your account, and delight with that noble girl, thus pursuing paternal vengeance. Yes, Albert, from whatever source the blow may have proceeded—it may be from an enemy, but that enemy is only the agent of providence." Albert held his head between his hands; he raised his face, red with shame and bathed in tears, and seizing Beauchamp's arm, "My friend," said he, "my life is ended. I cannot calmly say with you, 'Providence has struck the blow;' but I must discover who pursues me with this hatred, and when I have found him I shall kill him, or he will kill me. I rely on your friendship to assist me, Beauchamp, if contempt has not banished it from your heart."

"Contempt, my friend? How does this misfortune affect you? No, happily that unjust prejudice is forgotten which made the son responsible for the father's actions. Review your life, Albert; although it is only just beginning, did a lovely summer's day ever dawn with greater purity than has marked the commencement of your career? No, Albert, take my advice. You are young and rich—leave Paris—all is soon forgotten in this great Babylon of excitement and changing tastes. You will return after three or four years with a Russian princess for a bride, and no one will think more of what occurred yesterday than if it had happened sixteen years ago."

"Thank you, my dear Beauchamp, thank you for the excellent feeling which prompts your advice; but it cannot be. I have told you my wish, or rather my determination. You understand that, interested as I am in this affair, I cannot see it in the same light as you do. What appears to you to emanate from a celestial source, seems to me to proceed from one far less pure. Providence appears to me to have no share in this affair; and happily so, for instead of the invisible, impalpable agent of celestial rewards and punishments, I shall find one both palpable and visible, on whom I shall revenge myself, I assure you, for all I have suffered during the last month. Now, I repeat, Beauchamp, I wish to return to human and material existence, and if you are still the friend you profess to be, help me to discover the hand that struck the blow."

"Be it so," said Beauchamp; "if you must have me descend to earth, I submit; and if you will seek your enemy,

I will assist you, and I will engage to find him, my honor being almost as deeply interested as yours."

"Well, then, you understand, Beauchamp, that we begin our search immediately. Each moment's delay is an eternity for me. The calumniator is not yet punished, and he may hope that he will not be; but, on my honor, if he thinks so, he deceives himself."

"Well, listen, Morcerf."

"Ah, Beauchamp, I see you know something already; you will restore me to life."

"I do not say there is any truth in what I am going to tell you, but it is, at least, a ray of light in a dark night; by following it we may, perhaps, discover something more certain."

"Tell me; satisfy my impatience."

"Well, I will tell you what I did not like to mention on my return from Yanina."

"Say on."

"I went, of course, to the chief banker of the town to make inquiries. At the first word, before I had even mentioned your father's name"—

"'Ah,' said he. 'I guess what brings you here.'

"'How, and why?'

"'Because a fortnight since I was questioned on the same subject.'

"'By whom?'—'By a Paris banker, my correspondent.'

"'Whose name is'—

"'Danglars.'"

"He!" cried Albert; "yes, it is indeed he who has so long pursued my father with jealous hatred. He, the man who would be popular, cannot forgive the Count of Morcerf for being created a peer; and this marriage broken off without a reason being assigned—yes, it is all from the same cause."

"Make inquiries, Albert, but do not be angry without reason; make inquiries, and if it be true"—

"Oh, yes, if it be true," cried the young man, "he shall pay me all I have suffered."

"Beware, Morcerf, he is already an old man."

"I will respect his age as he has respected the honor of my family; if my father had offended him, why did he not attack him personally? Oh, no, he was afraid to encounter him face to face."

"I do not condemn you, Albert; I only restrain you. Act prudently."

"Oh, do not fear; besides, you will accompany me. Beauchamp, solemn transactions should be sanctioned by a witness. Before this day closes, if M. Danglars is guilty, he shall cease to live, or I shall die. Pardieu, Beauchamp, mine shall be a splendid funeral!"

"When such resolutions are made, Albert, they should be promptly executed. Do you wish to go to M. Danglars? Let us go immediately." They sent for a cabriolet. On entering the banker's mansion, they perceived the phaeton and servant of M. Andrea Cavalcanti. "Ah, parbleu, that's good," said Albert, with a gloomy tone. "If M. Danglars will not fight with me, I will kill his son-in-law; Cavalcanti will certainly fight." The servant announced the young man; but the banker, recollecting what had transpired the day before, did not wish him admitted. It was, however, too late; Albert had followed the footman, and, hearing the order given, forced the door open, and followed by Beauchamp found himself in the banker's study. "Sir," cried the latter, "am I no longer at liberty to receive whom I choose in my house? You appear to forget yourself sadly."

"No, sir," said Albert, coldly; "there are circumstances in which one cannot, except through cowardice,—I offer you that refuge,—refuse to admit certain persons at least."

"What is your errand, then, with me, sir?"

"I mean," said Albert, drawing near, and without apparently noticing Cavalcanti, who stood with his back towards the fireplace—"I mean to propose a meeting in some retired corner where no one will interrupt us for ten minutes; that will be sufficient—where two men having met, one of them will remain on the ground." Danglars turned pale; Cavalcanti moved a step forward, and Albert turned towards him. "And you, too," said he, "come, if you like, monsieur; you have a claim, being almost one of the family, and I will give as many rendezvous of that kind as I can find persons willing to accept them." Cavalcanti looked at Danglars with a stupefied air, and the latter, making an effort, arose and stepped between the two young men. Albert's attack on Andrea had placed him on a different footing, and he hoped this visit had another cause than that he had at first supposed.

"Indeed, sir," said he to Albert, "if you are come to quarrel with this gentleman because I have preferred him to you, I shall resign the case to the king's attorney."

"You mistake, sir," said Morcerf with a gloomy smile; "I am not referring in the least to matrimony, and I only addressed myself to M. Cavalcanti because he appeared disposed to interfere between us. In one respect you are right, for I am ready to quarrel with every one to-day; but you have the first claim, M. Danglars."

"Sir," replied Danglars, pale with anger and fear, "I warn you, when I have the misfortune to meet with a mad dog, I kill it; and far from thinking myself guilty of a crime, I believe I do society a kindness. Now, if you are mad and try to bite me, I will kill you without pity. Is it my fault that your father has dishonored himself?"

"Yes, miserable wretch!" cried Morcerf, "it is your fault." Danglars retreated a few steps. "My fault?" said he; "you must be mad! What do I know of the Grecian affair? Have I travelled in that country? Did I advise your father to sell the castle of Yanina—to betray"—

"Silence!" said Albert, with a thundering voice. "No; it is not you who have directly made this exposure and brought this sorrow on us, but you hypocritically provoked it."

"I?"

"Yes; you! How came it known?"

"I suppose you read it in the paper in the account from Yanina?"

"Who wrote to Yanina?"

"To Yanina?"

"Yes. Who wrote for particulars concerning my father?"

"I imagine any one may write to Yanina."

"But one person only wrote!"

"One only?"

"Yes; and that was you!"

"I, doubtless, wrote. It appears to me that when about to marry your daughter to a young man, it is right to make some inquiries respecting his family; it is not only a right, but a duty."

"You wrote, sir, knowing what answer you would receive."

"I, indeed? I assure you," cried Danglars, with a confidence and security proceeding less from fear than from the interest he really felt for the young man, "I solemnly declare to you, that I should never have thought of writing to Yanina, did I know anything of Ali Pasha's misfortunes."

"Who, then, urged you to write? Tell me."

"Pardieu, it was the most simple thing in the world. I was speaking of your father's past history. I said the origin of his fortune remained obscure. The person to whom I addressed my scruples asked me where your father had acquired his property? I answered, 'In Greece.'—'Then,' said he, 'write to Yanina.'"

"And who thus advised you?"

"No other than your friend, Monte Cristo."

"The Count of Monte Cristo told you to write to Yanina?"

"Yes; and I wrote, and will show you my correspondence, if you like." Albert and Beauchamp looked at each other. "Sir," said Beauchamp, who had not yet spoken, "you appear to accuse the count, who is absent from Paris at this moment, and cannot justify himself."

"I accuse no one, sir," said Danglars; "I relate, and I will repeat before the count what I have said to you."

"Does the count know what answer you received?"

"Yes; I showed it to him."

"Did he know my father's Christian name was Fernand, and his family name Mondego?"

"Yes, I had told him that long since, and I did only what any other would have done in my circumstances, and perhaps less. When, the day after the arrival of this answer, your father came by the advice of Monte Cristo to ask my daughter's hand for you, I decidedly refused him, but without any explanation or exposure. In short, why should I have any more to do with the affair? How did the honor or disgrace of M. de Morcerf affect me? It neither increased nor decreased my income."

Albert felt the blood mounting to his brow; there was no doubt upon the subject. Danglars defended himself with the baseness, but at the same time with the assurance, of a man who speaks the truth, at least in part, if not wholly—not for conscience' sake, but through fear. Besides, what was Morcerf seeking? It was not whether Danglars or Monte Cristo was more or less guilty; it was a man who would answer for the offence, whether trifling or serious; it was a man who would fight, and it was evident Danglars would not fight. And, in addition to this, everything forgotten or unperceived before presented itself now to his recollection. Monte Cristo knew everything, as he had bought the daughter of Ali Pasha; and, knowing everything, he had advised Danglars to write to Yanina. The answer known, he had yielded to Albert's wish to be introduced to Haidee, and allowed the conversation to turn on the death of Ali, and had not opposed Haidee's recital (but having, doubtless, warned the young girl, in the few Romaic words he spoke to her, not to implicate Morcerf's father). Besides, had he not begged of Morcerf not to mention his father's name before Haidee? Lastly, he had taken Albert to Normandy when he knew the final blow was near. There could be no doubt that all had been calculated and previously arranged; Monte Cristo then was in league with his father's enemies. Albert took Beauchamp aside, and communicated these ideas to him.

"You are right," said the latter; "M. Danglars has only been a secondary agent in this sad affair, and it is of M. de Monte Cristo that you must demand an explanation." Albert turned. "Sir," said he to Danglars, "understand that I do not take a final leave of you; I must ascertain if your insinuations are just, and am going now to inquire of the Count of Monte Cristo." He bowed to the banker, and went out with Beauchamp, without appearing to notice Cavalcanti. Danglars accompanied him to the door, where he again assured Albert that no motive of personal hatred had influenced him against the Count of Morcerf.

CHAPTER 88.
THE INSULT.

At the banker's door Beauchamp stopped Morcerf. "Listen," said he; "just now I told you it was of M. de Monte Cristo you must demand an explanation."

"Yes; and we are going to his house."

"Reflect, Morcerf, one moment before you go."

"On what shall I reflect?"

"On the importance of the step you are taking."

"Is it more serious than going to M. Danglars?"

"Yes; M. Danglars is a money-lover, and those who love money, you know, think too much of what they risk to be easily induced to fight a duel. The other is, on the contrary, to all appearance a true nobleman; but do you not fear to find him a bully?"

"I only fear one thing; namely, to find a man who will not fight."

"Do not be alarmed," said Beauchamp; "he will meet you. My only fear is that he will be too strong for you."

"My friend," said Morcerf, with a sweet smile, "that is what I wish. The happiest thing that could occur to me, would be to die in my father's stead; that would save us all."

"Your mother would die of grief."

"My poor mother!" said Albert, passing his hand across his eyes, "I know she would; but better so than die of shame."

"Are you quite decided, Albert?"

"Yes; let us go."

"But do you think we shall find the count at home?"

"He intended returning some hours after me, and doubtless he is now at home." They ordered the driver to take them to No. 30 Champs-Elysees. Beauchamp wished to go in alone, but Albert observed that as this was an unusual circumstance he might be allowed to deviate from the usual etiquette in affairs of honor. The cause which the young man espoused was one so sacred that Beauchamp had only to comply with all his wishes; he yielded and contented himself with following Morcerf. Albert sprang from the porter's lodge to the steps. He was received by Baptistin. The count had, indeed, just arrived, but he was in his bath, and had forbidden that any one should be admitted. "But after his bath?" asked Morcerf.

"My master will go to dinner."

"And after dinner?"

"He will sleep an hour."

"Then?"

"He is going to the opera."

"Are you sure of it?" asked Albert.

"Quite, sir; my master has ordered his horses at eight o'clock precisely."

"Very good," replied Albert; "that is all I wished to know." Then, turning towards Beauchamp, "If you have anything to attend to, Beauchamp, do it directly; if you have any appointment for this evening, defer it till tomorrow. I depend on you to accompany me to the opera; and if you can, bring Chateau-Renaud with you."

Beauchamp availed himself of Albert's permission, and left him, promising to call for him at a quarter before eight. On his return home, Albert expressed his wish to Franz Debray, and Morrel, to see them at the opera that evening. Then he went to see his mother, who since the events of the day before had refused to see any one, and had kept her room. He found her in bed, overwhelmed with grief at this public humiliation. The sight of Albert produced the effect which might naturally be expected on Mercedes; she pressed her son's hand and sobbed aloud, but her tears relieved her. Albert stood one moment speechless by the side of his mother's bed. It was evident from his pale face and knit brows that his resolution to revenge himself was growing weaker. "My dear mother," said he, "do you know if M. de Morcerf has any enemy?" Mercedes started; she noticed that the young man did not say "my father." "My son," she said, "persons in the count's situation have many secret enemies. Those who are known are not the most dangerous."

"I know it, and appeal to your penetration. You are of so superior a mind, nothing escapes you."

"Why do you say so?"

"Because, for instance, you noticed on the evening of the ball we gave, that M. de Monte Cristo would eat nothing in our house." Mercedes raised herself on her feverish arm. "M. de Monte Cristo!" she exclaimed; "and how is he connected with the question you asked me?"

"You know, mother, M. de Monte Cristo is almost an Oriental, and it is customary with the Orientals to secure full liberty for revenge by not eating or drinking in the houses of their enemies."

"Do you say M. de Monte Cristo is our enemy?" replied Mercedes, becoming paler than the sheet which covered her. "Who told you so? Why, you are mad, Albert! M. de Monte Cristo has only shown us kindness. M. de Monte Cristo saved your life; you yourself presented him to us. Oh, I entreat you, my son, if you had entertained such an idea, dispel it; and my counsel to you—nay, my prayer—is to retain his friendship."

"Mother," replied the young man, "you have especial reasons for telling me to conciliate that man."

"I?" said Mercedes, blushing as rapidly as she had turned pale, and again becoming paler than ever.

"Yes, doubtless; and is it not that he may never do us any harm?" Mercedes shuddered, and, fixing on her son a scrutinizing gaze, "You speak strangely," said she to Albert, "and you appear to have some singular prejudices. What has the count done? Three days since you were with him in Normandy; only three days since we looked on him as our best friend."

An ironical smile passed over Albert's lips. Mercedes saw it and with the double instinct of woman and mother guessed all; but as she was prudent and strong-minded she concealed both her sorrows and her fears. Albert was silent; an instant after, the countess resumed: "You came to inquire after my health; I will candidly acknowledge that I am not well. You should install yourself here, and cheer my solitude. I do not wish to be left alone."

"Mother," said the young man, "you know how gladly I would obey your wish, but an urgent and important affair obliges me to leave you for the whole evening."

"Well," replied Mercedes, sighing, "go, Albert; I will not make you a slave to your filial piety." Albert pretended he did not hear, bowed to his mother, and quitted her. Scarcely had he shut her door, when Mercedes called a confidential servant, and ordered him to follow Albert wherever he should go that evening, and to come and tell her immediately what he observed. Then she rang for her lady's maid, and, weak as she was, she dressed, in order to be ready for whatever might happen. The footman's mission was an easy one. Albert went to his room, and dressed with unusual care. At ten minutes to eight Beauchamp arrived; he had seen Chateau-Renaud, who had promised to be in the orchestra before the curtain was raised. Both got into Albert's coupe; and, as the young man had no reason to conceal where he was going, he called aloud, "To the opera." In his impatience he arrived before the beginning of the performance.

Chateau-Renaud was at his post; apprised by Beauchamp of the circumstances, he required no explanation from Albert. The conduct of the son in seeking to avenge his father was so natural that Chateau-Renaud did not seek to dissuade him, and was content with renewing his assurances of devotion. Debray was not yet come, but Albert knew that he seldom lost a scene at the opera. Albert wandered about the theatre until the curtain was drawn up. He hoped to meet with M. de Monte Cristo either in the lobby or on the stairs. The bell summoned him to his seat, and he entered the orchestra with Chateau-Renaud and Beauchamp. But his eyes scarcely quitted the box between the columns, which remained obstinately closed during the whole of the first act. At last, as Albert was looking at his watch for about the hundredth time, at the beginning of the second act the door opened, and Monte Cristo entered, dressed in black, and, leaning over the front of the box, looked around the pit. Morrel followed him, and looked also for his sister and brother in-law; he soon discovered them in another box, and kissed his hand to them.

The count, in his survey of the pit, encountered a pale face and threatening eyes, which evidently sought to gain his attention. He recognized Albert, but thought it better not to notice him, as he looked so angry and discomposed. Without communicating his thoughts to his companion, he sat down, drew out his opera-glass, and looked another way. Although apparently not noticing Albert, he did not, however, lose sight of him, and when the curtain fell at the end of the second act, he saw him leave the orchestra with his two friends. Then his head was seen passing at the back of the boxes, and the count knew that the approaching storm was intended to fall on him. He was at the moment conversing cheerfully with Morrel, but he was well prepared for what might happen. The door opened, and Monte Cristo, turning round, saw Albert, pale and trembling, followed by Beauchamp and Chateau-Renaud.

"Well," cried he, with that benevolent politeness which distinguished his salutation from the common civilities of the world, "my cavalier has attained his object. Good-evening, M. de Morcerf." The countenance of this man, who possessed such extraordinary control over his feelings, expressed the most perfect cordiality. Morrel only then recollected the letter he had received from the viscount, in which, without assigning any reason, he begged him to go to the opera, but he understood that something terrible was brooding.

"We are not come here, sir, to exchange hypocritical expressions of politeness, or false professions of friendship," said Albert, "but to demand an explanation." The young man's trembling voice was scarcely audible. "An explanation at the opera?" said the count, with that calm tone and penetrating eye which characterize the man who knows his cause is good. "Little acquainted as I am with the habits of Parisians, I should not have thought this the place for such a demand."

"Still, if people will shut themselves up," said Albert, "and cannot be seen because they are bathing, dining, or asleep, we must avail ourselves of the opportunity whenever they are to be seen."

"I am not difficult of access, sir; for yesterday, if my memory does not deceive me, you were at my house."

"Yesterday I was at your house, sir," said the young man; "because then I knew not who you were." In pronouncing these words Albert had raised his voice so as to be heard by those in the adjoining boxes and in the lobby. Thus the attention of many was attracted by this altercation. "Where are you come from, sir? You do not appear to be in the possession of your senses."

"Provided I understand your perfidy, sir, and succeed in making you understand that I will be revenged, I shall be reasonable enough," said Albert furiously.

"I do not understand you, sir," replied Monte Cristo; "and if I did, your tone is too high. I am at home here, and I alone have a right to raise my voice above another's. Leave the box, sir!" Monte Cristo pointed towards the door with the most commanding dignity. "Ah, I shall know how to make you leave your home!" replied Albert, clasping in his convulsed grasp the glove, which Monte Cristo did not lose sight of.

"Well, well," said Monte Cristo quietly, "I see you wish to quarrel with me; but I would give you one piece of advice, which you will do well to keep in mind. It is in poor taste to make a display of a challenge. Display is not becoming to every one, M. de Morcerf."

At this name a murmur of astonishment passed around the group of spectators of this scene. They had talked of no one but Morcerf the whole day. Albert understood the allusion in a moment, and was about to throw his glove at the count, when Morrel seized his hand, while Beauchamp and Chateau-Renaud, fearing the scene would surpass the limits of a challenge, held him back. But Monte Cristo, without rising, and leaning forward in his chair, merely stretched out his arm and, taking the damp, crushed glove from the clinched hand of the young man, "Sir," said he in a solemn tone, "I consider your glove thrown, and will return it to you wrapped around a bullet. Now leave me or I will summon my servants to throw you out at the door."

Wild, almost unconscious, and with eyes inflamed, Albert stepped back, and Morrel closed the door. Monte Cristo took up his glass again as if nothing had happened; his face was like marble, and his heart was like bronze. Morrel whispered, "What have you done to him?"

"I? Nothing—at least personally," said Monte Cristo.

"But there must be some cause for this strange scene."

"The Count of Morcerf's adventure exasperates the young man."

"Have you anything to do with it?"

"It was through Haidee that the Chamber was informed of his father's treason."

"Indeed?" said Morrel. "I had been told, but would not credit it, that the Grecian slave I have seen with you here in this very box was the daughter of Ali Pasha."

"It is true, nevertheless."

"Then," said Morrel, "I understand it all, and this scene was premeditated."

"How so?"

"Yes. Albert wrote to request me to come to the opera, doubtless that I might be a witness to the insult he meant to offer you."

"Probably," said Monte Cristo with his imperturbable tranquillity.

"But what shall you do with him?"

"With whom?"

"With Albert."

"What shall I do with Albert? As certainly, Maximilian, as I now press your hand, I shall kill him before ten o'clock to-morrow morning." Morrel, in his turn, took Monte Cristo's hand in both of his, and he shuddered to feel how cold and steady it was.

"Ah, Count," said he, "his father loves him so much!"

"Do not speak to me of that," said Monte Cristo, with the first movement of anger he had betrayed; "I will make him suffer." Morrel, amazed, let fall Monte Cristo's hand. "Count, count!" said he.

"Dear Maximilian," interrupted the count, "listen how adorably Duprez is singing that line,—

'O Mathilde! idole de mon ame!'

"I was the first to discover Duprez at Naples, and the first to applaud him. Bravo, bravo!" Morrel saw it was useless to say more, and refrained. The curtain, which had risen at the close of the scene with Albert, again fell, and a rap was heard at the door.

"Come in," said Monte Cristo with a voice that betrayed not the least emotion; and immediately Beauchamp appeared. "Good-evening, M. Beauchamp," said Monte Cristo, as if this was the first time he had seen the journalist that evening; "be seated."

Beauchamp bowed, and, sitting down, "Sir," said he, "I just now accompanied M. de Morcerf, as you saw."

"And that means," replied Monte Cristo, laughing, "that you had, probably, just dined together. I am happy to see, M. Beauchamp, that you are more sober than he was."

"Sir," said M. Beauchamp, "Albert was wrong, I acknowledge, to betray so much anger, and I come, on my own account, to apologize for him. And having done so, entirely on my own account, be it understood, I would add that I believe you too gentlemanly to refuse giving him some explanation concerning your connection with Yanina. Then I will add two words about the young Greek girl." Monte Cristo motioned him to be silent. "Come," said he, laughing, "there are all my hopes about to be destroyed."

"How so?" asked Beauchamp.

"Doubtless you wish to make me appear a very eccentric character. I am, in your opinion, a Lara, a Manfred, a Lord Ruthven; then, just as I am arriving at the climax, you defeat your own end, and seek to make an ordinary man of me. You bring me down to your own level, and demand explanations! Indeed, M. Beauchamp, it is quite laughable."

"Yet," replied Beauchamp haughtily, "there are occasions when probity commands"—

"M. Beauchamp," interposed this strange man, "the Count of Monte Cristo bows to none but the Count of

Monte Cristo himself. Say no more, I entreat you. I do what I please, M. Beauchamp, and it is always well done."

"Sir," replied the young man, "honest men are not to be paid with such coin. I require honorable guaranties."

"I am, sir, a living guaranty," replied Monte Cristo, motionless, but with a threatening look; "we have both blood in our veins which we wish to shed—that is our mutual guaranty. Tell the viscount so, and that to-morrow, before ten o'clock, I shall see what color his is."

"Then I have only to make arrangements for the duel," said Beauchamp.

"It is quite immaterial to me," said Monte Cristo, "and it was very unnecessary to disturb me at the opera for such a trifle. In France people fight with the sword or pistol, in the colonies with the carbine, in Arabia with the dagger. Tell your client that, although I am the insulted party, in order to carry out my eccentricity, I leave him the choice of arms, and will accept without discussion, without dispute, anything, even combat by drawing lots, which is always stupid, but with me different from other people, as I am sure to gain."

"Sure to gain!" repeated Beauchamp, looking with amazement at the count.

"Certainly," said Monte Cristo, slightly shrugging his shoulders; "otherwise I would not fight with M. de Morcerf. I shall kill him—I cannot help it. Only by a single line this evening at my house let me know the arms and the hour; I do not like to be kept waiting."

"Pistols, then, at eight o'clock, in the Bois de Vincennes," said Beauchamp, quite disconcerted, not knowing if he was dealing with an arrogant braggadocio or a supernatural being.

"Very well, sir," said Monte Cristo. "Now all that is settled, do let me see the performance, and tell your friend Albert not to come any more this evening; he will hurt himself with all his ill-chosen barbarisms: let him go home and go to sleep." Beauchamp left the box, perfectly amazed. "Now," said Monte Cristo, turning towards Morrel, "I may depend upon you, may I not?"

"Certainly," said Morrel, "I am at your service, count; still"—

"What?"

"It is desirable I should know the real cause."

"That is to say, you would rather not?"

"No."

"The young man himself is acting blindfolded, and knows not the true cause, which is known only to God and to me; but I give you my word, Morrel, that God, who does know it, will be on our side."

"Enough," said Morrel; "who is your second witness?"

"I know no one in Paris, Morrel, on whom I could confer that honor besides you and your brother Emmanuel. Do you think Emmanuel would oblige me?"

"I will answer for him, count."

"Well? that is all I require. To-morrow morning, at seven o'clock, you will be with me, will you not?"

"We will."

"Hush, the curtain is rising. Listen! I never lose a note of this opera if I can avoid it; the music of William Tell is so sweet."

CHAPTER 89.
A NOCTURNAL INTERVIEW.

Monte Cristo waited, according to his usual custom, until Duprez had sung his famous "Suivez-moi;" then he rose and went out. Morrel took leave of him at the door, renewing his promise to be with him the next morning at seven o'clock, and to bring Emmanuel. Then he stepped into his coupe, calm and smiling, and was at home in five minutes. No one who knew the count could mistake his expression when, on entering, he said, "Ali, bring me my pistols with the ivory cross."

Ali brought the box to his master, who examined the weapons with a solicitude very natural to a man who is about to intrust his life to a little powder and shot. These were pistols of an especial pattern, which Monte Cristo had had made for target practice in his own room. A cap was sufficient to drive out the bullet, and from the adjoining room no one would have suspected that the count was, as sportsmen would say, keeping his hand in. He was just taking one up and looking for the point to aim at on a little iron plate which served him as a target, when his study door opened, and Baptistin entered. Before he had spoken a word, the count saw in the next room a veiled woman, who had followed closely after Baptistin, and now, seeing the count with a pistol in his hand and swords on the table, rushed in. Baptistin looked at his master, who made a sign to him, and he went out, closing the door after him. "Who are you, madame?" said the count to the veiled woman.

The stranger cast one look around her, to be certain that they were quite alone; then bending as if she would have knelt, and joining her hands, she said with an accent of despair, "Edmond, you will not kill my son?" The count retreated a step, uttered a slight exclamation, and let fall the pistol he held. "What name did you pronounce then, Madame de Morcerf?" said he. "Yours!" cried she, throwing back her veil,—"yours, which I alone, perhaps, have not forgotten. Edmond, it is not Madame de Morcerf who is come to you, it is Mercedes."

"Mercedes is dead, madame," said Monte Cristo; "I know no one now of that name."

"Mercedes lives, sir, and she remembers, for she alone recognized you when she saw you, and even before she saw you, by your voice, Edmond,—by the simple sound of your voice; and from that moment she has followed your steps, watched you, feared you, and she needs not to inquire what hand has dealt the blow which now strikes M. de Morcerf."

"Fernand, do you mean?" replied Monte Cristo, with bitter irony; "since we are recalling names, let us remember them all." Monte Cristo had pronounced the name of Fernand with such an expression of hatred that Mercedes felt a thrill of horror run through every vein. "You see, Edmond, I am not mistaken, and have cause to say, 'Spare my son!'"

"And who told you, madame, that I have any hostile intentions against your son?"

"No one, in truth; but a mother has twofold sight. I guessed all; I followed him this evening to the opera, and, concealed in a parquet box, have seen all."

"If you have seen all, madame, you know that the son of Fernand has publicly insulted me," said Monte Cristo with awful calmness.

"Oh, for pity's sake!"

"You have seen that he would have thrown his glove in my face if Morrel, one of my friends, had not stopped him."

"Listen to me, my son has also guessed who you are,— he attributes his father's misfortunes to you."

"Madame, you are mistaken, they are not misfortunes,— it is a punishment. It is not I who strike M. de Morcerf; it is providence which punishes him."

"And why do you represent providence?" cried Mercedes. "Why do you remember when it forgets? What are Yanina and its vizier to you, Edmond? What injury his Fernand Mondego done you in betraying Ali Tepelini?"

"Ah, madame," replied Monte Cristo, "all this is an affair between the French captain and the daughter of Vasiliki. It does not concern me, you are right; and if I have sworn to revenge myself, it is not on the French captain, or the Count of Morcerf, but on the fisherman Fernand, the husband of Mercedes the Catalane."

"Ah, sir!" cried the countess, "how terrible a vengeance for a fault which fatality made me commit!—for I am the only culprit, Edmond, and if you owe revenge to any one, it is to me, who had not fortitude to bear your absence and my solitude."

"But," exclaimed Monte Cristo, "why was I absent? And why were you alone?"

"Because you had been arrested, Edmond, and were a prisoner."

"And why was I arrested? Why was I a prisoner?"

"I do not know," said Mercedes. "You do not, madame; at least, I hope not. But I will tell you. I was arrested and became a prisoner because, under the arbor of La Reserve, the day before I was to marry you, a man named Danglars wrote this letter, which the fisherman Fernand himself posted." Monte Cristo went to a secretary, opened a drawer by a spring, from which he took a paper which had lost its original color, and the ink of which had become of a rusty hue—this he placed in the hands of Mercedes. It was Danglars' letter to the king's attorney, which the Count of Monte Cristo, disguised as a clerk from the house of Thomson & French, had taken from the file against

Edmond Dantes, on the day he had paid the two hundred thousand francs to M. de Boville. Mercedes read with terror the following lines:—

"The king's attorney is informed by a friend to the throne and religion that one Edmond Dantes, second in command on board the Pharaon, this day arrived from Smyrna, after having touched at Naples and Porto-Ferrajo, is the bearer of a letter from Murat to the usurper, and of another letter from the usurper to the Bonapartist club in Paris. Ample corroboration of this statement may be obtained by arresting the above-mentioned Edmond Dantes, who either carries the letter for Paris about with him, or has it at his father's abode. Should it not be found in possession of either father or son, then it will assuredly be discovered in the cabin belonging to the said Dantes on board the Pharaon."

"How dreadful!" said Mercedes, passing her hand across her brow, moist with perspiration; "and that letter"—

"I bought it for two hundred thousand francs, madame," said Monte Cristo; "but that is a trifle, since it enables me to justify myself to you."

"And the result of that letter"—

"You well know, madame, was my arrest; but you do not know how long that arrest lasted. You do not know that I remained for fourteen years within a quarter of a league of you, in a dungeon in the Chateau d'If. You do not know that every day of those fourteen years I renewed the vow of vengeance which I had made the first day; and yet I was not aware that you had married Fernand, my calumniator, and that my father had died of hunger!"

"Can it be?" cried Mercedes, shuddering.

"That is what I heard on leaving my prison fourteen years after I had entered it; and that is why, on account of the living Mercedes and my deceased father, I have sworn to revenge myself on Fernand, and—I have revenged myself."

"And you are sure the unhappy Fernand did that?"

"I am satisfied, madame, that he did what I have told you; besides, that is not much more odious than that a Frenchman by adoption should pass over to the English; that a Spaniard by birth should have fought against the Spaniards; that a stipendiary of Ali should have betrayed and murdered Ali. Compared with such things, what is the letter you have just read?—a lover's deception, which the woman who has married that man ought certainly to forgive; but not so the lover who was to have married her. Well, the French did not avenge themselves on the traitor, the Spaniards did not shoot the traitor, Ali in his tomb left the traitor unpunished; but I, betrayed, sacrificed, buried, have risen from my tomb, by the grace of God, to punish that man. He sends me for that purpose, and here I am."
The poor woman's head and arms fell; her legs bent under

her, and she fell on her knees. "Forgive, Edmond, forgive for my sake, who love you still!"

The dignity of the wife checked the fervor of the lover and the mother. Her forehead almost touched the carpet, when the count sprang forward and raised her. Then seated on a chair, she looked at the manly countenance of Monte Cristo, on which grief and hatred still impressed a threatening expression. "Not crush that accursed race?" murmured he; "abandon my purpose at the moment of its accomplishment? Impossible, madame, impossible!"

"Edmond," said the poor mother, who tried every means, "when I call you Edmond, why do you not call me Mercedes?"

"Mercedes!" repeated Monte Cristo; "Mercedes! Well yes, you are right; that name has still its charms, and this is the first time for a long period that I have pronounced it so distinctly. Oh, Mercedes, I have uttered your name with the sigh of melancholy, with the groan of sorrow, with the last effort of despair; I have uttered it when frozen with cold, crouched on the straw in my dungeon; I have uttered it, consumed with heat, rolling on the stone floor of my prison. Mercedes, I must revenge myself, for I suffered fourteen years,—fourteen years I wept, I cursed; now I tell you, Mercedes, I must revenge myself."

The count, fearing to yield to the entreaties of her he had so ardently loved, called his sufferings to the assistance of his hatred. "Revenge yourself, then, Edmond," cried the poor mother; "but let your vengeance fall on the culprits,— on him, on me, but not on my son!"

"It is written in the good book," said Monte Cristo, "that the sins of the fathers shall fall upon their children to the third and fourth generation. Since God himself dictated those words to his prophet, why should I seek to make myself better than God?"

"Edmond," continued Mercedes, with her arms extended towards the count, "since I first knew you, I have adored your name, have respected your memory. Edmond, my friend, do not compel me to tarnish that noble and pure image reflected incessantly on the mirror of my heart. Edmond, if you knew all the prayers I have addressed to God for you while I thought you were living and since I have thought you must be dead! Yes, dead, alas! I imagined your dead body buried at the foot of some gloomy tower, or cast to the bottom of a pit by hateful jailers, and I wept! What could I do for you, Edmond, besides pray and weep? Listen; for ten years I dreamed each night the same dream. I had been told that you had endeavored to escape; that you had taken the place of another prisoner; that you had slipped into the winding sheet of a dead body; that you had been thrown alive from the top of the Chateau d'If, and that the cry you uttered as you dashed upon the rocks first revealed to your jailers that they were your murderers. Well, Edmond,

I swear to you, by the head of that son for whom I entreat your pity,—Edmond, for ten years I saw every night every detail of that frightful tragedy, and for ten years I heard every night the cry which awoke me, shuddering and cold. And I, too, Edmond—oh! believe me—guilty as I was—oh, yes, I, too, have suffered much!"

"Have you known what it is to have your father starve to death in your absence?" cried Monte Cristo, thrusting his hands into his hair; "have you seen the woman you loved giving her hand to your rival, while you were perishing at the bottom of a dungeon?"

"No," interrupted Mercedes, "but I have seen him whom I loved on the point of murdering my son." Mercedes uttered these words with such deep anguish, with an accent of such intense despair, that Monte Cristo could not restrain a sob. The lion was daunted; the avenger was conquered. "What do you ask of me?" said he,—"your son's life? Well, he shall live!" Mercedes uttered a cry which made the tears start from Monte Cristo's eyes; but these tears disappeared almost instantaneously, for, doubtless, God had sent some angel to collect them—far more precious were they in his eyes than the richest pearls of Guzerat and Ophir.

"Oh," said she, seizing the count's hand and raising it to her lips; "oh, thank you, thank you, Edmond! Now you are exactly what I dreamt you were,—the man I always loved. Oh, now I may say so!"

"So much the better," replied Monte Cristo; "as that poor Edmond will not have long to be loved by you. Death is about to return to the tomb, the phantom to retire in darkness."

"What do you say, Edmond?"

"I say, since you command me, Mercedes, I must die."

"Die? and why so? Who talks of dying? Whence have you these ideas of death?"

"You do not suppose that, publicly outraged in the face of a whole theatre, in the presence of your friends and those of your son—challenged by a boy who will glory in my forgiveness as if it were a victory—you do not suppose that I can for one moment wish to live. What I most loved after you, Mercedes, was myself, my dignity, and that strength which rendered me superior to other men; that strength was my life. With one word you have crushed it, and I die."

"But the duel will not take place, Edmond, since you forgive?"

"It will take place," said Monte Cristo, in a most solemn tone; "but instead of your son's blood to stain the ground, mine will flow." Mercedes shrieked, and sprang towards Monte Cristo, but, suddenly stopping, "Edmond," said she, "there is a God above us, since you live and since I have seen you again; I trust to him from my heart. While waiting his assistance I trust to your word; you have said that my son should live, have you not?"

"Yes, madame, he shall live," said Monte Cristo, surprised that without more emotion Mercedes had accepted the heroic sacrifice he made for her. Mercedes extended her hand to the count.

"Edmond," said she, and her eyes were wet with tears while looking at him to whom she spoke, "how noble it is of you, how great the action you have just performed, how sublime to have taken pity on a poor woman who appealed to you with every chance against her, Alas, I am grown old with grief more than with years, and cannot now remind my Edmond by a smile, or by a look, of that Mercedes whom he once spent so many hours in contemplating. Ah, believe me, Edmond, as I told you, I too have suffered much; I repeat, it is melancholy to pass one's life without having one joy to recall, without preserving a single hope; but that proves that all is not yet over. No, it is not finished; I feel it by what remains in my heart. Oh, I repeat it, Edmond; what you have just done is beautiful—it is grand; it is sublime."

"Do you say so now, Mercedes?—then what would you say if you knew the extent of the sacrifice I make to you? Suppose that the Supreme Being, after having created the world and fertilized chaos, had paused in the work to spare an angel the tears that might one day flow for mortal sins from her immortal eyes; suppose that when everything was in readiness and the moment had come for God to look upon his work and see that it was good—suppose he had snuffed out the sun and tossed the world back into eternal night—then—even then, Mercedes, you could not imagine what I lose in sacrificing my life at this moment." Mercedes looked at the count in a way which expressed at the same time her astonishment, her admiration, and her gratitude. Monte Cristo pressed his forehead on his burning hands, as if his brain could no longer bear alone the weight of its thoughts. "Edmond," said Mercedes, "I have but one word more to say to you." The count smiled bitterly. "Edmond," continued she, "you will see that if my face is pale, if my eyes are dull, if my beauty is gone; if Mercedes, in short, no longer resembles her former self in her features, you will see that her heart is still the same. Adieu, then, Edmond; I have nothing more to ask of heaven—I have seen you again, and have found you as noble and as great as formerly you were. Adieu, Edmond, adieu, and thank you."

But the count did not answer. Mercedes opened the door of the study and had disappeared before he had recovered from the painful and profound revery into which his thwarted vengeance had plunged him. The clock of the Invalides struck one when the carriage which conveyed Madame de Morcerf away rolled on the pavement of the Champs-Elysees, and made Monte Cristo raise his head. "What a fool I was," said he, "not to tear my heart out on the day when I resolved to avenge myself!"

CHAPTER 90.
THE MEETING.

After Mercedes had left Monte Cristo, he fell into profound gloom. Around him and within him the flight of thought seemed to have stopped; his energetic mind slumbered, as the body does after extreme fatigue. "What?" said he to himself, while the lamp and the wax lights were nearly burnt out, and the servants were waiting impatiently in the anteroom; "what? this edifice which I have been so long preparing, which I have reared with so much care and toil, is to be crushed by a single touch, a word, a breath! Yes, this self, of whom I thought so much, of whom I was so proud, who had appeared so worthless in the dungeons of the Chateau d'If, and whom I had succeeded in making so great, will be but a lump of clay to-morrow. Alas, it is not the death of the body I regret; for is not the destruction of the vital principle, the repose to which everything is tending, to which every unhappy being aspires,—is not this the repose of matter after which I so long sighed, and which I was seeking to attain by the painful process of starvation when Faria appeared in my dungeon? What is death for me? One step farther into rest,—two, perhaps, into silence.

"No, it is not existence, then, that I regret, but the ruin of projects so slowly carried out, so laboriously framed.

285

Providence is now opposed to them, when I most thought it would be propitious. It is not God's will that they should be accomplished. This burden, almost as heavy as a world, which I had raised, and I had thought to bear to the end, was too great for my strength, and I was compelled to lay it down in the middle of my career. Oh, shall I then, again become a fatalist, whom fourteen years of despair and ten of hope had rendered a believer in providence? And all this—all this, because my heart, which I thought dead, was only sleeping; because it has awakened and has begun to beat again, because I have yielded to the pain of the emotion excited in my breast by a woman's voice. Yet," continued the count, becoming each moment more absorbed in the anticipation of the dreadful sacrifice for the morrow, which Mercedes had accepted, "yet, it is impossible that so noble-minded a woman should thus through selfishness consent to my death when I am in the prime of life and strength; it is impossible that she can carry to such a point maternal love, or rather delirium. There are virtues which become crimes by exaggeration. No, she must have conceived some pathetic scene; she will come and throw herself between us; and what would be sublime here will there appear ridiculous." The blush of pride mounted to the count's forehead as this thought passed through his mind. "Ridiculous?" repeated he; "and the ridicule will fall on me. I ridiculous? No, I would rather die."

By thus exaggerating to his own mind the anticipated ill-fortune of the next day, to which he had condemned himself by promising Mercedes to spare her son, the count at last exclaimed, "Folly, folly, folly!—to carry generosity so far as to put myself up as a mark for that young man to aim at. He will never believe that my death was suicide; and yet it is important for the honor of my memory,—and this surely is not vanity, but a justifiable pride,—it is important the world should know that I have consented, by my free will, to stop my arm, already raised to strike, and that with the arm which has been so powerful against others I have struck myself. It must be; it shall be."

Seizing a pen, he drew a paper from a secret drawer in his desk, and wrote at the bottom of the document (which was no other than his will, made since his arrival in Paris) a sort of codicil, clearly explaining the nature of his death. "I do this, O my God," said he, with his eyes raised to heaven, "as much for thy honor as for mine. I have during ten years considered myself the agent of thy vengeance, and other wretches, like Morcerf, Danglars, Villefort, even Morcerf himself, must not imagine that chance has freed them from their enemy. Let them know, on the contrary, that their punishment, which had been decreed by providence, is only delayed by my present determination, and although they escape it in this world, it awaits them in another, and that they are only exchanging time for eternity."

While he was thus agitated by gloomy uncertainties,—wretched waking dreams of grief,—the first rays of morning pierced his windows, and shone upon the pale blue paper on which he had just inscribed his justification of providence. It was just five o'clock in the morning when a slight noise like a stifled sigh reached his ear. He turned his head, looked around him, and saw no one; but the sound was repeated distinctly enough to convince him of its reality.

He arose, and quietly opening the door of the drawing-room, saw Haidee, who had fallen on a chair, with her arms hanging down and her beautiful head thrown back. She had been standing at the door, to prevent his going out without seeing her, until sleep, which the young cannot resist, had overpowered her frame, wearied as she was with watching. The noise of the door did not awaken her, and Monte Cristo gazed at her with affectionate regret. "She remembered that she had a son," said he; "and I forgot I had a daughter." Then, shaking his head sorrowfully, "Poor Haidee," said he; "she wished to see me, to speak to me; she has feared or guessed something. Oh, I cannot go without taking leave of her; I cannot die without confiding her to some one." He quietly regained his seat, and wrote under the other lines:—

"I bequeath to Maximilian Morrel, captain of Spahis,—and son of my former patron, Pierre Morrel, shipowner at Marseilles,—the sum of twenty millions, a part of which may be offered to his sister Julia and brother-in-law Emmanuel, if he does not fear this increase of fortune may mar their happiness. These twenty millions are concealed in my grotto at Monte Cristo, of which Bertuccio knows the secret. If his heart is free, and he will marry Haidee, the daughter of Ali Pasha of Yanina, whom I have brought up with the love of a father, and who has shown the love and tenderness of a daughter for me, he will thus accomplish my last wish. This will has already constituted Haidee heiress of the rest of my fortune, consisting of lands, funds in England, Austria, and Holland, furniture in my different palaces and houses, and which without the twenty millions and the legacies to my servants, may still amount to sixty millions."

He was finishing the last line when a cry behind him made him start, and the pen fell from his hand. "Haidee," said he, "did you read it?"

"Oh, my lord," said she, "why are you writing thus at such an hour? Why are you bequeathing all your fortune to me? Are you going to leave me?"

"I am going on a journey, dear child," said Monte Cristo, with an expression of infinite tenderness and melancholy; "and if any misfortune should happen to me."

The count stopped. "Well?" asked the young girl, with an authoritative tone the count had never observed before, and which startled him. "Well, if any misfortune happen to me," replied Monte Cristo, "I wish my daughter to be happy." Haidee smiled sorrowfully, and shook her head. "Do you think of dying, my lord?" said she.

"The wise man, my child, has said, 'It is good to think of death.'"

"Well, if you die," said she, "bequeath your fortune to others, for if you die I shall require nothing;" and, taking the paper, she tore it in four pieces, and threw it into the middle of the room. Then, the effort having exhausted her strength, she fell not asleep this time, but fainting on the floor. The count leaned over her and raised her in his arms; and seeing that sweet pale face, those lovely eyes closed, that beautiful form motionless and to all appearance lifeless, the idea occurred to him for the first time, that perhaps she loved him otherwise than as a daughter loves a father.

"Alas," murmured he, with intense suffering, "I might, then, have been happy yet." Then he carried Haidee to her room, resigned her to the care of her attendants, and returning to his study, which he shut quickly this time, he again copied the destroyed will. As he was finishing, the sound of a cabriolet entering the yard was heard. Monte Cristo approached the window, and saw Maximilian and Emmanuel alight. "Good," said he; "it was time,"—and he sealed his will with three seals. A moment afterwards he heard a noise in the drawing-room, and went to open the door himself. Morrel was there; he had come twenty minutes before the time appointed. "I am perhaps come too soon, count," said he, "but I frankly acknowledge that I have not closed my eyes all night, nor has any one in my house. I need to see you strong in your courageous assurance, to recover myself." Monte Cristo could not resist this proof of affection; he not only extended his hand to the young man, but flew to him with open arms. "Morrel," said he, "it is a happy day for me, to feel that I am beloved by such a man as you. Good-morning, Emmanuel; you will come with me then, Maximilian?"

"Did you doubt it?" said the young captain.

"But if I were wrong"—

"I watched you during the whole scene of that challenge yesterday; I have been thinking of your firmness all night, and I said to myself that justice must be on your side, or man's countenance is no longer to be relied on."

"But, Morrel, Albert is your friend?"

"Simply an acquaintance, sir."

"You met on the same day you first saw me?"

"Yes, that is true; but I should not have recollected it if you had not reminded me."

"Thank you, Morrel." Then ringing the bell once, "Look." said he to Ali, who came immediately, "take that to my solicitor. It is my will, Morrel. When I am dead, you will go and examine it."

"What?" said Morrel, "you dead?"

"Yes; must I not be prepared for everything, dear friend? But what did you do yesterday after you left me?"

"I went to Tortoni's, where, as I expected, I found Beauchamp and Chateau-Renaud. I own I was seeking them."

"Why, when all was arranged?"

"Listen, count; the affair is serious and unavoidable."

"Did you doubt it!"

"No; the offence was public, and every one is already talking of it."

"Well?"

"Well, I hoped to get an exchange of arms,—to substitute the sword for the pistol; the pistol is blind."

"Have you succeeded?" asked Monte Cristo quickly, with an imperceptible gleam of hope.

"No; for your skill with the sword is so well known."

"Ah?—who has betrayed me?"

"The skilful swordsman whom you have conquered."

"And you failed?"

"They positively refused."

"Morrel," said the count, "have you ever seen me fire a pistol?"

"Never."

"Well, we have time; look." Monte Cristo took the pistols he held in his hand when Mercedes entered, and fixing an ace of clubs against the iron plate, with four shots he successively shot off the four sides of the club. At each shot Morrel turned pale. He examined the bullets with which Monte Cristo performed this dexterous feat, and saw that they were no larger than buckshot. "It is astonishing," said he. "Look, Emmanuel." Then turning towards Monte Cristo, "Count," said he, "in the name of all that is dear to you, I entreat you not to kill Albert!—the unhappy youth has a mother."

"You are right," said Monte Cristo; "and I have none." These words were uttered in a tone which made Morrel shudder. "You are the offended party, count."

"Doubtless; what does that imply?"

"That you will fire first."

"I fire first?"

"Oh, I obtained, or rather claimed that; we had conceded enough for them to yield us that."

"And at what distance?"

"Twenty paces." A smile of terrible import passed over the count's lips. "Morrel," said he, "do not forget what you have just seen."

"The only chance for Albert's safety, then, will arise from your emotion."

"I suffer from emotion?" said Monte Cristo.

"Or from your generosity, my friend; to so good a marksman as you are, I may say what would appear absurd to another."

"What is that?"

"Break his arm—wound him—but do not kill him."

"I will tell you, Morrel," said the count, "that I do not need entreating to spare the life of M. de Morcerf; he shall be so well spared, that he will return quietly with his two friends, while I"—

"And you?"

"That will be another thing; I shall be brought home."

"No, no," cried Maximilian, quite unable to restrain his feelings.

"As I told you, my dear Morrel, M. de Morcerf will kill me." Morrel looked at him in utter amazement. "But what has happened, then, since last evening, count?"

"The same thing that happened to Brutus the night before the battle of Philippi; I have seen a ghost."

"And that ghost"—

"Told me, Morrel, that I had lived long enough." Maximilian and Emmanuel looked at each other. Monte Cristo drew out his watch. "Let us go," said he; "it is five minutes past seven, and the appointment was for eight o'clock." A carriage was in readiness at the door. Monte Cristo stepped into it with his two friends. He had stopped a moment in the passage to listen at a door, and Maximilian and Emmanuel, who had considerately passed forward a few steps, thought they heard him answer by a sigh to a sob from within. As the clock struck eight they drove up to the place of meeting. "We are first," said Morrel, looking out of the window. "Excuse me, sir," said Baptistin, who had followed his master with indescribable terror, "but I think I see a carriage down there under the trees."

Monte Cristo sprang lightly from the carriage, and offered his hand to assist Emmanuel and Maximilian. The latter retained the count's hand between his. "I like," said he, "to feel a hand like this, when its owner relies on the goodness of his cause."

"It seems to me," said Emmanuel, "that I see two young men down there, who are evidently, waiting." Monte Cristo drew Morrel a step or two behind his brother-in-law. "Maximilian," said he, "are your affections disengaged?" Morrel looked at Monte Cristo with astonishment. "I do not seek your confidence, my dear friend. I only ask you a simple question; answer it;—that is all I require."

"I love a young girl, count."

"Do you love her much?"

"More than my life."

"Another hope defeated!" said the count. Then, with a sigh, "Poor Haidee!" murmured he.

"To tell the truth, count, if I knew less of you, I should think that you were less brave than you are."

"Because I sigh when thinking of some one I am leaving? Come, Morrel, it is not like a soldier to be so bad a judge of courage. Do I regret life? What is it to me, who have passed twenty years between life and death? Moreover, do not alarm yourself, Morrel; this weakness, if it is such, is betrayed to you alone. I know the world is a drawing-room, from which we must retire politely and honestly; that is, with a bow, and our debts of honor paid."

"That is to the purpose. Have you brought your arms?"

"I?—what for? I hope these gentlemen have theirs."

"I will inquire," said Morrel.

"Do; but make no treaty—you understand me?"

"You need not fear." Morrel advanced towards Beauchamp and Chateau-Renaud, who, seeing his intention, came to meet him. The three young men bowed to each other courteously, if not affably.

"Excuse me, gentlemen," said Morrel, "but I do not see M. de Morcerf."

"He sent us word this morning," replied Chateau-Renaud, "that he would meet us on the ground."

"Ah," said Morrel. Beauchamp pulled out his watch. "It is only five minutes past eight," said he to Morrel; "there is not much time lost yet."

"Oh, I made no allusion of that kind," replied Morrel.

"There is a carriage coming," said Chateau-Renaud. It advanced rapidly along one of the avenues leading towards the open space where they were assembled. "You are doubtless provided with pistols, gentlemen? M. de Monte Cristo yields his right of using his."

"We had anticipated this kindness on the part of the count," said Beauchamp, "and I have brought some weapons which I bought eight or ten days since, thinking to want them on a similar occasion. They are quite new, and have not yet been used. Will you examine them."

"Oh, M. Beauchamp, if you assure me that M. de Morcerf does not know these pistols, you may readily believe that your word will be quite sufficient."

"Gentlemen," said Chateau-Renaud, "it is not Morcerf coming in that carriage;—faith, it is Franz and Debray!" The two young men he announced were indeed approaching. "What chance brings you here, gentlemen?" said Chateau-Renaud, shaking hands with each of them. "Because," said Debray, "Albert sent this morning to request us to come." Beauchamp and Chateau-Renaud exchanged looks of astonishment. "I think I understand his reason," said Morrel.

"What is it?"

"Yesterday afternoon I received a letter from M. de Morcerf, begging me to attend the opera."

"And I," said Debray.

"And I also," said Franz.

"And we, too," added Beauchamp and Chateau-Renaud.

"Having wished you all to witness the challenge, he now wishes you to be present at the combat."

"Exactly so," said the young men; "you have probably guessed right."

"But, after all these arrangements, he does not come himself," said Chateau-Renaud. "Albert is ten minutes after time."

"There he comes," said Beauchamp, "on horseback, at full gallop, followed by a servant."

"How imprudent," said Chateau-Renaud, "to come on horseback to fight a duel with pistols, after all the instructions I had given him."

"And besides," said Beauchamp, "with a collar above his cravat, an open coat and white waistcoat! Why has he not painted a spot upon his heart?—it would have been more simple." Meanwhile Albert had arrived within ten paces of the group formed by the five young men. He jumped from his horse, threw the bridle on his servant's arms, and joined them. He was pale, and his eyes were red and swollen; it was evident that he had not slept. A shade of melancholy gravity overspread his countenance, which was not natural to him. "I thank you, gentlemen," said he, "for having complied with my request; I feel extremely grateful for this mark of friendship." Morrel had stepped back as Morcerf approached, and remained at a short distance. "And to you also, M. Morrel, my thanks are due. Come, there cannot be too many."

"Sir," said Maximilian, "you are not perhaps aware that I am M. de Monte Cristo's friend?"

"I was not sure, but I thought it might be so. So much the better; the more honorable men there are here the better I shall be satisfied."

"M. Morrel," said Chateau-Renaud, "will you apprise the Count of Monte Cristo that M. de Morcerf is arrived, and we are at his disposal?" Morrel was preparing to fulfil his commission. Beauchamp had meanwhile drawn the box of pistols from the carriage. "Stop, gentlemen," said Albert; "I have two words to say to the Count of Monte Cristo."

"In private?" asked Morrel.

"No, sir; before all who are here."

Albert's witnesses looked at each other. Franz and Debray exchanged some words in a whisper, and Morrel, rejoiced at this unexpected incident, went to fetch the count, who was walking in a retired path with Emmanuel. "What does he want with me?" said Monte Cristo.

"I do not know, but he wishes to speak to you."

"Ah?" said Monte Cristo, "I trust he is not going to tempt me by some fresh insult!"

"I do not think that such is his intention," said Morrel.

The count advanced, accompanied by Maximilian and Emmanuel. His calm and serene look formed a singular contrast to Albert's grief-stricken face, who approached also, followed by the other four young men. When at three paces distant from each other, Albert and the count stopped.

"Approach, gentlemen," said Albert; "I wish you not to lose one word of what I am about to have the honor of saying to the Count of Monte Cristo, for it must be repeated by you to all who will listen to it, strange as it may appear to you."

"Proceed, sir," said the count.

"Sir," said Albert, at first with a tremulous voice, but which gradually became firmer, "I reproached you with exposing the conduct of M. de Morcerf in Epirus, for guilty as I knew he was, I thought you had no right to punish him; but I have since learned that you had that right. It is not Fernand Mondego's treachery towards Ali Pasha which induces me so readily to excuse you, but the treachery of the fisherman Fernand towards you, and the almost unheard-of miseries which were its consequences; and I say, and proclaim it publicly, that you were justified in revenging yourself on my father, and I, his son, thank you for not using greater severity."

Had a thunderbolt fallen in the midst of the spectators of this unexpected scene, it would not have surprised them more than did Albert's declaration. As for Monte Cristo, his eyes slowly rose towards heaven with an expression of infinite gratitude. He could not understand how Albert's fiery nature, of which he had seen so much among the Roman bandits, had suddenly stooped to this humiliation. He recognized the influence of Mercedes, and saw why her noble heart had not opposed the sacrifice she knew beforehand would be useless. "Now, sir," said Albert, "if you think my apology sufficient, pray give me your hand. Next to the merit of infallibility which you appear to possess, I rank that of candidly acknowledging a fault. But this confession concerns me only. I acted well as a man, but you have acted better than man. An angel alone could have saved one of us from death—that angel came from heaven, if not to make us friends (which, alas, fatality renders impossible), at least to make us esteem each other."

Monte Cristo, with moistened eye, heaving breast, and lips half open, extended to Albert a hand which the latter pressed with a sentiment resembling respectful fear. "Gentlemen," said he, "M. de Monte Cristo receives my apology. I had acted hastily towards him. Hasty actions are generally bad ones. Now my fault is repaired. I hope the world will not call me cowardly for acting as my conscience dictated. But if any one should entertain a false opinion of me," added he, drawing himself up as if he would challenge both friends and enemies, "I shall endeavor to correct his mistake."

"What happened during the night?" asked Beauchamp of Chateau-Renaud; "we appear to make a very sorry figure here."

"In truth, what Albert has just done is either very despicable or very noble," replied the baron.

"What can it mean?" said Debray to Franz. "The Count of Monte Cristo acts dishonorably to M. de Morcerf, and is justified by his son! Had I ten Yaninas in my family, I should only consider myself the more bound to fight ten times." As for Monte Cristo, his head was bent down, his arms were powerless. Bowing under the weight of twenty-four years' reminiscences, he thought not of Albert, of Beauchamp, of Chateau-Renaud, or of any of that group; but he thought of that courageous woman who had come to plead for her son's life, to whom he had offered his, and who had now saved it by the revelation of a dreadful family secret, capable of destroying forever in that young man's heart every feeling of filial piety.

"Providence still," murmured he; "now only am I fully convinced of being the emissary of God!"

CHAPTER 91.
MOTHER AND SON.

The Count of Monte Cristo bowed to the five young men with a melancholy and dignified smile, and got into his carriage with Maximilian and Emmanuel. Albert, Beauchamp, and Chateau-Renaud remained alone. Albert looked at his two friends, not timidly, but in a way that appeared to ask their opinion of what he had just done.

"Indeed, my dear friend," said Beauchamp first, who had either the most feeling or the least dissimulation, "allow me to congratulate you; this is a very unhoped-for conclusion of a very disagreeable affair."

Albert remained silent and wrapped in thought. Chateau-Renaud contented himself with tapping his boot with his flexible cane. "Are we not going?" said he, after this embarrassing silence. "When you please," replied Beauchamp; "allow me only to compliment M. de Morcerf, who has given proof to-day of rare chivalric generosity."

"Oh, yes," said Chateau-Renaud.

"It is magnificent," continued Beauchamp, "to be able to exercise so much self-control!"

"Assuredly; as for me, I should have been incapable of it," said Chateau-Renaud, with most significant coolness.

"Gentlemen," interrupted Albert, "I think you did not understand that something very serious had passed between M. de Monte Cristo and myself."

"Possibly, possibly," said Beauchamp immediately; "but every simpleton would not be able to understand your heroism, and sooner or later you will find yourself compelled to explain it to them more energetically than would be convenient to your bodily health and the duration of your life. May I give you a friendly counsel? Set out for Naples, the Hague, or St. Petersburg—calm countries, where the point of honor is better understood than among our hot-headed Parisians. Seek quietude and oblivion, so that you may return peaceably to France after a few years. Am I not right, M. de Chateau-Renaud?"

"That is quite my opinion," said the gentleman; "nothing induces serious duels so much as a duel forsworn."

"Thank you, gentlemen," replied Albert, with a smile of indifference; "I shall follow your advice—not because you give it, but because I had before intended to quit France. I thank you equally for the service you have rendered me in being my seconds. It is deeply engraved on my heart, and, after what you have just said, I remember that only." Chateau-Renaud and Beauchamp looked at each other; the impression was the same on both of them, and the tone in which Morcerf had just expressed his thanks was so determined that the position would have become embarrassing for all if the conversation had continued.

"Good-by, Albert," said Beauchamp suddenly, carelessly extending his hand to the young man. The latter did not appear to arouse from his lethargy; in fact, he did not notice the offered hand. "Good-by," said Chateau-Renaud in his turn, keeping his little cane in his left hand, and saluting with his right. Albert's lips scarcely whispered "Good-by," but his look was more explicit; it expressed a whole poem of restrained anger, proud disdain, and generous indignation. He preserved his melancholy and motionless position for some time after his two friends had regained their carriage; then suddenly unfastening his horse from the little tree to which his servant had tied it, he mounted and galloped off in the direction of Paris.

In a quarter of an hour he was entering the house in the Rue du Helder. As he alighted, he thought he saw his father's pale face behind the curtain of the count's bedroom. Albert turned away his head with a sigh, and went to his own apartments. He cast one lingering look on all the luxuries which had rendered life so easy and so happy since his infancy; he looked at the pictures, whose faces seemed to smile, and the landscapes, which appeared painted in brighter colors. Then he took away his mother's portrait, with its oaken frame, leaving the gilt frame from which he took it black and empty. Then he arranged all his beautiful

Turkish arms, his fine English guns, his Japanese china, his cups mounted in silver, his artistic bronzes by Feucheres and Barye; examined the cupboards, and placed the key in each; threw into a drawer of his secretary, which he left open, all the pocket-money he had about him, and with it the thousand fancy jewels from his vases and his jewel-boxes; then he made an exact inventory of everything, and placed it in the most conspicuous part of the table, after putting aside the books and papers which had collected there.

At the beginning of this work, his servant, notwithstanding orders to the contrary, came to his room. "What do you want?" asked he, with a more sorrowful than angry tone. "Pardon me, sir," replied the valet; "you had forbidden me to disturb you, but the Count of Morcerf has called me."

"Well!" said Albert.

"I did not like to go to him without first seeing you."

"Why?"

"Because the count is doubtless aware that I accompanied you to the meeting this morning."

"It is probable," said Albert.

"And since he has sent for me, it is doubtless to question me on what happened there. What must I answer?"

"The truth."

"Then I shall say the duel did not take place?"

"You will say I apologized to the Count of Monte Cristo. Go."

The valet bowed and retired, and Albert returned to his inventory. As he was finishing this work, the sound of horses prancing in the yard, and the wheels of a carriage shaking his window, attracted his attention. He approached the window, and saw his father get into it, and drive away. The door was scarcely closed when Albert bent his steps to his mother's room; and, no one being there to announce him, he advanced to her bed-chamber, and distressed by what he saw and guessed, stopped for one moment at the door. As if the same idea had animated these two beings, Mercedes was doing the same in her apartments that he had just done in his. Everything was in order,—laces, dresses, jewels, linen, money, all were arranged in the drawers, and the countess was carefully collecting the keys. Albert saw all these preparations and understood them, and exclaiming, "My mother!" he threw his arms around her neck.

The artist who could have depicted the expression of these two countenances would certainly have made of them a beautiful picture. All these proofs of an energetic resolution, which Albert did not fear on his own account, alarmed him for his mother. "What are you doing?" asked he.

"What were you doing?" replied she.

"Oh, my mother!" exclaimed Albert, so overcome he could scarcely speak; "it is not the same with you and me—you cannot have made the same resolution I have, for I have come to warn you that I bid adieu to your house, and—and to you."

"I also," replied Mercedes, "am going, and I acknowledge I had depended on your accompanying me; have I deceived myself?"

"Mother," said Albert with firmness. "I cannot make you share the fate I have planned for myself. I must live henceforth without rank and fortune, and to begin this hard apprenticeship I must borrow from a friend the loaf I shall eat until I have earned one. So, my dear mother, I am going at once to ask Franz to lend me the small sum I shall require to supply my present wants."

"You, my poor child, suffer poverty and hunger? Oh, do not say so; it will break my resolutions."

"But not mine, mother," replied Albert. "I am young and strong; I believe I am courageous, and since yesterday I have learned the power of will. Alas, my dear mother, some have suffered so much, and yet live, and have raised a new fortune on the ruin of all the promises of happiness which heaven had made them—on the fragments of all the hope which God had given them! I have seen that, mother; I know that from the gulf in which their enemies have plunged them they have risen with so much vigor and glory that in their turn they have ruled their former conquerors, and have punished them. No, mother; from this moment I have done with the past, and accept nothing from it—not even a name, because you can understand that your son cannot bear the name of a man who ought to blush for it before another."

"Albert, my child," said Mercedes, "if I had a stronger heart, that is the counsel I would have given you; your conscience has spoken when my voice became too weak; listen to its dictates. You had friends, Albert; break off their acquaintance. But do not despair; you have life before you, my dear Albert, for you are yet scarcely twenty-two years old; and as a pure heart like yours wants a spotless name, take my father's—it was Herrera. I am sure, my dear Albert, whatever may be your career, you will soon render that name illustrious. Then, my son, return to the world still more brilliant because of your former sorrows; and if I am wrong, still let me cherish these hopes, for I have no future to look forward to. For me the grave opens when I pass the threshold of this house."

"I will fulfil all your wishes, my dear mother," said the young man. "Yes, I share your hopes; the anger of heaven will not pursue us, since you are pure and I am innocent. But, since our resolution is formed, let us act promptly. M. de Morcerf went out about half an hour ago; the opportunity is favorable to avoid an explanation."

"I am ready, my son," said Mercedes. Albert ran to fetch a carriage. He recollected that there was a small furnished house to let in the Rue de Saints Peres, where his mother would find a humble but decent lodging, and thither he intended conducting the countess. As the carriage stopped at the door, and Albert was alighting, a man approached and gave him a letter. Albert recognized the bearer. "From the count," said Bertuccio. Albert took the letter, opened, and read it, then looked round for Bertuccio, but he was gone. He returned to Mercedes with tears in his eyes and heaving breast, and without uttering a word he gave her the letter. Mercedes read:—

Albert,—While showing you that I have discovered your plans, I hope also to convince you of my delicacy. You are free, you leave the count's house, and you take your mother to your home; but reflect, Albert, you owe her more than your poor noble heart can pay her. Keep the struggle for yourself, bear all the suffering, but spare her the trial of poverty which must accompany your first efforts; for she deserves not even the shadow of the misfortune which has this day fallen on her, and providence is not willing that the innocent should suffer for the guilty. I know you are going to leave the Rue du Helder without taking anything with you. Do not seek to know how I discovered it; I know it—that is sufficient.

Now, listen, Albert. Twenty-four years ago I returned, proud and joyful, to my country. I had a betrothed, Albert, a lovely girl whom I adored, and I was bringing to my betrothed a hundred and fifty louis, painfully amassed by ceaseless toil. This money was for her; I destined it for her, and, knowing the treachery of the sea I buried our treasure in the little garden of the house my father lived in at Marseilles, on the Allees de Meillan. Your mother, Albert, knows that poor house well. A short time since I passed through Marseilles, and went to see the old place, which revived so many painful recollections; and in the evening I took a spade and dug in the corner of the garden where I had concealed my treasure. The iron box was there—no one had touched it—under a beautiful fig-tree my father had planted the day I was born, which overshadowed the spot. Well, Albert, this money, which was formerly designed to promote the comfort and tranquillity of the woman I adored, may now, through strange and painful circumstances, be devoted to the same purpose. Oh, feel for me, who could offer millions to that poor woman, but who return her only the piece of black bread forgotten under my poor roof since the day I was torn from her I loved. You are a generous man, Albert, but perhaps you may be blinded by pride or resentment; if you refuse me, if you ask another for what I have a right to offer you, I will say it is ungenerous of you to refuse the life of your mother at the hands of a man whose father was allowed by your father to die in all the horrors of poverty and despair.

Albert stood pale and motionless to hear what his mother would decide after she had finished reading this letter. Mercedes turned her eyes with an ineffable look towards heaven. "I accept it," said she; "he has a right to pay the dowry, which I shall take with me to some convent!" Putting the letter in her bosom, she took her son's arm, and with a firmer step than she even herself expected she went down-stairs.

CHAPTER 92.
THE SUICIDE.

Meanwhile Monte Cristo had also returned to town with Emmanuel and Maximilian. Their return was cheerful. Emmanuel did not conceal his joy at the peaceful termination of the affair, and was loud in his expressions of delight. Morrel, in a corner of the carriage, allowed his brother-in-law's gayety to expend itself in words, while he felt equal inward joy, which, however, betrayed itself only in his countenance. At the Barriere du Trone they met Bertuccio, who was waiting there, motionless as a sentinel at his post. Monte Cristo put his head out of the window, exchanged a few words with him in a low tone, and the steward disappeared. "Count," said Emmanuel, when they were at the end of the Place Royale, "put me down at my door, that my wife may not have a single moment of needless anxiety on my account or yours."

"If it were not ridiculous to make a display of our triumph, I would invite the count to our house; besides that, he doubtless has some trembling heart to comfort. So we will take leave of our friend, and let him hasten home."

"Stop a moment," said Monte Cristo; "do not let me lose both my companions. Return, Emmanuel, to your charming wife, and present my best compliments to her; and do you, Morrel, accompany me to the Champs Elysees."

"Willingly," said Maximilian; "particularly as I have business in that quarter."

"Shall we wait breakfast for you?" asked Emmanuel.

"No," replied the young man. The door was closed, and the carriage proceeded. "See what good fortune I brought you!" said Morrel, when he was alone with the count. "Have you not thought so?"

"Yes," said Monte Cristo; "for that reason I wished to keep you near me."

"It is miraculous!" continued Morrel, answering his own thoughts.

"What?" said Monte Cristo.

"What has just happened."

"Yes," said the Count, "you are right—it is miraculous."

"For Albert is brave," resumed Morrel.

"Very brave," said Monte Cristo; "I have seen him sleep with a sword suspended over his head."

"And I know he has fought two duels," said Morrel. "How can you reconcile that with his conduct this morning?"

"All owing to your influence," replied Monte Cristo, smiling.

"It is well for Albert he is not in the army," said Morrel.

"Why?"

"An apology on the ground!" said the young captain, shaking his head.

"Come," said the count mildly, "do not entertain the prejudices of ordinary men, Morrel! Acknowledge, that if Albert is brave, he cannot be a coward; he must then have had some reason for acting as he did this morning, and confess that his conduct is more heroic than otherwise."

"Doubtless, doubtless," said Morrel; "but I shall say, like the Spaniard, 'He has not been so brave to-day as he was yesterday.'"

"You will breakfast with me, will you not, Morrel?" said the count, to turn the conversation.

"No; I must leave you at ten o'clock."

"Your engagement was for breakfast, then?" said the count.

Morrel smiled, and shook his head. "Still you must breakfast somewhere."

"But if I am not hungry?" said the young man.

"Oh," said the count, "I only know two things which destroy the appetite,—grief—and as I am happy to see you very cheerful, it is not that—and love. Now after what you told me this morning of your heart, I may believe"—

"Well, count," replied Morrel gayly, "I will not dispute it."

"But you will not make me your confidant, Maximilian?" said the count, in a tone which showed how gladly he would have been admitted to the secret.

"I showed you this morning that I had a heart, did I not, count?" Monte Cristo only answered by extending his hand to the young man. "Well," continued the latter, "since that heart is no longer with you in the Bois de Vincennes, it is elsewhere, and I must go and find it."

"Go," said the count deliberately; "go, dear friend, but promise me if you meet with any obstacle to remember that I have some power in this world, that I am happy to use that power in the behalf of those I love, and that I love you, Morrel."

"I will remember it," said the young man, "as selfish children recollect their parents when they want their aid. When I need your assistance, and the moment arrives, I will come to you, count."

"Well, I rely upon your promise. Good-by, then."

"Good-by, till we meet again." They had arrived in the Champs Elysees. Monte Cristo opened the carriage-door, Morrel sprang out on the pavement, Bertuccio was waiting on the steps. Morrel disappeared down the Avenue de Marigny, and Monte Cristo hastened to join Bertuccio.

"Well?" asked he.

"She is going to leave her house," said the steward.

"And her son?"

"Florentin, his valet, thinks he is going to do the same."

"Come this way." Monte Cristo took Bertuccio into his study, wrote the letter we have seen, and gave it to the steward. "Go," said he quickly. "But first, let Haidee be informed that I have returned."

"Here I am," said the young girl, who at the sound of the carriage had run down-stairs and whose face was radiant with joy at seeing the count return safely. Bertuccio left. Every transport of a daughter finding a father, all the delight of a mistress seeing an adored lover, were felt by Haidee during the first moments of this meeting, which she had so eagerly expected. Doubtless, although less evident, Monte Cristo's joy was not less intense. Joy to hearts which have suffered long is like the dew on the ground after a long drought; both the heart and the ground absorb that beneficent moisture falling on them, and nothing is outwardly apparent.

Monte Cristo was beginning to think, what he had not for a long time dared to believe, that there were two Mercedes in the world, and he might yet be happy. His eye, elate with happiness, was reading eagerly the tearful gaze of Haidee, when suddenly the door opened. The count knit his brow. "M. de Morcerf!" said Baptistin, as if that name sufficed for his excuse. In fact, the count's face brightened.

"Which," asked he, "the viscount or the count?"

"The count."

"Oh," exclaimed Haidee, "is it not yet over?"

"I know not if it is finished, my beloved child," said Monte Cristo, taking the young girl's hands; "but I do know you have nothing more to fear."

"But it is the wretched"——

"That man cannot injure me, Haidee," said Monte Cristo; "it was his son alone that there was cause to fear."

"And what I have suffered," said the young girl, "you shall never know, my lord." Monte Cristo smiled. "By my father's tomb," said he, extending his hand over the head of the young girl, "I swear to you, Haidee, that if any misfortune happens, it will not be to me."

"I believe you, my lord, as implicitly as if God had spoken to me," said the young girl, presenting her forehead to him. Monte Cristo pressed on that pure beautiful forehead a kiss which made two hearts throb at once, the one violently, the other heavily. "Oh," murmured the count, "shall I then be permitted to love again? Ask M. de Morcerf into the drawing-room," said he to Baptistin, while he led the beautiful Greek girl to a private staircase.

We must explain this visit, which although expected by Monte Cristo, is unexpected to our readers. While Mercedes, as we have said, was making a similar inventory of her property to Albert's, while she was arranging her jewels, shutting her drawers, collecting her keys, to leave everything in perfect order, she did not perceive a pale and sinister face at a glass door which threw light into the passage, from which everything could be both seen and heard. He who was thus looking, without being heard or seen, probably heard and saw all that passed in Madame de Morcerf's apartments. From that glass door the pale-faced man went to the count's bedroom and raised with a constricted hand the curtain of a window overlooking the court-yard. He remained there ten minutes, motionless and dumb, listening to the beating of his own heart. For him those ten minutes were very long. It was then Albert, returning from his meeting with the count, perceived his father watching for his arrival behind a curtain, and turned aside. The count's eye expanded; he knew Albert had insulted the count dreadfully, and that in every country in the world such an insult would lead to a deadly duel. Albert returned safely—then the count was revenged.

An indescribable ray of joy illumined that wretched countenance like the last ray of the sun before it disappears behind the clouds which bear the aspect, not of a downy couch, but of a tomb. But as we have said, he waited in vain for his son to come to his apartment with the account of his triumph. He easily understood why his son did not come to see him before he went to avenge his father's honor; but when that was done, why did not his son come and throw himself into his arms?

It was then, when the count could not see Albert, that he sent for his servant, who he knew was authorized not to conceal anything from him. Ten minutes afterwards, General Morcerf was seen on the steps in a black coat with a military collar, black pantaloons, and black gloves. He had apparently given previous orders, for as he reached the bottom step his carriage came from the coach-house ready for him. The valet threw into the carriage his military cloak, in which two swords were wrapped, and, shutting the door, he took his seat by the side of the coachman. The coachman stooped down for his orders.

"To the Champs Elysees," said the general; "the Count of Monte Cristo's. Hurry!" The horses bounded beneath the whip; and in five minutes they stopped before the count's door. M. de Morcerf opened the door himself, and as the carriage rolled away he passed up the walk, rang, and entered the open door with his servant.

A moment afterwards, Baptistin announced the Count of Morcerf to Monte Cristo, and the latter, leading Haidee aside, ordered that Morcerf be asked into the drawing-room. The general was pacing the room the third time when, in turning, he perceived Monte Cristo at the door. "Ah, it is M. de Morcerf," said Monte Cristo quietly; "I thought I had not heard aright."

"Yes, it is I," said the count, whom a frightful contraction of the lips prevented from articulating freely.

"May I know the cause which procures me the pleasure of seeing M. de Morcerf so early?"

"Had you not a meeting with my son this morning?" asked the general.

"I had," replied the count.

"And I know my son had good reasons to wish to fight with you, and to endeavor to kill you."

"Yes, sir, he had very good ones; but you see that in spite of them he has not killed me, and did not even fight."

"Yet he considered you the cause of his father's dishonor, the cause of the fearful ruin which has fallen on my house."

"It is true, sir," said Monte Cristo with his dreadful calmness; "a secondary cause, but not the principal."

"Doubtless you made, then, some apology or explanation?"

"I explained nothing, and it is he who apologized to me."

"But to what do you attribute this conduct?"

"To the conviction, probably, that there was one more guilty than I."

"And who was that?"

"His father."

"That may be," said the count, turning pale; "but you know the guilty do not like to find themselves convicted."

"I know it, and I expected this result."

"You expected my son would be a coward?" cried the count.

"M. Albert de Morcerf is no coward!" said Monte Cristo.

"A man who holds a sword in his hand, and sees a mortal enemy within reach of that sword, and does not fight, is a coward! Why is he not here that I may tell him so?"

"Sir." replied Monte Cristo coldly, "I did not expect that you had come here to relate to me your little family affairs. Go and tell M. Albert that, and he may know what to answer you."

"Oh, no, no," said the general, smiling faintly, "I did not come for that purpose; you are right. I came to tell you that I also look upon you as my enemy. I came to tell you that I hate you instinctively; that it seems as if I had always known you, and always hated you; and, in short, since the young people of the present day will not fight, it remains for us to do so. Do you think so, sir?"

"Certainly. And when I told you I had foreseen the result, it is the honor of your visit I alluded to."

"So much the better. Are you prepared?"

"Yes, sir."

"You know that we shall fight till one of us is dead," said the general, whose teeth were clinched with rage. "Until one of us dies," repeated Monte Cristo, moving his head slightly up and down.

"Let us start, then; we need no witnesses."

"Very true," said Monte Cristo; "it is unnecessary, we know each other so well!"

"On the contrary," said the count, "we know so little of each other."

"Indeed?" said Monte Cristo, with the same indomitable coolness; "let us see. Are you not the soldier Fernand who deserted on the eve of the battle of Waterloo? Are you not the Lieutenant Fernand who served as guide and spy to the French army in Spain? Are you not the Captain Fernand who betrayed, sold, and murdered his benefactor, Ali? And have not all these Fernands, united, made Lieutenant-General, the Count of Morcerf, peer of France?"

"Oh," cried the general, as if branded with a hot iron, "wretch,—to reproach me with my shame when about, perhaps, to kill me! No, I did not say I was a stranger to you. I know well, demon, that you have penetrated into the darkness of the past, and that you have read, by the light of what torch I know not, every page of my life; but perhaps I may be more honorable in my shame than you under your pompous coverings. No—no, I am aware you know me; but I know you only as an adventurer sewn up in gold and jewellery. You call yourself in Paris the Count of Monte Cristo; in Italy, Sinbad the Sailor; in Malta, I forget what. But it is your real name I want to know, in the midst of your hundred names, that I may pronounce it when we meet to fight, at the moment when I plunge my sword through your heart."

The Count of Monte Cristo turned dreadfully pale; his eye seemed to burn with a devouring fire. He leaped towards a dressing-room near his bedroom, and in less than a moment, tearing off his cravat, his coat and waistcoat, he put on a sailor's jacket and hat, from beneath which rolled his long black hair. He returned thus, formidable and implacable, advancing with his arms crossed on his breast, towards the general, who could not understand why he had disappeared, but who on seeing him again, and feeling his teeth chatter and his legs sink under him, drew back, and only stopped when he found a table to support his clinched hand. "Fernand," cried he, "of my hundred names I need only tell you one, to overwhelm you! But you guess it now, do you not?—or, rather, you remember it? For, notwithstanding all my sorrows and my tortures, I show you to-day a face which the happiness of revenge makes young again—a face you must often have seen in your dreams since your marriage with Mercedes, my betrothed!"

The general, with his head thrown back, hands extended, gaze fixed, looked silently at this dreadful apparition; then seeking the wall to support him, he glided along close to it until he reached the door, through which he went out backwards, uttering this single mournful, lamentable, distressing cry,—"Edmond Dantes!" Then, with sighs which were unlike any human sound, he dragged himself to the door, reeled across the court-yard, and falling into the arms of his valet, he said in a voice scarcely intelligible,—"Home, home." The fresh air and the shame he felt at having exposed himself before his servants, partly recalled his senses, but the ride was short, and as he drew near his house all his wretchedness revived. He stopped at a short distance from the house and alighted.

The door was wide open, a hackney-coach was standing in the middle of the yard—a strange sight before so noble a mansion; the count looked at it with terror, but without daring to inquire its meaning, he rushed towards his apartment. Two persons were coming down the stairs; he had only time to creep into an alcove to avoid them. It was Mercedes leaning on her son's arm and leaving the house. They passed close by the unhappy being, who, concealed behind the damask curtain, almost felt Mercedes dress brush past him, and his son's warm breath, pronouncing these words,—"Courage, mother! Come, this is no longer our home!" The words died away, the steps were lost in the distance. The general drew himself up, clinging to the curtain; he uttered the most dreadful sob which ever escaped from the bosom of a father abandoned at the same time by his wife and son. He soon heard the clatter of the iron step of the hackney-coach, then the coachman's voice, and then the rolling of the heavy vehicle shook the windows.

He darted to his bedroom to see once more all he had loved in the world; but the hackney-coach drove on and the head of neither Mercedes nor her son appeared at the window to take a last look at the house or the deserted father and husband. And at the very moment when the wheels of that coach crossed the gateway a report was heard, and a thick smoke escaped through one of the panes of the window, which was broken by the explosion.

CHAPTER 93.
VALENTINE.

We may easily conceive where Morrel's appointment was. On leaving Monte Cristo he walked slowly towards Villefort's; we say slowly, for Morrel had more than half an hour to spare to go five hundred steps, but he had hastened to take leave of Monte Cristo because he wished to be alone with his thoughts. He knew his time well—the hour when Valentine was giving Noirtier his breakfast, and was sure not to be disturbed in the performance of this pious duty. Noirtier and Valentine had given him leave to go twice a week, and he was now availing himself of that permission. He had arrived; Valentine was expecting him. Uneasy and almost crazed, she seized his hand and led him to her grandfather. This uneasiness, amounting almost to frenzy, arose from the report Morcerf's adventure had made in the world, for the affair at the opera was generally known. No one at Villefort's doubted that a duel would ensue from it. Valentine, with her woman's instinct, guessed that Morrel would be Monte Cristo's second, and from the young man's well-known courage and his great affection for the count, she feared that he would not content himself with the passive part assigned to him. We may easily understand how eagerly the particulars were asked for, given, and received;

and Morrel could read an indescribable joy in the eyes of his beloved, when she knew that the termination of this affair was as happy as it was unexpected.

"Now," said Valentine, motioning to Morrel to sit down near her grandfather, while she took her seat on his footstool,—"now let us talk about our own affairs. You know, Maximilian, grandpapa once thought of leaving this house, and taking an apartment away from M. de Villefort's."

"Yes," said Maximilian, "I recollect the project, of which I highly approved."

"Well," said Valentine, "you may approve again, for grandpapa is again thinking of it."

"Bravo," said Maximilian.

"And do you know," said Valentine, "what reason grandpapa gives for leaving this house." Noirtier looked at Valentine to impose silence, but she did not notice him; her looks, her eyes, her smile, were all for Morrel.

"Oh, whatever may be M. Noirtier's reason," answered Morrel, "I can readily believe it to be a good one."

"An excellent one," said Valentine. "He pretends the air of the Faubourg St. Honore is not good for me."

"Indeed?" said Morrel; "in that M. Noirtier may be right; you have not seemed to be well for the last fortnight."

"Not very," said Valentine. "And grandpapa has become my physician, and I have the greatest confidence in him, because he knows everything."

"Do you then really suffer?" asked Morrel quickly.

"Oh, it must not be called suffering; I feel a general uneasiness, that is all. I have lost my appetite, and my stomach feels as if it were struggling to get accustomed to something." Noirtier did not lose a word of what Valentine said. "And what treatment do you adopt for this singular complaint?"

"A very simple one," said Valentine. "I swallow every morning a spoonful of the mixture prepared for my grandfather. When I say one spoonful, I began by one— now I take four. Grandpapa says it is a panacea." Valentine smiled, but it was evident that she suffered.

Maximilian, in his devotedness, gazed silently at her. She was very beautiful, but her usual pallor had increased; her eyes were more brilliant than ever, and her hands, which were generally white like mother-of-pearl, now more resembled wax, to which time was adding a yellowish hue. From Valentine the young man looked towards Noirtier. The latter watched with strange and deep interest the young girl, absorbed by her affection, and he also, like Morrel, followed those traces of inward suffering which was so little perceptible to a common observer that they escaped the notice of every one but the grandfather and the lover.

"But," said Morrel, "I thought this mixture, of which you now take four spoonfuls, was prepared for M. Noirtier?"

"I know it is very bitter," said Valentine; "so bitter, that all I drink afterwards appears to have the same taste." Noirtier looked inquiringly at his granddaughter. "Yes, grandpapa," said Valentine; "it is so. Just now, before I came down to you, I drank a glass of sugared water; I left half, because it seemed so bitter." Noirtier turned pale, and made a sign that he wished to speak. Valentine rose to fetch the dictionary. Noirtier watched her with evident anguish. In fact, the blood was rushing to the young girl's head already, her cheeks were becoming red. "Oh," cried she, without losing any of her cheerfulness, "this is singular! I can't see! Did the sun shine in my eyes?" And she leaned against the window.

"The sun is not shining," said Morrel, more alarmed by Noirtier's expression than by Valentine's indisposition. He ran towards her. The young girl smiled. "Cheer up," said she to Noirtier. "Do not be alarmed, Maximilian; it is nothing, and has already passed away. But listen! Do I not hear a carriage in the court-yard?" She opened Noirtier's door, ran to a window in the passage, and returned hastily. "Yes," said she, "it is Madame Danglars and her daughter, who have come to call on us. Good-by;—I must run away, for they would send here for me, or, rather, farewell till I see you again. Stay with grandpapa, Maximilian; I promise you not to persuade them to stay."

Morrel watched her as she left the room; he heard her ascend the little staircase which led both to Madame de Villefort's apartments and to hers. As soon as she was gone, Noirtier made a sign to Morrel to take the dictionary. Morrel obeyed; guided by Valentine, he had learned how to understand the old man quickly. Accustomed, however, as he was to the work, he had to repeat most of the letters of the alphabet and to find every word in the dictionary, so that it was ten minutes before the thought of the old man was translated by these words, "Fetch the glass of water and the decanter from Valentine's room."

Morrel rang immediately for the servant who had taken Barrois's situation, and in Noirtier's name gave that order. The servant soon returned. The decanter and the glass were completely empty. Noirtier made a sign that he wished to speak. "Why are the glass and decanter empty?" asked he; "Valentine said she only drank half the glassful." The translation of this new question occupied another five minutes. "I do not know," said the servant, "but the housemaid is in Mademoiselle Valentine's room: perhaps she has emptied them."

"Ask her," said Morrel, translating Noirtier's thought this time by his look. The servant went out, but returned almost immediately. "Mademoiselle Valentine passed through the room to go to Madame de Villefort's," said he; "and in passing, as she was thirsty, she drank what remained in the glass; as for the decanter, Master Edward had emptied that to make a pond for his ducks." Noirtier raised his eyes to heaven, as a gambler does who stakes his all on one stroke. From that moment the old man's eyes were fixed on the door, and did not quit it.

It was indeed Madame Danglars and her daughter whom Valentine had seen; they had been ushered into Madame de Villefort's room, who had said she would receive them there. That is why Valentine passed through her room, which was on a level with Valentine's, and only separated from it by Edward's. The two ladies entered the drawing-room with that sort of official stiffness which preludes a formal communication. Among worldly people manner is contagious. Madame de Villefort received them with equal solemnity. Valentine entered at this moment, and the formalities were resumed. "My dear friend," said the baroness, while the two young people were shaking hands, "I and Eugenie are come to be the first to announce to you the approaching marriage of my daughter with Prince Cavalcanti." Danglars kept up the title of prince. The popular banker found that it answered better than count. "Allow me to present you my sincere congratulations," replied Madame de Villefort. "Prince Cavalcanti appears to be a young man of rare qualities."

"Listen," said the baroness, smiling; "speaking to you as a friend I can say that the prince does not yet appear all he will be. He has about him a little of that foreign manner by which French persons recognize, at first sight, the Italian or German nobleman. Besides, he gives evidence of great kindness of disposition, much keenness of wit, and as to suitability, M. Danglars assures me that his fortune is majestic—that is his word."

"And then," said Eugenie, while turning over the leaves of Madame de Villefort's album, "add that you have taken a great fancy to the young man."

"And," said Madame de Villefort, "I need not ask you if you share that fancy."

"I?" replied Eugenie with her usual candor. "Oh, not the least in the world, madame! My wish was not to confine myself to domestic cares, or the caprices of any man, but to be an artist, and consequently free in heart, in person, and in thought." Eugenie pronounced these words with so firm a tone that the color mounted to Valentine's cheeks. The timid girl could not understand that vigorous nature which appeared to have none of the timidities of woman.

"At any rate," said she, "since I am to be married whether I will or not, I ought to be thankful to providence for having released me from my engagement with M. Albert de Morcerf, or I should this day have been the wife of a dishonored man."

"It is true," said the baroness, with that strange simplicity sometimes met with among fashionable ladies, and of which plebeian intercourse can never entirely deprive them,—"it is very true that had not the Morcerfs hesitated, my daughter would have married Monsieur Albert. The general depended much on it; he even came to force M. Danglars. We have had a narrow escape."

"But," said Valentine, timidly, "does all the father's shame revert upon the son? Monsieur Albert appears to me quite innocent of the treason charged against the general."

"Excuse me," said the implacable young girl, "Monsieur Albert claims and well deserves his share. It appears that after having challenged M. de Monte Cristo at the Opera yesterday, he apologized on the ground to-day."

"Impossible," said Madame de Villefort.

"Ah, my dear friend," said Madame Danglars, with the same simplicity we before noticed, "it is a fact. I heard it from M. Debray, who was present at the explanation." Valentine also knew the truth, but she did not answer. A single word had reminded her that Morrel was expecting her in M. Noirtier's room. Deeply engaged with a sort of inward contemplation, Valentine had ceased for a moment to join in the conversation. She would, indeed, have found it impossible to repeat what had been said the last few minutes, when suddenly Madame Danglars' hand, pressed on her arm, aroused her from her lethargy.

"What is it?" said she, starting at Madame Danglars' touch as she would have done from an electric shock. "It is, my dear Valentine," said the baroness, "that you are, doubtless, suffering."

"I?" said the young girl, passing her hand across her burning forehead.

"Yes, look at yourself in that glass; you have turned pale and then red successively, three or four times in one minute."

"Indeed," cried Eugenie, "you are very pale!"

"Oh, do not be alarmed; I have been so for many days." Artless as she was, the young girl knew that this was an opportunity to leave, and besides, Madame de Villefort came to her assistance. "Retire, Valentine," said she; "you are really suffering, and these ladies will excuse you; drink a glass of pure water, it will restore you." Valentine kissed Eugenie, bowed to Madame Danglars, who had already risen to take her leave, and went out. "That poor child," said Madame de Villefort when Valentine was gone, "she makes me very uneasy, and I should not be astonished if she had some serious illness."

Meanwhile, Valentine, in a sort of excitement which she could not quite understand, had crossed Edward's room without noticing some trick of the child, and through her own had reached the little staircase. She was within three steps of the bottom; she already heard Morrel's voice, when suddenly a cloud passed over her eyes, her stiffened foot missed the step, her hands had no power to hold the baluster, and falling against the wall she lost her balance wholly and toppled to the floor. Morrel bounded to the door, opened it, and found Valentine stretched out at the bottom of the stairs. Quick as a flash, he raised her in his arms and placed her in a chair. Valentine opened her eyes.

"Oh, what a clumsy thing I am," said she with feverish volubility; "I don't know my way. I forgot there were three more steps before the landing."

"You have hurt yourself, perhaps," said Morrel. "What can I do for you, Valentine?" Valentine looked around her; she saw the deepest terror depicted in Noirtier's eyes. "Don't worry, dear grandpapa," said she, endeavoring to smile; "it is nothing—it is nothing; I was giddy, that is all."

"Another attack of giddiness," said Morrel, clasping his hands. "Oh, attend to it, Valentine, I entreat you."

"But no," said Valentine,—"no, I tell you it is all past, and it was nothing. Now, let me tell you some news; Eugenie is to be married in a week, and in three days there is to be a grand feast, a betrothal festival. We are all invited, my father, Madame de Villefort, and I—at least, I understood it so."

"When will it be our turn to think of these things? Oh, Valentine, you who have so much influence over your grandpapa, try to make him answer—Soon."

"And do you," said Valentine, "depend on me to stimulate the tardiness and arouse the memory of grandpapa?"

"Yes," cried Morrel, "make haste. So long as you are not mine, Valentine, I shall always think I may lose you."

"Oh," replied Valentine with a convulsive movement, "oh, indeed, Maximilian, you are too timid for an officer, for a soldier who, they say, never knows fear. Ah, ha, ha!" she burst into a forced and melancholy laugh, her arms stiffened and twisted, her head fell back on her chair, and she remained motionless. The cry of terror which was stopped on Noirtier's lips, seemed to start from his eyes. Morrel understood it; he knew he must call assistance. The young man rang the bell violently; the housemaid who had been in Mademoiselle Valentine's room, and the servant who had replaced Barrois, ran in at the same moment. Valentine was so pale, so cold, so inanimate that without listening to what was said to them they were seized with the fear which pervaded that house, and they flew into the passage crying for help. Madame Danglars and Eugenie were going out at that moment; they heard the cause of the disturbance. "I told you so!" exclaimed Madame de Villefort. "Poor child!"

CHAPTER 94.
MAXIMILIAN'S AVOWAL.

At the same moment M. de Villefort's voice was heard calling from his study, "What is the matter?" Morrel looked at Noirtier who had recovered his self-command, and with a glance indicated the closet where once before under somewhat similar circumstances, he had taken refuge. He had only time to get his hat and throw himself breathless into the closet when the procureur's footstep was heard in the passage. Villefort sprang into the room, ran to Valentine, and took her in his arms. "A physician, a physician,—M. d'Avrigny!" cried Villefort; "or rather I will go for him myself." He flew from the apartment, and Morrel at the same moment darted out at the other door. He had been struck to the heart by a frightful recollection—the conversation he had heard between the doctor and Villefort the night of Madame de Saint-Meran's death, recurred to him; these symptoms, to a less alarming extent, were the same which had preceded the death of Barrois. At the same time Monte Cristo's voice seemed to resound in his ear with the words he had heard only two hours before, "Whatever you want, Morrel, come to me; I have great power." More rapidly than thought, he darted down the Rue Matignon, and thence to the Avenue des Champs Elysees.

Meanwhile M. de Villefort arrived in a hired cabriolet
at M. d'Avrigny's door. He rang so violently that the porter
was alarmed. Villefort ran up-stairs without saying a word.
The porter knew him, and let him pass, only calling to him,
"In his study, Monsieur Procureur—in his study!" Villefort
pushed, or rather forced, the door open. "Ah," said the
doctor, "is it you?"

"Yes," said Villefort, closing the door after him, "it is
I, who am come in my turn to ask you if we are quite alone.
Doctor, my house is accursed!"

"What?" said the latter with apparent coolness, but
with deep emotion, "have you another invalid?"

"Yes, doctor," cried Villefort, clutching his hair, "yes!"

D'Avrigny's look implied, "I told you it would be so."
Then he slowly uttered these words, "Who is now dying
in your house? What new victim is going to accuse you
of weakness before God?" A mournful sob burst from
Villefort's heart; he approached the doctor, and seizing his
arm,—"Valentine," said he, "it is Valentine's turn!"

"Your daughter?" cried d'Avrigny with grief and
surprise.

"You see you were deceived," murmured the magistrate;
"come and see her, and on her bed of agony entreat her
pardon for having suspected her."

"Each time you have applied to me," said the doctor,
"it has been too late; still I will go. But let us make haste,

sir; with the enemies you have to do with there is no time to be lost."

"Oh, this time, doctor, you shall not have to reproach me with weakness. This time I will know the assassin, and will pursue him."

"Let us try first to save the victim before we think of revenging her," said d'Avrigny. "Come." The same cabriolet which had brought Villefort took them back at full speed, and at this moment Morrel rapped at Monte Cristo's door. The count was in his study and was reading with an angry look something which Bertuccio had brought in haste. Hearing the name of Morrel, who had left him only two hours before, the count raised his head, arose, and sprang to meet him. "What is the matter, Maximilian?" asked he; "you are pale, and the perspiration rolls from your forehead." Morrel fell into a chair. "Yes," said he, "I came quickly; I wanted to speak to you."

"Are all your family well?" asked the count, with an affectionate benevolence, whose sincerity no one could for a moment doubt.

"Thank you, count—thank you," said the young man, evidently embarrassed how to begin the conversation; "yes, every one in my family is well."

"So much the better; yet you have something to tell me?" replied the count with increased anxiety.

"Yes," said Morrel, "it is true; I have but now left a house where death has just entered, to run to you."

"Are you then come from M. de Morcerf's?" asked Monte Cristo.

"No," said Morrel; "is some one dead in his house?"

"The general has just blown his brains out," replied Monte Cristo with great coolness.

"Oh, what a dreadful event!" cried Maximilian.

"Not for the countess, or for Albert," said Monte Cristo; "a dead father or husband is better than a dishonored one,—blood washes out shame."

"Poor countess," said Maximilian, "I pity her very much; she is so noble a woman!"

"Pity Albert also, Maximilian; for believe me he is the worthy son of the countess. But let us return to yourself. You have hastened to me—can I have the happiness of being useful to you?"

"Yes, I need your help: that is I thought like a madman that you could lend me your assistance in a case where God alone can succor me."

"Tell me what it is," replied Monte Cristo.

"Oh," said Morrel, "I know not, indeed, if I may reveal this secret to mortal ears, but fatality impels me, necessity constrains me, count"—Morrel hesitated. "Do you think I love you?" said Monte Cristo, taking the young man's hand affectionately in his.

"Oh, you encourage me, and something tells me there," placing his hand on his heart, "that I ought to have no secret from you."

"You are right, Morrel; God is speaking to your heart, and your heart speaks to you. Tell me what it says."

"Count, will you allow me to send Baptistin to inquire after some one you know?"

"I am at your service, and still more my servants."

"Oh, I cannot live if she is not better."

"Shall I ring for Baptistin?"

"No, I will go and speak to him myself." Morrel went out, called Baptistin, and whispered a few words to him. The valet ran directly. "Well, have you sent?" asked Monte Cristo, seeing Morrel return.

"Yes, and now I shall be more calm."

"You know I am waiting," said Monte Cristo, smiling.

"Yes, and I will tell you. One evening I was in a garden; a clump of trees concealed me; no one suspected I was there. Two persons passed near me—allow me to conceal their names for the present; they were speaking in an undertone, and yet I was so interested in what they said that I did not lose a single word."

"This is a gloomy introduction, if I may judge from your pallor and shuddering, Morrel."

"Oh, yes, very gloomy, my friend. Some one had just died in the house to which that garden belonged. One

342

of the persons whose conversation I overheard was the master of the house; the other, the physician. The former was confiding to the latter his grief and fear, for it was the second time within a month that death had suddenly and unexpectedly entered that house which was apparently destined to destruction by some exterminating angel, as an object of God's anger."

"Ah, indeed?" said Monte Cristo, looking earnestly at the young man, and by an imperceptible movement turning his chair, so that he remained in the shade while the light fell full on Maximilian's face. "Yes," continued Morrel, "death had entered that house twice within one month."

"And what did the doctor answer?" asked Monte Cristo.

"He replied—he replied, that the death was not a natural one, and must be attributed"—

"To what?"

"To poison."

"Indeed?" said Monte Cristo with a slight cough which in moments of extreme emotion helped him to disguise a blush, or his pallor, or the intense interest with which he listened; "indeed, Maximilian, did you hear that?"

"Yes, my dear count, I heard it; and the doctor added that if another death occurred in a similar way he must appeal to justice." Monte Cristo listened, or appeared to do so, with the greatest calmness. "Well," said Maximilian, "death came a third time, and neither the master of the house nor the doctor said a word. Death is now, perhaps, striking a fourth blow. Count, what am I bound to do, being in possession of this secret?"

"My dear friend," said Monte Cristo, "you appear to be relating an adventure which we all know by heart. I know the house where you heard it, or one very similar to it; a house with a garden, a master, a physician, and where there have been three unexpected and sudden deaths. Well, I have not intercepted your confidence, and yet I know all that as well as you, and I have no conscientious scruples. No, it does not concern me. You say an exterminating angel appears to have devoted that house to God's anger—well, who says your supposition is not reality? Do not notice things which those whose interest it is to see them pass over. If it is God's justice, instead of his anger, which is walking through that house, Maximilian, turn away your face and let his justice accomplish its purpose." Morrel shuddered. There was something mournful, solemn, and terrible in the count's manner. "Besides," continued he, in so changed a tone that no one would have supposed it was the same person speaking—"besides, who says that it will begin again?"

"It has returned, count," exclaimed Morrel; "that is why I hastened to you."

"Well, what do you wish me to do? Do you wish me, for instance, to give information to the procureur?" Monte

Cristo uttered the last words with so much meaning that Morrel, starting up, cried out, "You know of whom I speak, count, do you not?"

"Perfectly well, my good friend; and I will prove it to you by putting the dots to the 'i,' or rather by naming the persons. You were walking one evening in M. de Villefort's garden; from what you relate, I suppose it to have been the evening of Madame de Saint-Meran's death. You heard M. de Villefort talking to M. d'Avrigny about the death of M. de Saint-Meran, and that no less surprising, of the countess. M. d'Avrigny said he believed they both proceeded from poison; and you, honest man, have ever since been asking your heart and sounding your conscience to know if you ought to expose or conceal this secret. Why do you torment them? 'Conscience, what hast thou to do with me?' as Sterne said. My dear fellow, let them sleep on, if they are asleep; let them grow pale in their drowsiness, if they are disposed to do so, and pray do you remain in peace, who have no remorse to disturb you." Deep grief was depicted on Morrel's features; he seized Monte Cristo's hand. "But it is beginning again, I say!"

"Well," said the Count, astonished at his perseverance, which he could not understand, and looking still more earnestly at Maximilian, "let it begin again,—it is like the house of the Atreidae; [*] God has condemned them, and they must submit to their punishment. They will all disappear, like the fabrics children build with cards, and which fall, one by one, under the breath of their builder, even if there are two hundred of them. Three months since it was M. de Saint-Meran; Madame de Saint-Meran two months since; the other day it was Barrois; to-day, the old Noirtier, or young Valentine."

* In the old Greek legend the Atreidae, or children of Atreus, were doomed to punishment because of the abominable crime of their father. The Agamemnon of Aeschylus is based on this legend.

"You knew it?" cried Morrel, in such a paroxysm of terror that Monte Cristo started,—he whom the falling heavens would have found unmoved; "you knew it, and said nothing?"

"And what is it to me?" replied Monte Cristo, shrugging his shoulders; "do I know those people? and must I lose the one to save the other? Faith, no, for between the culprit and the victim I have no choice."

"But I," cried Morrel, groaning with sorrow, "I love her!"

"You love?—whom?" cried Monte Cristo, starting to his feet, and seizing the two hands which Morrel was raising towards heaven.

"I love most fondly—I love madly—I love as a man who would give his life-blood to spare her a tear—I love Valentine de Villefort, who is being murdered at this moment! Do you understand me? I love her; and I ask God and you how I can save her?" Monte Cristo uttered a cry which those only can conceive who have heard the roar of a wounded lion. "Unhappy man," cried he, wringing his hands in his turn; "you love Valentine,—that daughter of an accursed race!" Never had Morrel witnessed such an expression—never had so terrible an eye flashed before his face—never had the genius of terror he had so often seen, either on the battle-field or in the murderous nights of Algeria, shaken around him more dreadful fire. He drew back terrified.

As for Monte Cristo, after this ebullition he closed his eyes as if dazzled by internal light. In a moment he restrained himself so powerfully that the tempestuous heaving of his breast subsided, as turbulent and foaming waves yield to the sun's genial influence when the cloud has passed. This silence, self-control, and struggle lasted about twenty seconds, then the count raised his pallid face. "See," said he, "my dear friend, how God punishes the most thoughtless and unfeeling men for their indifference, by presenting dreadful scenes to their view. I, who was looking on, an eager and curious spectator,—I, who was watching the working of this mournful tragedy,—I, who like a wicked angel was laughing at the evil men committed protected by secrecy (a secret is easily kept by the rich and powerful), I am in my turn bitten by the serpent whose tortuous course I was watching, and bitten to the heart!"

Morrel groaned. "Come, come," continued the count, "complaints are unavailing, be a man, be strong, be full of hope, for I am here and will watch over you." Morrel shook his head sorrowfully. "I tell you to hope. Do you understand me?" cried Monte Cristo. "Remember that I never uttered a falsehood and am never deceived. It is twelve o'clock, Maximilian; thank heaven that you came at noon rather than in the evening, or to-morrow morning. Listen, Morrel—it is noon; if Valentine is not now dead, she will not die."

"How so?" cried Morrel, "when I left her dying?" Monte Cristo pressed his hands to his forehead. What was passing in that brain, so loaded with dreadful secrets? What does the angel of light or the angel of darkness say to that mind, at once implacable and generous? God only knows.

Monte Cristo raised his head once more, and this time he was calm as a child awaking from its sleep. "Maximilian," said he, "return home. I command you not to stir—attempt nothing, not to let your countenance betray a thought, and I will send you tidings. Go."

"Oh, count, you overwhelm me with that coolness. Have you, then, power against death? Are you superhuman? Are you an angel?" And the young man, who had never shrunk from danger, shrank before Monte Cristo with indescribable terror. But Monte Cristo looked at him with so melancholy and sweet a smile, that Maximilian felt the tears filling his eyes. "I can do much for you, my friend," replied the count. "Go; I must be alone." Morrel, subdued by the extraordinary ascendancy Monte Cristo exercised over everything around him, did not endeavor to resist it. He pressed the count's hand and left. He stopped one moment at the door for Baptistin, whom he saw in the Rue Matignon, and who was running.

Meanwhile, Villefort and d'Avrigny had made all possible haste, Valentine had not revived from her fainting fit on their arrival, and the doctor examined the invalid with all the care the circumstances demanded, and with an interest which the knowledge of the secret intensified twofold. Villefort, closely watching his countenance and his lips, awaited the result of the examination. Noirtier, paler than even the young girl, more eager than Villefort for the decision, was watching also intently and affectionately. At last d'Avrigny slowly uttered these words:—"she is still alive!"

"Still?" cried Villefort; "oh, doctor, what a dreadful word is that."

"Yes," said the physician, "I repeat it; she is still alive, and I am astonished at it."

"But is she safe?" asked the father.

"Yes, since she lives." At that moment d'Avrigny's glance met Noirtier's eye. It glistened with such extraordinary joy, so rich and full of thought, that the physician was struck. He placed the young girl again on the chair,—her lips were scarcely discernible, they were so pale and white, as well as her whole face,—and remained motionless, looking at Noirtier, who appeared to anticipate and commend all he did. "Sir," said d'Avrigny to Villefort, "call Mademoiselle Valentine's maid, if you please." Villefort went himself to find her; and d'Avrigny approached Noirtier. "Have you something to tell me?" asked he. The old man winked his eyes expressively, which we may remember was his only way of expressing his approval.

"Privately?"

"Yes."

"Well, I will remain with you." At this moment Villefort returned, followed by the lady's maid; and after her came Madame de Villefort.

"What is the matter, then, with this dear child? she has just left me, and she complained of being indisposed, but I did not think seriously of it." The young woman with tears in her eyes and every mark of affection of a true mother, approached Valentine and took her hand. D'Avrigny continued to look at Noirtier; he saw the eyes of the old man dilate and become round, his cheeks turn pale and tremble; the perspiration stood in drops upon his forehead. "Ah," said he, involuntarily following Noirtier's eyes, which were fixed on Madame de Villefort, who repeated,—"This poor child would be better in bed. Come, Fanny, we will put her to bed." M. d'Avrigny, who saw that would be a means of his remaining alone with Noirtier, expressed his opinion that it was the best thing that could be done; but he forbade that anything should be given to her except what he ordered.

They carried Valentine away; she had revived, but could scarcely move or speak, so shaken was her frame by the attack. She had, however, just power to give one parting look to her grandfather, who in losing her seemed to be resigning his very soul. D'Avrigny followed the invalid, wrote a prescription, ordered Villefort to take a cabriolet, go in person to a chemist's to get the prescribed medicine, bring it himself, and wait for him in his daughter's room. Then, having renewed his injunction not to give Valentine anything, he went down again to Noirtier, shut the doors carefully, and after convincing himself that no one was listening,—"Do you," said he, "know anything of this young lady's illness?"

"Yes," said the old man.

"We have no time to lose; I will question, and do you answer me." Noirtier made a sign that he was ready to answer. "Did you anticipate the accident which has happened to your granddaughter?"

"Yes." D'Avrigny reflected a moment; then approaching Noirtier,—"Pardon what I am going to say," added he, "but no indication should be neglected in this terrible situation. Did you see poor Barrois die?" Noirtier raised his eyes to heaven. "Do you know of what he died!" asked d'Avrigny, placing his hand on Noirtier's shoulder.

"Yes," replied the old man.

"Do you think he died a natural death?" A sort of smile was discernible on the motionless lips of Noirtier.

"Then you have thought that Barrois was poisoned?"

"Yes."

"Do you think the poison he fell a victim to was intended for him?"

"No."

"Do you think the same hand which unintentionally struck Barrois has now attacked Valentine?"

"Yes."

"Then will she die too?" asked d'Avrigny, fixing his penetrating gaze on Noirtier. He watched the effect of this question on the old man. "No," replied he with an air of triumph which would have puzzled the most clever diviner. "Then you hope?" said d'Avrigny, with surprise.

"Yes."

"What do you hope?" The old man made him understand with his eyes that he could not answer. "Ah, yes, it is true," murmured d'Avrigny. Then, turning to Noirtier,—"Do you hope the assassin will be tried?"

"No."

"Then you hope the poison will take no effect on Valentine?"

"Yes."

"It is no news to you," added d'Avrigny, "to tell you that an attempt has been made to poison her?" The old man made a sign that he entertained no doubt upon the subject. "Then how do you hope Valentine will escape?" Noirtier kept his eyes steadfastly fixed on the same spot. D'Avrigny followed the direction and saw that they were fixed on a bottle containing the mixture which he took every morning. "Ah, indeed?" said d'Avrigny, struck with a sudden thought, "has it occurred to you"—Noirtier did not let him finish. "Yes," said he. "To prepare her system to resist poison?"

"Yes."

"By accustoming her by degrees"—

"Yes, yes, yes," said Noirtier, delighted to be understood.

"Of course. I had told you that there was brucine in the mixture I give you."

"Yes."

"And by accustoming her to that poison, you have endeavored to neutralize the effect of a similar poison?" Noirtier's joy continued. "And you have succeeded," exclaimed d'Avrigny. "Without that precaution Valentine would have died before assistance could have been procured. The dose has been excessive, but she has only been shaken by it; and this time, at any rate, Valentine will not die." A superhuman joy expanded the old man's eyes, which were raised towards heaven with an expression of infinite gratitude. At this moment Villefort returned. "Here, doctor," said he, "is what you sent me for."

"Was this prepared in your presence?"

"Yes," replied the procureur.

"Have you not let it go out of your hands?"

"No." D'Avrigny took the bottle, poured some drops of the mixture it contained in the hollow of his hand, and swallowed them. "Well," said he, "let us go to Valentine; I will give instructions to every one, and you, M. de Villefort, will yourself see that no one deviates from them."

At the moment when d'Avrigny was returning to Valentine's room, accompanied by Villefort, an Italian priest, of serious demeanor and calm and firm tone, hired for his use the house adjoining the hotel of M. de Villefort. No one knew how the three former tenants of that house left it. About two hours afterwards its foundation was reported to be unsafe; but the report did not prevent the new occupant establishing himself there with his modest furniture the same day at five o'clock. The lease was drawn up for three, six, or nine years by the new tenant, who, according to the rule of the proprietor, paid six months in advance. This new tenant, who, as we have said, was an Italian, was called Il Signor Giacomo Busoni. Workmen were immediately called in, and that same night the passengers at the end of the faubourg saw with surprise that carpenters and masons were occupied in repairing the lower part of the tottering house.

CHAPTER 95.
FATHER AND DAUGHTER.

We saw in a preceding chapter how Madame Danglars went formally to announce to Madame de Villefort the approaching marriage of Eugenie Danglars and M. Andrea Cavalcanti. This announcement, which implied or appeared to imply, the approval of all the persons concerned in this momentous affair, had been preceded by a scene to which our readers must be admitted. We beg them to take one step backward, and to transport themselves, the morning of that day of great catastrophes, into the showy, gilded salon we have before shown them, and which was the pride of its owner, Baron Danglars. In this room, at about ten o'clock in the morning, the banker himself had been walking to and fro for some minutes thoughtfully and in evident uneasiness, watching both doors, and listening to every sound. When his patience was exhausted, he called his valet. "Etienne," said he, "see why Mademoiselle Eugenie has asked me to meet her in the drawing-room, and why she makes me wait so long."

Having given this vent to his ill-humor, the baron became more calm; Mademoiselle Danglars had that morning requested an interview with her father, and had fixed on the gilded drawing-room as the spot. The singularity of this step, and above all its formality, had not a little surprised the banker, who had immediately obeyed his daughter by repairing first to the drawing-room. Etienne soon returned from his errand. "Mademoiselle's lady's maid says, sir, that mademoiselle is finishing her toilette, and will be here shortly."

Danglars nodded, to signify that he was satisfied. To the world and to his servants Danglars assumed the character of the good-natured man and the indulgent father. This was one of his parts in the popular comedy he was performing,—a make-up he had adopted and which suited him about as well as the masks worn on the classic stage by paternal actors, who seen from one side, were the image of geniality, and from the other showed lips drawn down in chronic ill-temper. Let us hasten to say that in private the genial side descended to the level of the other, so that generally the indulgent man disappeared to give place to the brutal husband and domineering father. "Why the devil does that foolish girl, who pretends to wish to speak to me, not come into my study? and why on earth does she want to speak to me at all?"

He was turning this thought over in his brain for the twentieth time, when the door opened and Eugenie appeared, attired in a figured black satin dress, her hair dressed and gloves on, as if she were going to the Italian Opera. "Well,

Eugenie, what is it you want with me? and why in this solemn drawing-room when the study is so comfortable?"

"I quite understand why you ask, sir," said Eugenie, making a sign that her father might be seated, "and in fact your two questions suggest fully the theme of our conversation. I will answer them both, and contrary to the usual method, the last first, because it is the least difficult. I have chosen the drawing-room, sir, as our place of meeting, in order to avoid the disagreeable impressions and influences of a banker's study. Those gilded cashbooks, drawers locked like gates of fortresses, heaps of bank-bills, come from I know not where, and the quantities of letters from England, Holland, Spain, India, China, and Peru, have generally a strange influence on a father's mind, and make him forget that there is in the world an interest greater and more sacred than the good opinion of his correspondents. I have, therefore, chosen this drawing-room, where you see, smiling and happy in their magnificent frames, your portrait, mine, my mother's, and all sorts of rural landscapes and touching pastorals. I rely much on external impressions; perhaps, with regard to you, they are immaterial, but I should be no artist if I had not some fancies."

"Very well," replied M. Danglars, who had listened to all this preamble with imperturbable coolness, but without understanding a word, since like every man burdened with thoughts of the past, he was occupied with seeking the thread of his own ideas in those of the speaker.

"There is, then, the second point cleared up, or nearly so," said Eugenie, without the least confusion, and with that masculine pointedness which distinguished her gesture and her language; "and you appear satisfied with the explanation. Now, let us return to the first. You ask me why I have requested this interview; I will tell you in two words, sir; I will not marry count Andrea Cavalcanti."

Danglars leaped from his chair and raised his eyes and arms towards heaven.

"Yes, indeed, sir," continued Eugenie, still quite calm; "you are astonished, I see; for since this little affair began, I have not manifested the slightest opposition, and yet I am always sure, when the opportunity arrives, to oppose a determined and absolute will to people who have not consulted me, and things which displease me. However, this time, my tranquillity, or passiveness as philosophers say, proceeded from another source; it proceeded from a wish, like a submissive and devoted daughter" (a slight smile was observable on the purple lips of the young girl), "to practice obedience."

"Well?" asked Danglars.

"Well, sir," replied Eugenie, "I have tried to the very last and now that the moment has come, I feel in spite of all my efforts that it is impossible."

"But," said Danglars, whose weak mind was at first quite overwhelmed with the weight of this pitiless logic, marking evident premeditation and force of will, "what is your reason for this refusal, Eugenie? what reason do you assign?"

"My reason?" replied the young girl. "Well, it is not that the man is more ugly, more foolish, or more disagreeable than any other; no, M. Andrea Cavalcanti may appear to those who look at men's faces and figures as a very good specimen of his kind. It is not, either, that my heart is less touched by him than any other; that would be a schoolgirl's reason, which I consider quite beneath me. I actually love no one, sir; you know it, do you not? I do not then see why, without real necessity, I should encumber my life with a perpetual companion. Has not some sage said, 'Nothing too much'? and another, 'I carry all my effects with me'? I have been taught these two aphorisms in Latin and in Greek; one is, I believe, from Phaedrus, and the other from Bias. Well, my dear father, in the shipwreck of life—for life is an eternal shipwreck of our hopes—I cast into the sea my useless encumbrance, that is all, and I remain with my own will, disposed to live perfectly alone, and consequently perfectly free."

"Unhappy girl, unhappy girl!" murmured Danglars, turning pale, for he knew from long experience the solidity of the obstacle he had so suddenly encountered.

"Unhappy girl," replied Eugenie, "unhappy girl, do you say, sir? No, indeed; the exclamation appears quite theatrical and affected. Happy, on the contrary, for what am I in want of! The world calls me beautiful. It is something to be well received. I like a favorable reception; it expands the countenance, and those around me do not then appear so ugly. I possess a share of wit, and a certain relative sensibility, which enables me to draw from life in general, for the support of mine, all I meet with that is good, like the monkey who cracks the nut to get at its contents. I am rich, for you have one of the first fortunes in France. I am your only daughter, and you are not so exacting as the fathers of the Porte Saint-Martin and Gaiete, who disinherit their daughters for not giving them grandchildren. Besides, the provident law has deprived you of the power to disinherit me, at least entirely, as it has also of the power to compel me to marry Monsieur This or Monsieur That. And so—being, beautiful, witty, somewhat talented, as the comic operas say, and rich—and that is happiness, sir—why do you call me unhappy?"

Danglars, seeing his daughter smiling, and proud even to insolence, could not entirely repress his brutal feelings, but they betrayed themselves only by an exclamation. Under the fixed and inquiring gaze levelled at him from under those beautiful black eyebrows, he prudently turned away, and calmed himself immediately, daunted by the power of a resolute mind. "Truly, my daughter," replied he with a smile, "you are all you boast of being, excepting one thing; I will not too hastily tell you which, but would rather leave you to guess it." Eugenie looked at Danglars, much surprised that one flower of her crown of pride, with which she had so superbly decked herself, should be disputed. "My daughter," continued the banker, "you have perfectly explained to me the sentiments which influence a girl like you, who is determined she will not marry; now it remains for me to tell you the motives of a father like me, who has decided that his daughter shall marry." Eugenie bowed, not as a submissive daughter, but as an adversary prepared for a discussion.

"My daughter," continued Danglars, "when a father asks his daughter to choose a husband, he has always some reason for wishing her to marry. Some are affected with the mania of which you spoke just now, that of living again in their grandchildren. This is not my weakness, I tell you at once; family joys have no charm for me. I may acknowledge this to a daughter whom I know to be philosophical enough to understand my indifference, and not to impute it to me as a crime."

"This is not to the purpose," said Eugenie; "let us speak candidly, sir; I admire candor."

"Oh," said Danglars, "I can, when circumstances render it desirable, adopt your system, although it may not be my general practice. I will therefore proceed. I have proposed to you to marry, not for your sake, for indeed I did not think of you in the least at the moment (you admire candor, and will now be satisfied, I hope); but because it suited me to marry you as soon as possible, on account of certain commercial speculations I am desirous of entering into." Eugenie became uneasy.

"It is just as I tell you, I assure you, and you must not be angry with me, for you have sought this disclosure. I do not willingly enter into arithmetical explanations with an artist like you, who fears to enter my study lest she should imbibe disagreeable or anti-poetic impressions and sensations. But in that same banker's study, where you very willingly presented yourself yesterday to ask for the thousand francs I give you monthly for pocket-money, you must know, my dear young lady, that many things may be learned, useful even to a girl who will not marry. There one may learn, for instance, what, out of regard to your nervous susceptibility, I will inform you of in the drawing-room, namely, that the credit of a banker is his physical and moral life; that credit sustains him as breath animates the body; and M. de Monte Cristo once gave me a lecture on that subject, which I have never forgotten. There we may learn that as credit sinks, the body becomes a corpse, and this is what must happen very soon to the banker who is proud to own so good a logician as you for his daughter." But Eugenie, instead of stooping, drew herself up under the blow. "Ruined?" said she.

"Exactly, my daughter; that is precisely what I mean," said Danglars, almost digging his nails into his breast, while he preserved on his harsh features the smile of the heartless though clever man; "ruined—yes, that is it."

"Ah!" said Eugenie.

"Yes, ruined! Now it is revealed, this secret so full of horror, as the tragic poet says. Now, my daughter, learn from my lips how you may alleviate this misfortune, so far as it will affect you."

"Oh," cried Eugenie, "you are a bad physiognomist, if you imagine I deplore on my own account the catastrophe of which you warn me. I ruined? and what will that signify to me? Have I not my talent left? Can I not, like Pasta, Malibran, Grisi, acquire for myself what you would never have given me, whatever might have been your fortune, a hundred or a hundred and fifty thousand livres per annum, for which I shall be indebted to no one but myself; and which, instead of being given as you gave me those poor twelve thousand francs, with sour looks and reproaches for my prodigality, will be accompanied with acclamations, with bravos, and with flowers? And if I do not possess that talent, which your smiles prove to me you doubt, should I not still have that ardent love of independence, which will be a substitute for wealth, and which in my mind supersedes even the instinct of self-preservation? No, I grieve not on my own account, I shall always find a resource; my books, my pencils, my piano, all the things which cost but little, and which I shall be able to procure, will remain my own.

"Do you think that I sorrow for Madame Danglars? Undeceive yourself again; either I am greatly mistaken, or she has provided against the catastrophe which threatens you, and, which will pass over without affecting her. She has taken care for herself,—at least I hope so,—for her attention has not been diverted from her projects by watching over me. She has fostered my independence by professedly indulging my love for liberty. Oh, no, sir; from my childhood I have seen too much, and understood too much, of what has passed around me, for misfortune to have an undue power over me. From my earliest recollections, I have been beloved by no one—so much the worse; that has naturally led me to love no one—so much the better—now you have my profession of faith."

"Then," said Danglars, pale with anger, which was not at all due to offended paternal love,—"then, mademoiselle, you persist in your determination to accelerate my ruin?"

"Your ruin? I accelerate your ruin? What do you mean? I do not understand you."

"So much the better, I have a ray of hope left; listen."

"I am all attention," said Eugenie, looking so earnestly at her father that it was an effort for the latter to endure her unrelenting gaze.

"M. Cavalcanti," continued Danglars, "is about to marry you, and will place in my hands his fortune, amounting to three million livres."

"That is admirable!" said Eugenie with sovereign contempt, smoothing her gloves out one upon the other.

"You think I shall deprive you of those three millions," said Danglars; "but do not fear it. They are destined to produce at least ten. I and a brother banker have obtained a grant of a railway, the only industrial enterprise which in these days promises to make good the fabulous prospects that Law once held out to the eternally deluded Parisians, in the fantastic Mississippi scheme. As I look at it, a millionth part of a railway is worth fully as much as an acre of waste land on the banks of the Ohio. We make in our case a deposit, on a mortgage, which is an advance, as you see, since we gain at least ten, fifteen, twenty, or a hundred livres' worth of iron in exchange for our money. Well, within a week I am to deposit four millions for my share; the four millions, I promise you, will produce ten or twelve."

"But during my visit to you the day before yesterday, sir, which you appear to recollect so well," replied Eugenie, "I saw you arranging a deposit—is not that the term?—of five millions and a half; you even pointed it out to me in two drafts on the treasury, and you were astonished that so valuable a paper did not dazzle my eyes like lightning."

"Yes, but those five millions and a half are not mine, and are only a proof of the great confidence placed in me; my title of popular banker has gained me the confidence of charitable institutions, and the five millions and a half belong to them; at any other time I should not have hesitated to make use of them, but the great losses I have recently sustained are well known, and, as I told you, my credit is rather shaken. That deposit may be at any moment withdrawn, and if I had employed it for another purpose, I should bring on me a disgraceful bankruptcy. I do not despise bankruptcies, believe me, but they must be those which enrich, not those which ruin. Now, if you marry M. Cavalcanti, and I get the three millions, or even if it is thought I am going to get them, my credit will be restored, and my fortune, which for the last month or two has been swallowed up in gulfs which have been opened in my path by an inconceivable fatality, will revive. Do you understand me?"

"Perfectly; you pledge me for three millions, do you not?"

"The greater the amount, the more flattering it is to you; it gives you an idea of your value."

"Thank you. One word more, sir; do you promise me to make what use you can of the report of the fortune M. Cavalcanti will bring without touching the money? This is no act of selfishness, but of delicacy. I am willing to help rebuild your fortune, but I will not be an accomplice in the ruin of others."

"But since I tell you," cried Danglars, "that with these three million"—

"Do you expect to recover your position, sir, without touching those three million?"

"I hope so, if the marriage should take place and confirm my credit."

"Shall you be able to pay M. Cavalcanti the five hundred thousand francs you promise for my dowry?"

"He shall receive them on returning from the mayor's." [*]

* The performance of the civil marriage.

"Very well!"

"What next? what more do you want?"

"I wish to know if, in demanding my signature, you leave me entirely free in my person?"

"Absolutely."

"Then, as I said before, sir,—very well; I am ready to marry M. Cavalcanti."

"But what are you up to?"

"Ah, that is my affair. What advantage should I have over you, if knowing your secret I were to tell you mine?" Danglars bit his lips. "Then," said he, "you are ready to pay the official visits, which are absolutely indispensable?"

"Yes," replied Eugenie.

"And to sign the contract in three days?"

"Yes."

"Then, in my turn, I also say, very well!" Danglars pressed his daughter's hand in his. But, extraordinary to relate, the father did not say, "Thank you, my child," nor did the daughter smile at her father. "Is the conference ended?" asked Eugenie, rising. Danglars motioned that he had nothing more to say. Five minutes afterwards the piano resounded to the touch of Mademoiselle d'Armilly's fingers, and Mademoiselle Danglars was singing Brabantio's malediction on Desdemona. At the end of the piece Etienne entered, and announced to Eugenie that the horses were in the carriage, and that the baroness was waiting for her to pay her visits. We have seen them at Villefort's; they proceeded then on their course.